# HOW TO SAVE THE WORLD

By Lexie Dunne

Superheroes Anonymous
Supervillains Anonymous
How to Save the World

# HOW TO SAVE THE WORLD

## LEXIE DUNNE

HARPER
VOYAGER
IMPULSE

*An Imprint of HarperCollins Publishers*

HOW TO SAVE THE WORLD. Copyright © 2016 by Lexie Dunne. All rights reserved under International and Pan-American Copyright Conventions. By payment of the required fees, you have been granted the nonexclusive, nontransferable right to access and read the text of this e-book on-screen. No part of this text may be reproduced, transmitted, downloaded, decompiled, reverse-engineered, or stored in or introduced into any information storage and retrieval system, in any form or by any means, whether electronic or mechanical, now known or hereafter invented, without the express written permission of HarperCollins e-books. For information, address HarperCollins Publishers, 195 Broadway, New York, NY 10007.

EPub Edition OCTOBER 2016 ISBN: 9780062471703

Print Edition ISBN: 9780062471833

10 9 8 7 6 5 4 3 2 1

*For the girls who were stuck playing Lois Lane and April O'Neil (awesome though they are). You've always been a superhero.*

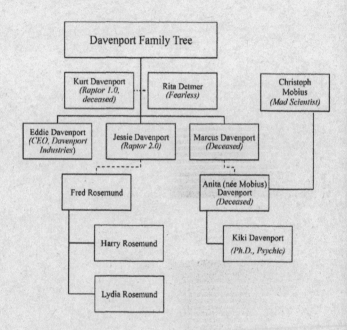

## Davenport Family Tree

Kurt Davenport
*(Raptor 1.0, deceased)*

Rita Detmer
*(Fearless)*

Christoph Mobius
*(Mad Scientist)*

Eddie Davenport
*(CEO, Davenport Industries)*

Jessie Davenport
*(Raptor 2.0)*

Marcus Davenport
*(Deceased)*

Fred Rosemund

Anita (née Mobius) Davenport
*(Deceased)*

Harry Rosemund

Kiki Davenport
*(Ph.D., Psychic)*

Lydia Rosemund

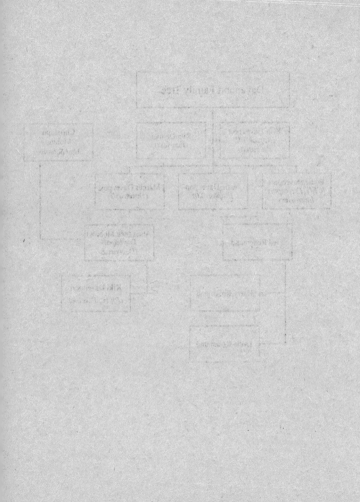

## THE FEARED FIVE
## (WORLD'S FIRST SUPERHEROES):

Raptor (Kurt Davenport, Entrepreneur)
Phantom Fuel (Sarah Mann, Engineer)
Invisible Victor (Victor Singh, Metaphysicist)
The Cheetah (Nigel Calibrese, Pizza Delivery)
Gail Garson (News reporter)

# ACKNOWLEDGMENTS

They say it takes a village to raise a child, and the same holds true for writing a book. I tried to get the village to actually write the book for me, but no luck. There are several people without whom this book would not be complete, my family first among them. Thank you to my parents for being loving and supportive, to my siblings—especially Hannah, forced to listen to every plot point in nauseating detail—for the ride-or-die attitude that's propelled us this far in life.

To my cheerleading squad Jennifer Shew, Marian McGraw, Erica Lilly, Camille Schlesinger, Islay Bell-Webb, Maximus "C.C." Powers, and Ayefah: you lifted me up through writing, editing, and the panic attacks, so thank you. To the other Impulse authors: you've been a rock in the storm of anxiety, and you're lovely. Thank you, Rosalyn Foster and Samantha Brody, for beta reading and talking plot with me, you wonderful dames. Thanks also to my new editor, Anna Will, who came in at the last moment and patiently guided us through the growing pains.

Most of all, thank you to Team Rebecca (i.e. Rebecca Strauss and Rebecca Lucash) for being the engine that started and keeps this world going. Every day I count myself lucky to know you and to work with you.

Finally, to all of my internet friends: I love you all, you remarkable weirdos.

# CHAPTER 1

**H**alfway to the Chinese place, something grabbed
me by the scruff of the neck and sent me flying. It was
a toss-up over which hurt worse: the landing, or my
pride. I hadn't even heard her coming.

"Seriously?" is probably not the correct response to
seeing a supervillain standing over you in an alleyway.
Most people might scream or run. I chose to glare,
even though the woman standing in front of me was
armed to the teeth—which she'd recently had capped,
apparently. They were a great deal less pointy than the
last time I'd seen them. I brushed snow off of the knees
of my jeans. "What was that for?"

Razor X, one of Chicago's up-and-coming supervillains, probably glared right back at me. It was a hard
to see her eyebrows under the visor on her bulbous
helmet. Her half cape fluttered in the icy wind. "I
called you three times last week!"

"I've been busy. And dodging a phone call is no reason to pick me up and throw me."

She raised the ray gun at her side and I saw her arm shake a little. The idiot wasn't even wearing her winter suit. "I had to get your attention somehow. You weren't going to call me back, were you?"

"I totally was," I said.

"Liar."

"Raze, I'm trying to get dinner."

"When you agree to a public battle, it makes me look really stupid when I put it out on the network and I'm the only one that shows up." Raze stomped her foot.

"Raze," I said again. "I've got a job now, and you know there are complications with the—"

Her voice took on a whining edge. "You need to get a uniform and a proper hero name. What does it say about me as a villain if my nemesis is named *Hostage Girl*? Huh? Like, that name alone does all the work for me. And come to think of it, girl is really a demeaning term when you're—you're what? Thirty?"

"Twenty-seven." I folded my arms over my light-weight jacket. Though I considered myself a native—five years in the city officially as of last week—to most Chicagoans I looked like an idiot, braving snow-piled November streets without a parka. But I wasn't exactly a normal Chicagoan anymore. Or, hell, even a normal human anymore, which was why flying freaks in masks and capes thought tossing me into an alley was a situational appropriate greeting. "And I will make it to a battle, I will, when I have an actual identity set up, but you know how the last few months have been."

"I got out of Detmer so we could be enemies, Gail. I did that for us." Raze's lip quivered. She flipped her visor up to give me a pitiful look.

People made of sterner stuff than me would have crumpled under the pressure of those puppy-dog eyes, even though the woman in the alley had personally put me in the hospital seventeen times. I reached out and gripped her shoulder, giving it a reassuring squeeze. "I know, and I'm sorry. Do you want to come over? I'm picking up Chinese."

She brightened temporarily. "Can I poison it? I've got this new formula I'm working on, almost worked out the bugs with the projectile v—"

"Absolutely not," I said.

"Hard pass, then," she said. "Answer a text every once in a while, Gail. Show an enemy some love for once."

"Fine, fine," I said. "You wouldn't want to give me a lift, would you?"

"As heavy as you are? No." She took off with a whir of her rocket boots and a blast of exhaust that made me cough and wave at the air in front of my face.

"Jerk," I said under my breath, though she had a point. I might be barely taller than five feet and lean with muscle, but I weighed six times what I looked like I should weigh. Just one of the side effects of no longer being carbon-based.

With my enemy off to sulk in her lair, I stepped

back onto the street, hoping that nobody had seen me get grabbed. When you earn the moniker Hostage Girl because villains can't seem to keep their hands off of you, a witnessed kidnapping could lead to an article on the Domino at the very least. And I was doing my best to keep my face off of the internet these days. I didn't want people looking too closely at Gail Godwin, Hostage Girl, because they might start to question a few things. Like the new physique, the fact that I no longer had to wear winter coats, or the man I had been spending a great deal of time with lately.

Of course, with my luck, the minute I stepped clear of the alley, my ears picked up the whir-click of a hoverboard. My shoulders sagged. "I just want to get food, whoever you are," I said without looking behind me. "Leave me alone."

"Hostage Girl."

I turned to look: a man in red-and-blue interlocking armor with a robotic face mask. A giant crack that I happened to know had been caused by War Hammer bisected the helmet. Yellow circles glowed where the man's eyes should have been. I watched the backdraft from his hoverboard send ripples in a puddle of dirty sludge.

"Captain Cracked," I said. "It's been a while. What do you want? If you're here to kidnap me, it won't go well."

For him at least. Maybe he was one of the villains who hadn't entirely gotten the memo yet.

"There are rumors," he said, the voice modulator making his words sound twice as sinister. I wondered idly what his villain name had been before Sam punched the giant crack in his mask. "About you."

"Buzz off," I said, as those rumors were kind of a sore subject.

"People think you're not Class D anymore." He raised his ray gun, which was not nearly as elegant as Raze's. "State your class rating."

I eyed the muzzle, debated if I wanted to run a zigzag pattern and get my boots wet in the slush, and decided against it. I ran full tilt at him and hit him like a linebacker instead. My shoulder drove into the midsection of his armor with enough force that I heard the *crack* of something in his armor breaking. With a shout and a whoosh, we flew backward. His weird computerized voice sounded even stranger when it was screaming curse words as he struggled to dislodge me.

I, on the other hand, was trying to reach the control panel between his shoulder blades. I'd seen it when he'd first held me hostage years ago, and thanks to my enhanced hearing now, I could hear it purring softly. No doubt it held his processor. I scrabbled with my fingernails, trying to wedge my fingers in and pull the wiring out.

He panicked and took off, leaving me with no choice but to hold on.

The hoverboard protested under all of the extra weight. With me clinging to him, Captain Cracked couldn't use the zappers in his hands without shocking himself, too, so he flailed his arms and tried to dislodge me. My grip was too strong for him to knock me off, so we swung wildly through the air. At one point, it would have made me dizzy; now I just tried harder for the panel.

"Everything is not proceeding as I have foreseen," Captain Cracked said. Panic sounded incredibly strange through the voice modulator.

I finally got my fingers around the panel and he let out an electronically flattened shout. He pitched forward so suddenly that it knocked my equilibrium off enough to send us both careening onto a fourth-story rooftop. We landed in a dirty puddle—so much for my boots—and the force of our impact sent me rolling.

I sprang right back to my feet and squared off against him. It was a point of some pride when he skittered back on his rocket sledge in obvious shock. "The rumors are true. You're no longer Class D," he said.

"Gee, you think?" I said, and he shot at me.

I jumped in time, landing on the other side of the now-smoking hole in the roof. I charged at him once more, ducked under a second blast, and skidded on the ice for the last couple of feet, body-checking him hard. He tumbled backward and I drove my fist straight into his helmet. The crack in his mask made a crunching noise as it expanded.

"What I am is none of your business. All you need to know is Hostage Girl hits back now," I said, and tried to punch him again.

He dodged this time, shoving me off of him. While I scrambled to my feet, ready to deliver more pain, he took off into the sky, fleeing in terror. I considered jumping after him, but my stomach growled. I watched the man who usually terrorized Lincoln Park fly away into the slate-gray clouds and shook my head.

The supervillains needed a better communication network. When were they going to understand that Hostage Girl was no longer defenseless?

With Captain Cracked gone, I looked around to take stock of my situation. He'd dropped me on a roof close to the Chinese food place, so that was nice, but I was also on the fourth floor and I couldn't see any rooftop access anywhere. And when I peered into the still-smoking hole left by the ray gun, a very annoyed family stared back at me. "Sorry about that," I called. "Any chance of—no? I can't use your door? Okay."

Apparently I was stranded on the roof.

I wandered to the edge of the roof and judged the distance to the ground below. If I screwed up, four stories wouldn't kill me, but it would lead to a couple of painful days. I wasn't indestructible, not by a long shot, but I could take quite a bit more of a beating than a regular human. It was more that I didn't want to deal with my trainer scolding me.

Sometimes I wondered what it would be like to live a normal life. Not really the time to worry about that, though. My existential crisis could wait until I was on the ground. I took a deep breath, stepped off the roof, and tried to phase down to the ground, altering my momentum to let me land safely. Instead, I hit the dumpster hard enough for the impact to rattle in my bones. My foot went straight through a trash bag and into something sticky, which made me grimace. "Great," I said, hauling myself out of the dumpster. "Just fabulous."

I limped the rest of the way. The fact that my knees weren't throbbing told me I'd been a little successful at phasing, which was an ability I could mainly only use subconsciously, so at least there was that.

I stepped inside and ignored my growling stomach when the smell of soy sauce and fried noodles hit. "Mr. Shen," I said. "It's me, your favorite customer, and I forgot to beg for extra egg rolls, so—seriously? Is it something in the water?"

The robber and Mr. Shen both blinked at me at the same time. I put it down to startling them and not the fact that I looked and smelled like I'd landed in a dumpster. Or it could have been that I was a tiny woman who'd just walked into a robbery at gunpoint and was more annoyed than freaked out.

"Down on the ground!" the robber said, the gun in his hand twitching wildly. He wore a gray hoodie and a ski mask, and even through the *eau de dumpster* emanating from my shoes, I could smell nervous sweat on him. My ears picked up the rabbit-pulse of his heartbeat.

"Did you hear me, bitch?" he said, and I nearly rolled my eyes. Why that word? Why always that word? "Get on the ground!"

Mr. Shen gave me a panicked look and gestured frantically. I should have been more afraid, but annoy-

ance won out. Why had this guy picked *my* favorite
Chinese food place? The owners were kind, the crab
rangoon was to die for, and they'd finally stopped
side-eyeing my orders, which could comfortably feed
a family of forty.

"Sorry," I said, and I took a step closer. "I wasn't listening. You need to speak up."

Immediately, the gun swung in my direction. Much
better, in my opinion.

"You got a death wish or something?"

"No, I can safely say I don't. I mean, you could kill
me with that thing, you really could." Probably. We
hadn't exactly tested my healing ability lately. "But you
won't."

I saw the whites of the robber's eyes as he took an
involuntary half step back. "Oh, yeah?" he said, clearly
faking bravado. "And why is that?"

"Because I'm—" Like with Captain Cracked, I
struck first, launching into a roundhouse kick so fast
that I kicked the gun right out of his hand. I landed and
knocked him back, pulling my punch in case he was as
human as he seemed. "—going to do that. Stay down!"

I hadn't actually fought a regular-powered human
one-on-one before. Contrary to the evidence from the
past ten minutes of my life, I hadn't actually fought that
many people, powered or not. For most of my time in
Chicago, I'd been a hostage, not a hero. I cringed when
I heard something crack as the man's back hit the floor,
and stepped back.

That proved to be a mistake.

He leapt back to his feet. Instead of charging me, he grabbed a bamboo plant and chucked it at my head. I ducked; the next bamboo plant went hurtling toward my favorite provider of delicious crab rangoon, so I tackled Mr. Shen. He grunted as we both landed on the linoleum.

"I just needed the money!" the robber said. "You just had to give me the money, that was it."

"Oh, sure, he robs the place and he's the wronged party here," I said. To Mr. Shen, I said, "Stay down. I'll take care of him."

Mr. Shen looked at me with wide eyes and I wanted to sigh. I'd been hoping to keep him from copping wise to the fact that I didn't play for the regular human team. Not that he would judge me for it, but it was hard enough to find places to eat as Hostage Girl. Hostage Girl plus what I'd become? That was even worse.

"Seriously, stay put," I said.

When I rose to my feet, the robber caught me in a flying tackle. I tried to stand my ground, but the greasy floor made that impossible. We slid back into the kitchen, a place fraught with danger, open flames, and far too many knives for comfort. I dodged a wild swing toward my face. He ducked the haymaker that would have hopefully knocked him out, and snatched up a knife. It caught the edge of my jacket when he brandished it at me.

In retaliation, I threw a handful of dumplings in his face. I blocked the next strike with an elbow to his wrist, spun, and drove my other elbow under his chin. He

HOW TO SAVE THE WORLD 11

staggered back, clearly seeing stars, so I grabbed a cooling pan from the metal countertop and walloped him.

He hit the floor a little too hard.

"You might want to call 911," I said, panting. I looked at the rip in my jacket and frowned. "He needs medical attention."

While we waited for the police to show up, we left him crumpled up on the kitchen floor and I collected my food, carefully stacking the three bulging bags so that I could trot them back to my apartment. They were heavy, but that was the least of my worries.

"So . . . who are you really? What's your mask?" Mr. Shen asked as I pushed a generous tip in the jar. He wouldn't actually let me pay for the food itself.

I shook my head as we heard the wail of a siren and red and blue lights splashed along the walls. "No mask. Just . . . a local picking up dinner from the place down the street."

Mr. Shen gave me a skeptical look, which I supposed was fair.

"Sorry?" I said. "Good luck. And sorry about the bamboo plants."

"See you next time, Gail," Mr. Shen said.

"Looking forward to it."

A noise made me whirl, my arms laden with the bags of food, to see the robber groaning and pushing himself to his feet. Mr. Shen and the rest of the kitchen staff scrambled back in fear. I moved to drop the food, but even I wasn't fast enough to stop him before he snatched up a knife from the counter and flung it.

I saw it arc through the air, heard it rotate in slow motion, tumbling end over end toward my face—and then I was sitting on my couch with a headache.

"Oh, hey!" My very own superhero trainer and roommate, Angélica Rocha, looked up from her book as I let out a gasp and reeled backward. "You're back! That was fast. Did you do that on purpose?"

The man on my other side frowned, pausing in the middle of peeling out of his new uniform's gauntlets. "Gail?" Guy Bookman asked. "What happened?" He finished tugging off his War Hammer glove.

"Why do you smell like that?" Angélica asked.

I groaned and set the bags on the coffee table to rub my temples. "It's a long story, and you're going to yell."

"Why would I yell?" Angélica dove into the bag nearest her. "Whatever happened, you got the food here in record time. This is a miracle. Definitely—" This was said around a mouthful of lo mein noodles. "—something to celebrate."

"You say that now, but wait until I tell you about the robber," I said. "And the dumpster."

Guy wrapped an arm around my shoulders and kissed the side of my head. "I knew I should've picked up the food on my way over."

**A**n hour later, very little remained of the Chinese food and Guy and I were left alone in the living room, Angélica having ducked into her room after receiving a text message. I stretched out, bones popping in a way that made Guy wince.

"Is that healthy?" he asked, looking up from his tablet.

"I have no idea."

"I don't think it's healthy. It doesn't sound healthy." He set the tablet on the coffee table, which was only a little dented from the time Angélica had thrown me into it while wrestling over who had to go grocery shopping. "Maybe you should go to Davenport and get a checkup."

I popped my shoulders again. It wasn't to spite him—precisely. "Nope," I said. "I feel great. There's nothing to worry about. In fact, I think everything's finally calming down."

"You got in two fights and teleported nearly two miles," Guy said. "How does your head feel?"

In truth, it felt fine. Applying food to the injury, as Angélica liked to say, was usually the quickest cure for overextending myself and my new abilities. Now all I needed was a little sleep, and I'd be fine. Or I would be if I could stay out of trouble, a forecast that never looked promising.

But Guy, bless his kind and considerate soul, would always be a worrywart. He wasn't overly pushy about it, so I didn't mind. Besides, he was really easy to distract. Which I did now by putting down my magazine and crawling straight into his lap.

He leaned his head against the back of the couch.

"I know what you're doing," he said as I settled on his thighs.

I pushed his hair back so that the forelock wasn't falling into his eyes the way it usually did. "Mm-hmm. I'm not subtle. It's something everybody loves about me. Is it working?"

Guy lifted his hand and wiggled it in a so-so gesture, but I could hear the way his heartbeat had picked up and I could see a smile twitching at the edges of his lips. He had the barest hint of a five o'clock shadow going on and his skin was a little gray with exhaustion, but even tired from a long day in the office and foiling a few bank robberies, he was still pretty gorgeous.

I laughed when he finally broke, grinning and tugging me closer. "Thought so," I said, kissing him.

His hand slid under the back of my shirt as the other tangled in my hair, which was still messy from my Chinese food encounters. He kissed me like we hadn't just seen each other the night before, like we might never see each other again—

Or he did until we both heard thumping on the wall. I sighed, my head dropping onto Guy's shoulder. "What is it this time?" I called through the wall.

"I have an early meeting tomorrow and have no interest in listening to your sexual shenanigans. Take it to his place!"

Which would involve going downtown. Granted, his place was a *lot* nicer than mine, closer to work, and he loved cooking so there would be breakfast, but it would also require moving and I was perfectly happy to remain right where I was. "Just put some headphones on," I said back, not bothering to raise my voice. Angélica could hear me perfectly.

Just like I could hear her muttered Portuguese insult in reply perfectly as well.

I left my forehead resting against Guy's shoulder. "Why did I agree to move in with the bossiest woman on the planet?"

"Because you can't afford both food and rent," he said. "What's her deal right now?"

"She's got investors coming in tomorrow," I said. "I normally *wouldn't care*," I said, raising my voice for emphasis, "but since I know it's a big day for her, I'll be nice this once."

"You can have the apartment to yourself this weekend," Angélica said.

I turned to Guy. "See? She's being nice in return."

He shook his head, his eyes amused behind the glasses. "You know I can't hear her when you guys talk through walls at regular volume like that's something normal people do."

"She says we've got this place for the weekend," I said, and dropped next to Guy on the couch. "She's probably spending it with that mystery boyfriend of hers that she refuses to tell me anything about. And I heard you call me that, Angélica."

Guy put his arm around my shoulders and pulled me close. "I guess we could watch the news," he said.

Watching the news invariably meant that he'd get alerted about some catastrophe in progress and feel ob-

ligated to rush off and defend against it. Or there would
be another story wondering what had happened to
Blaze, which would only make Guy frown. His brother
Sam had quit being War Hammer and had driven into
the sunset on a motorcycle. Not that I blamed him: discovering that his ex-girlfriend—originally thought to
be dead—had instead been experimented on and tor-
tured for years had to weigh heavily on the soul. With
Sam off on his spiritual journey, it had made sense for
Guy to take over the identity and the Chicago territory. Heroes went on hiatus and switched masks more
than even I knew, so all of us were surprised when the
media had latched on. As far as the rest of the world
knew, Blaze, Guy's previous superhero identity, had
simply vanished from Miami. And his whereabouts
were the biggest mystery apart from the identity of
the villain who had turned the Statute of Liberty into
a disco mirror ball. *Where's Blaze?* had become a catch-
phrase tossed around by media pundits everywhere.
They refused to let it die, so the last thing I wanted to
do was watch the news right now. I raised an eyebrow
at him.

"Or . . . I could fly us to my place?" he offered.

I grinned. "Let me get my stuff."

# CHAPTER 2

Every superhero has an origin story. Every supervillain, too, but that's not as important since I don't hang out with as many of those these days.

Take my roommate, Angélica. Her bus to a soccer game had crashed outside of her hometown and she'd woken up with the ability to hurtle herself across distances in the blink of an eye. Her soccer career was over before it had started, but she'd found work as a trainer at Davenport—the umbrella corporation that secretly controlled all superhero interests. Guy and his siblings had gotten their powers from an explosion. For my friend Vicki Burroughs—yes, *that* Victoria Burroughs—well, I didn't actually know her origin story because it changed every time she told it.

Only three people on the planet could claim they were given their powers intentionally. Two of them lived in my apartment (Angélica's origin story hadn't ended on the soccer field—she was later dosed with the same superpower-inducing serum I had been hit with, in order to save her life after she'd been poisoned). The third was in prison. Synthetic superheroes, which made us pretty interesting in our own right. The fact that Angélica and I had cut ties with Davenport made life a little difficult. The corporation and I were still on vague speaking terms, but Davenport had been responsible for throwing me in prison for a crime I hadn't committed. Now I wanted nothing to do with them, even though they were primarily responsible for helping those with new powers acclimate. It made finding a balance and trying to live my life very difficult, as I was no longer normal.

The new powers were pretty cool, though. All of the carbon in my body had been replaced by a synthetic isotope called Mobium, named after the scientist who had invented it. My metabolism had sped up to ridiculous levels, and I'd been enhanced: stronger than the average human, faster, theoretically more intelligent, with the ability to absorb superpowers from others. Which was why I could involuntarily teleport and why I technically could use Angélica's original powers to shift my momentum and cross distances faster than the eye could follow. We had no idea how the Mobium worked or why I picked up the new powers that I did, considering that I spent a lot of time with Guy and he had a passel of intriguing abilities I wouldn't mind having for myself, and I had nothing to show for it.

Judge all you like, but flight would be a useful ability.

Unfortunately, there were downsides. Dr. Mobius had been inadvertently killed when I'd blown up a Lodi Corp building, which meant that Angélica and I had no idea how any of our powers actually worked. And cutting myself off from Davenport meant I had fewer resources. It led to a lot of nights sitting up in my room, wondering what I had become. Mad scientists rarely wrote instruction manuals for their crazy inventions, even when those inventions were actual people.

But still, being kidnapped by Dr. Mobius and changed into a superhero had almost been a blessing. My life before getting superpowers wasn't all that enviable. But the thing I'd hated the most had been my job at *Mirror Reality* magazine, which was why I couldn't explain to my friends now why I'd chosen to go back.

The main office for all of Angus P. Vanderfeld's many magazines hadn't changed much in the couple of months I'd been away in Detmer supervillain prison and on the run from the law. It was still in the Shrewsbury building downtown, and thanks to my history of being taken hostage, it still had a great deal more security than the surrounding buildings. Several of the same workers were even still present, though there was a rotating roster of pretty faces hoping for a break—that one day Angus might declare them perfect for a modeling gig. I estimated about seven people actually kept the office functional, and even then, not well.

When I had come and asked for my job back, I'd almost seen something like relief in Angus's patrician, closed-off face. For a man who prided himself on get-

ting as many Botox shots as possible, it was rare to
see an actual expression from him. He'd jetted off to
Fashion Week the next day, leaving me with a gigantic
docket of backlogged work the wannabe models had
left undone.

Two months later, I had things under control.
When the call from security buzzed up to my desk,
I was between tasks, debating what to eat for my sev-
enth morning snack.

"Ms. Godwin, there's a Ms. Gunn requesting access."

Naomi was here? That was interesting. I checked
my phone, which apparently had been set on SILENT,
and scrolled through the text messages that I'd missed.

*u there?*
*gail cmon*
*gail gail gail*
*plz be there need to talk to u*
*whatever dropping by anyway*
*tell security to buzz me up already*

For somebody who wrote prize-winning articles for
the Domino and other respected publications, she certainly believed strongly in text-speak. "It's okay," I said
to Roland the security guard. "Can you give her a guest
pass? She should be on my okay list from now on."

"Got it."

Roland and I went way back, given how many times
we'd nodded tiredly to each other getting off too late.
I tugged my shoes on from where I'd kicked them off
and peeked into the cubicle next to me. I had to stand
on my tiptoes. "Your favorite reporter's here," I said.

Portia McPeak grumbled and didn't look up from her solitaire game. "She keeps turning me down for coffee. She's missed her chance."

"Her loss."

I headed for the elevator to wait for Naomi, figuring she'd be a minute chatting with the guard. She talked to *everybody* if she could get a chance. It made her a good reporter, but it also made going anywhere with her a little annoying.

I was wrong this time. She stepped off the elevator almost immediately, which meant whatever she was dropping by for had to be important.

"That was you at the Chinese food place on the news, wasn't it?" she asked right away, skipping greetings.

"No comment."

"So, yes?"

"I hear the guy's going to make a full recovery. I didn't even hit him that—I mean, the woman in the video didn't hit him that hard, and he still had the strength to throw a knife at her afterward."

Naomi grinned. Her hair, which had been in dreads the last time I'd seen her, was now crimped and gathered in a twist at the back of her neck. "You need better media management skills."

"Or not to talk to the media, but she keeps texting me. You're not actually here about the Chinese food robber, are you?"

"Luckily for you, nope. Got a spare office or something? We need to talk."

We went to one of the glass-walled conference

rooms. It didn't afford that much privacy, but at least none of my coworkers could listen in. They weren't used to me having visitors, so I spotted a couple curious looks as we walked past the cubicle farm. Luckily, only Portia knew who Naomi was, as she'd helped me break Naomi out of a Davenport facility a few months back.

"What's so urgent?" I asked, digging in the cabinet for snacks. "Is something literally on fire? New threat of apocalypse?"

"Only in San Francisco, and I bet Shark-Man has that under control."

I raised my eyebrows. Shark-Man never had anything under control.

"There aren't any listening devices in here, are there? I would have told you to come to my office, but—" She waved a hand in my general direction, which was fair. Hostage Girl walking into the Domino headquarters would have raised a few eyebrows. "And I'm pretty sure they've got the place bugged. Part of the gag order."

"Yes, how's life as a shill?" I asked. As part of Naomi learning the identities of several of its major superheroes, Davenport had pulled a few strings to get her a better job. Unfortunately, she had to follow a certain set of rules. She chafed at them constantly. Usually through long text message screeds sent to my phone at two a.m.

"It sucks, but what can you do?" Naomi pulled a battered red file folder from her hipster messenger bag and dropped it on the table. "This isn't going to be pleasant for you."

"Is it about Jeremy?" My ex of over a year had been electrocuted while saving the day. It had been heroic and downright stupid on his part, but it had led to powers. I hoped. Jeremy's situation was a new definition of limbo for me, and I didn't like it.

"No," Naomi said, shaking her head. "This is something else."

Armed with some of the fancy crackers we kept stocked for meetings and peanut butter that I hoped wasn't expired—not that it would matter against my own special biology—I sat down at the conference room table. Naomi flipped the file open. It only took one glance at the top page for me to grimace.

"You look like you smelled something awful," Naomi said.

"It's not that far out of the realm of possibility, not with him." The top page was photocopied from what looked like some kind of official dossier. *Christoph Mobius*, it read across the top, and it showed a picture of what could either be a man's face or a Halloween mask that had taken a wrong turn somewhere. Since I'd met the man, I knew it was the former, but some days I still had my doubts. I scowled at the picture. "Where did you g—wait, what are you doing?"

"What are you talking about?" Naomi began spreading out pages.

"Are you supposed to be looking into this? I thought Davenport cut you a very specific deal, and that deal included no snooping on Lodi Corp." Lodi had once been a competitor of Davenport's, but when I'd blown up their building and revealed they had a mole inside one of Davenport's offices, Davenport had dismantled Lodi Corp with frightening efficiency. I got the feeling they wanted all of this buried quietly and deeply, which meant Naomi was treading on dangerous ground.

She proved it by nodding. "I'm not supposed to be looking into this, duh."

"Naomi."

"Gail." Naomi stole a cracker and popped the whole thing in her mouth.

"This is why we're both always in trouble," I said, rubbing my forehead.

"It's not like Davenport would ever tell you any of this. And this has everything to do with you."

Well, when she put it that way. I looked at the cornucopia of information she'd spread all over the conference table. It shouldn't have surprised me that she would look hard into Lodi, considering how closely she was connected to it. Lodi had—via Mobius and his serum—created Brooklyn, alias Chelsea, the superpowered woman who'd hired Naomi to find Guy's and his brother Sam's weaknesses. When Naomi had discovered her new boss was a supervillain, she'd refused to turn over the information she found, and Brook had then tried to kidnap her. The circumstances behind Mobius's involvement with Lodi, however, were still a mystery. And Naomi, with her nose for information, would never rest until she had answers.

Given that her hunt for answers had dragged me into trouble before, though, I didn't feel like the caution on my part was overrated.

"All right, all right, fine," I said.

Naomi grinned. "You cave too easily."

"Shut up. What's so important that you had to blow up my phone and then race over, anyway? And, ugh, get this thing out of my face. I hate that guy." I turned the page with Mobius's face on it over. I'd spent long enough staring at his ugly mug when he'd strapped me to a table and dosed me with his serum. "Where's the fire, anyway? And is it literal?"

"Not literal. This—" Naomi tapped a page "—is where the fire is."

I picked up the page and skimmed the page. "Lodi's lab results for Mobium? Davenport will want that."

"They can get it the same place I did, if they really want it. But here, take a look at this one, and this one." She shoved two more pages over, and I read those just as quickly. "Chels—Brook's lab work. Some of it."

"This means nothing to me," I said, frowning. "Lodi was experimenting on her for years. So there are test results, so what?"

"Look at the notes section at the bottom of the page."

"What about it?"

Naomi reached into her messenger bag and pulled out a little leather-bound notebook. Somebody's personal journal, I realized, and then the smell of it hit my nostrils. Mobius's personal journal. "Add the notes to this," Naomi said, waving the journal at me, "and it says some things."

I took it warily. "Where did you get this?"

Naomi waved a hand. That was fine; I hadn't actually expected her to tell me.

I flipped through the journal. Mobius's handwriting wasn't easy to read: spiky and cramped like he'd been thinking faster than he could write, it filled every page to the very edge. "Do you want me to read all of this?" I asked, feeling a little sick. Apparently my issues over what he'd done to me hadn't vanished. Oh, joy. "Is there a CliffsNotes or something?"

"Once you get through the science and ravings about the Bears, it boils down to him ranting about the thing he hated."

"Lodi?" I asked, since they'd kind of kept him captive and used him for his giant brain.

Naomi shook her head. "Superheroes."

I scrunched my nose up. "What?"

"I know, I thought it was strange, too. If the man hated superheroes so much, why make more?"

"Lodi made him do it?"

"I don't think even Lodi could get past this level of mania, Gail." Naomi took the journal and flipped through the pages, a frown etched into her features. "He really hated you supertypes. On a deep, visceral level."

"And yet he created a serum that's added three of us to the population," I said. "I still say Lodi made him do it."

Naomi groaned. "You'd think you of all people would embrace conspiracy theories."

I raised my eyebrows. "Did you somehow miss the part where I was kidnapped over and over again for four years and never really wondered why?"

Naomi paused. "Okay, point. But something's hinky."

I wasn't sure I agreed. I'd done my time—literally—and even if I had doubts about what I was now, life had reached at least a minor equilibrium. I didn't want to poke at the Jenga pieces and send the tower toppling over. Not for a man who was definitely dead. "Where'd you get all of this stuff, anyway?"

"That's not important."

"Oh, but I bet it is."

Naomi's smile showed most of her teeth. "Not revealing my sources. I feel like this is significant. Mobius gave you your powers for a reason, right?"

"Right," I said. The reason I'd ended up with superpowers was so convoluted that some days I didn't even understand it myself, not even with the enhanced intellect. I'd become the very important but powerless piece in a large game of chess, meant to get Mobius's granddaughter, my friend Kiki, away from a Lodi spy within Davenport. We'd been successful in the end, but it gave me a headache to think about how it had all panned out. Jeremy had been the one to pay the biggest price. "Mobius did it so I'd help save Kiki, sort of. I still don't see why it's significant."

"I just think it is, that's all. I made copies for you."

"Really? You aren't worried I'll take them straight to Davenport?"

Naomi just gave me a long look.

"Point," I said, and took the sheaf of papers she passed over. "I'll look over these. If nothing else, maybe they'll answer questions about the Mobium."

"Started growing a tail yet?"

"Ha, ha," I said.

"I'm just saying, it could happen any day now."

"You suck." My phone screen lit up with a call from Guy, which was surprising. He rarely called during office hours. "Hold on a sec." I picked up the phone. "Hello?"

"Gail. Hey. Are you busy? Like, is there anything you can't miss?"

"Uh, not particularly, why?"

"How soon can you get to Davenport Tower?"

I blinked. Davenport Tower was in New York City. "With or without a 'porter? Because I'm not exactly cleared for that."

"I'll get you cleared."

"Guy, what's wrong?"

"It'll be easier to explain when you get here," Guy said, sounding frustrated. "Hurry, though. Nobody's hurt, exactly. Just—yeah, hurry. See you soon."

And I was left with a dead call.

"Cryptic," I said, shoving the phone in my pocket. "I have to go."

"Is it trouble?" Naomi was already gathering her papers and shoving them back into the file folder. "Superhero trouble? Can I come?"

"Yeah, Davenport would take one look at your credentials and laugh."

"Their loss. I'll walk you out."

Which would only give her a chance to badger me, I knew, but whatever. "Let's swing by my desk on the way out. I have a feeling I'm going to need better shoes."

Because Guy had sounded urgent, I skipped the 'L' and took a cab. In the Willis Tower—which I still wanted to call the Sears Tower—I took the elevator to the forty-seventh floor and stepped into a lobby I'd once helped decimate with a close enemy and some even closer friends. It said DARTMOOR INCORPORATED on a large sign, but this was a Davenport facility. Everything was laid out exactly the same at each waystation, down to the grumpy guard blocking the way to non-Davenport personnel.

The security guard gave me an uninspired look. "ID?"

"Really, Marsh? We go through this every week."

"State your business." He made a come-on motion with his fingers, holding his hand out for my ID, which I passed over with a sigh.

"I'm going to Davenport Tower," I said. "Do we really have to go through the whole routine? I'm kind of in a hurry."

Marsh gave me another unimpressed look.

"Fine," I said. "Not my business if you want to

waste time giving Abbott and Costello a run for their money."

"State your business," Marsh said again, reaching for the taser on his belt.

"I'm traveling to headquarters," I said. "I'm on the approved list."

Marsh handed my ID back and looked at the screen in front of him. "Step up to the scanner."

I'd already stepped over, which made him glare at me. I held my palm over the scanner and let it prick the side of my finger. GODWIN, GAIL flashed over the little screen, listing my stats. I winced a little at my cholesterol count. The body scan and Marsh poking through my bag took a few seconds longer. I'd already learned to ditch anything he could find remotely suspicious, like the really cool-looking compact mirror I'd bought. Apparently gold lamé was a terrorist threat these days. Today, he shoved the bag back at me with a dissatisfied look.

"You're cleared," Marsh said, looking grumpy about the prospect. He handed over the same flimsy badge I wore every visit. "Go on through."

"A pleasure as always, Marsh."

Not even a single grunt from him in reply. Rude.

The 'porter responsible for zapping me from Chicago to New York, at least, was polite. 'Porting over long distances always left me buzzing and gave me a small headache, but I was able to pay attention when the receptionist instructed me to head to Medical. Oh, that was not good.

The first time they'd brought me into Davenport,

I'd been taken straight there. My appointment had been with Cooper—a man who, it turned out, was a Lodi Corp spy and was trying to find a way to discreetly kill me the entire time. Which partially explained the reason I always wanted to drag my feet on the way to this department.

The secretaries at the front waved me past. "Kiki said to send you straight in."

I nodded at them and headed back to Kiki's office. Seeing no sign of her, I moved on to the examination rooms.

Jackpot.

"Gail, hi." Guy, who was sitting on the cot with his elbows propped on his knees, looked up to give me a tight smile. He, Angélica, and Kiki were all gathered in the room, looking tense. "You made it."

"With only minimal harassment from my favorite security guard. What's going on?"

I looked at Kiki, as her heartbeat had elevated above the others. She wore her typical uniform—the white polo shirt that sneered at wrinkles, the dark blue Davenport pants—but, unusually, her hair was down from its athletic ponytail. It hung over her face now as she sat at the computer, body bowed forward as though somebody had punched her in the stomach. It made me belatedly freeze in my tracks.

"Is Jeremy okay?" I asked. The entire trip over, the only conclusion I had come to was that something must have changed with Jeremy's situation. Why else would they have called me to Medical?

Kiki raised her head, and the sight of her red-rimmed

eyes sent a bolt of fear straight through my gut. "He's fine. Or there's been no change, at any rate," she said, wiping at her eye with a thumb. "This is something else."

"Has somebody died?" I asked.

Angélica, who was watching Kiki's face carefully, said, "The opposite, actually."

Somebody had come back to life? There could only be one culprit, and it sent a curl of fear all the way down to my soles. The instinct to run came on surprisingly strong, considering I was surrounded by multiple people that I would trust to save my life in a heartbeat. "It's Cooper, isn't it?" I asked. "He's back?"

"No," Kiki said, shaking her head fervently.

I breathed out in relief.

"No, it's not Cooper," Angélica said. "But you won't like—"

She was interrupted by the hiss of the door opening behind me. Already on edge, I whipped about, my fists going up.

"Oh, roomie! You're here, too."

I looked up into the face of my mortal enemy as she was dragged into the room by two men in Detmer Prison uniforms. Brooklyn Gianelli—known to the world as the pink-and-white-clad supervillain named Chelsea—looked like the time in prison had actually done her some good, if the smirk and swagger were anything to judge by. She had her hands clasped palm-to-palm, locked in plastic cuffs of some type.

I turned and looked at my supposed friends and significant other. "Explain," I said.

# CHAPTER 3

"Long time, no see." Brook dropped onto a chair and kicked her feet out. How she managed to look completely nonchalant handcuffed and surrounded by security guards, I had no idea. Brook made seeming casual and bored in the face of danger look like a natural superpower.

Except the last time she'd been in the room with Guy, she hadn't looked bored or casual. She'd been doing her best to kill him, since she held a grudge against Guy's older brother Sam, and she hadn't been too picky about which Bookman she'd like to kill. I automatically took a step to the right, planting myself between Brook and Guy.

My ex-cellmate smiled at me, tilting her head. "The shrinks cleared that trigger right out of me."

"I don't believe you," I said. I'd been to Detmer Maximum Security Prison, Brook's current place of residence.

Granted, I'd been innocent—it was a long story, but it boiled down to Rita Detmer setting me up to look like a criminal, all so she could beat me up in the name of teaching me how to save Kiki—and Brook definitely wasn't. Either way, Detmer was more like a day spa than a prison. Not much focus had been placed on actually rehabilitating said supervillains, which was a shame. Brook, who'd spent years in a cage as Lodi Corp's science experiment, could have used some real therapy. "What is she doing here?" I looked around at the others in the room.

"You'll see." Kiki looked unsettled; I could hear her heartbeat speeding up slightly, which did nothing to reassure me. Kiki waved a hand to activate the monitor behind her. "This came in this morning. The techs are working on tracing the source."

A face filled the screen. Somebody had shoved the camera in close, grossly distorting its proportions, but my stomach still dropped. Dr. Christoph Mobius filled the entire screen, wearing a dirty flannel shirt and holding a newspaper. My breath stuttered to a halt in my chest. I had a copy of the same paper on my desk at work. I'd picked it up outside my 'L' stop that morning.

"You told me he was dead," I said. "You said that when I blew up Lodi—"

"I was wrong," Kiki said in a strangled voice, which made sense. The man on the screen was her grandfather, after all.

On the screen, a gloved hand reached in and poked Mobius's shoulder when his eyelids drooped. "Speak," said a modulated voice, and I frowned.

"To whoever gets this message," Dr. Mobius said, glaring into the camera and making sweat spring up on the back of my neck, "this is a ransom video. I demand to speak only to the one named—must I really stick to this mundane script?" He looked over the top of the camera and presumably at the person behind it. "Why are there so many words? It's utterly banal."

I didn't flinch when the hand appeared again, striking him across the face, though Kiki did.

"As I was saying," Mobius said, with a little spittle and blood trickling down his chin, "I will speak only with the one called Chelsea. I believe you can find her in Detmer. Any attempts to contact me made by anybody other than Chelsea will end with me—Dr. Christoph Mobius—losing my life."

This time, Kiki whimpered. I had to look away and remind myself that the man might be one of the worst people on the planet, but he was also her grandfather.

"I will be in touch within twenty-four hours. If anybody but Chelsea answers, there will be—"

A green-and-yellow blast hit the monitor, splitting it in half. Instantly, everybody in the room was on their feet, fists and other weapons pointed at Brook. She stood by the table, one arm up and extended toward the TV. Her chest heaved. She had gone bone-white and her eyes were suspiciously bright, but I ignored these details to focus on the fact that the whirling vortex in her palm, where her stinging power beams emerged, was wide open.

"Get on the ground!" one of the guards said, surging forward.

I saw Brook begin to turn and dove, tackling the guard to the ground. The beam washed over my back and did nothing but tickle. Of everybody in the room, I was the only one her stinging powers couldn't hurt.

Brook gasped and jumped back, pointing both hands toward the ceiling. "Davenport told me he was dead," she said.

I climbed off of the guard and exchanged a look with Guy. Anger was par for the course with Brook, but this was something different. This verged on hysteria. If she thought she could get away with it, I imagined, she would be barreling through the wall and flying for shelter.

"Any idea who has him?" I asked.

Kiki shook her head. "All we have is the video."

Angélica turned to Brook's guards. "You two wait outside until we're done. We've got one Class B and three Class Cs, we're more than capable of handling her."

They argued, which I felt was foolish—Detmer guards, traditionally, didn't have superpowers at all.

I tuned them out, sitting down so hard that the chair creaked underneath me. So Dr. Mobius was alive. We'd all thought he had been in the Lodi facility I had blown up while escaping from Cooper. The thought of having killed people—I knew I had, since there was no way the building had been completely empty—had given me more than a couple sleepless nights since. Learning that my creator had been among them had been such a mental minefield that I'd been better off suppressing the feelings, and had done so with vigor.

And now that he was alive and apparently being held for ransom, I *really* didn't know how to feel. I looked at where Angélica and Kiki were arguing with the guards. Brook stood behind them, breathing hard, rage plainly written on her face as she stared at the shattered remains of the TV.

"Brook's not taking this well," I said to Guy. "Not that I would expect her to. Mobius experimented on her for a long time. Somebody at least should have warned her."

"It's weird to hear you on Brook's side," Guy said.

"Cellmates for life," I said, though I wasn't feeling much humor. Purposely creating new superheroes was illegal. Holding people against their will and experimenting on them, as Mobius and Lodi had with Brook, was more than illegal: it was reprehensible. Seeing the last of Lodi hadn't exactly left me heartbroken.

But now somebody had Dr. Mobius and knew that somebody at Davenport would be willing to try to save him.

"Did they send this video straight to you?" I asked Kiki.

Angélica, Brook, and Kiki all turned to look at me in surprise.

"Well?" I asked.

Kiki shook her head. "No, to Davenport in general. Eddie brought me in on this one because of my family ties."

I wrinkled my nose. The CEO of Davenport Industries and I had a few issues with each other. They involved me telling him to go have sex with a goat, and him taking away my rights and sending me to prison. One time I'd puked on his shoes. It had been a highlight.

"Eddie also authorized Brook's temporary release," Kiki continued. "She doesn't have to participate—"

"Let him die," Brook said. "In fact, find him and I'll take care of it myself. Hell, I'll do it for free and then I'll fly myself back to Detmer for the extended sentence. Happily."

"What *is* it with that place?" Guy asked under his breath.

I hadn't gotten around to telling him that Detmer was more day spa than prison, but now wasn't the time to get into it.

Kiki cleared her throat. "Lodi was forcing Mobius—"

"I don't give a damn! He let them do this to me!" Brook said.

"And when he escaped, he took you with him," Kiki said.

"That doesn't make up for any of it."

"They can commute your prison sentence," Angélica said, her voice neutral. Brook knew I had Mobium—she'd discovered it when I'd proven immune to her angry stinging-bee beams—but she had no idea that Angélica did, too. "Dr. Mobius would be a valuable asset. If you or Gail get sick, he may be the only person who could help."

"Like I give a damn about *Gail* getting sick," Brook said.

"Right back at you," I said, and Brook glared at

me. "But I've got the upgraded, more stable version of Mobium he probably didn't want to give to Lodi. How long before you start breaking down into itty-bitty pieces?"

I didn't need superhearing to catch the obscenity Brook muttered at me. "That man should die," she said. "I want no part in saving him."

"What if I offer a trade?" Guy said, lifting his head.

"There's nothing you have that I want," Brook said, shifting her glare from me to him. "Nothing your brother has, either, so don't even try."

"Not him," Guy said, and this time the falling sensation in my stomach came from an entirely new source. I was not, I realized, going to like whatever he was about to say. "But Petra—"

Brook's hands clenched into fists. Petra Bookman, her best friend from high school and Guy's older sister, had been missing a year longer than she had. Everybody had thought Brook was dead. Nobody was sure Petra was. Sam had devoted his life to finding Petra, at the expense of Brook, who'd been kidnapped and had wound up at Lodi Corp when Sam had failed to save her. Since Sam had been the reason she'd been in trouble in the first place, I didn't blame her for hating his guts.

"You want to find her, don't you?" Guy asked. Brook's fists began to shake, but Guy's eyes remained steady on her face.

"Guy," I said. I really didn't like where this was going.

"You go along, help us retrieve Mobius, and we can look for her together," Guy said.

Brook's face was completely unreadable.

"Can I have a word?" I asked Guy, grabbing his wrist and pulling him to his feet with my not inconsequential strength. "Outside? In the hallway? We'll just be a minute."

I figured Kiki and Angélica could handle Brook in her current state. If not, well, we had bigger problems. Luckily, the hallway outside was completely empty of other Davenport staff, including the guards we'd kicked out of the room. I whipped around to look at Guy. "Do you have a death wish?"

He raised his eyebrows.

"Guy, that woman has a berserker switch that could go off at any second and it's definitely tripped by all things Bookman. Isn't that just a tiny bit disconcerting for you?"

"It's not exactly something that gives me the warm fuzzies," Guy said, frowning. "But she wants nothing to do with rescuing Mobius, and we need her."

"I barely want anything to do with rescuing Mobius," I said, "and he held her captive for a hell of a lot longer than he did for me. That doesn't mean you should offer to go on a wild-goose chase."

"It might not be a wild-goose chase," Guy said, but he didn't look like he really believed the words coming out of his mouth.

"Weren't you telling me Sam lost years of his life looking for Petra?" I asked.

"I'm a lot more levelheaded than my brother," Guy said. "Are you upset about that or upset I didn't consult you before making that offer?"

"I can be upset about multiple things," I said, as that was definitely the truth. "But in this case, I'm a little upset you didn't mention to me that you were thinking about working with the woman who nearly killed you, and who did in fact kill Angélica for a little while."

"She needs some closure about Petra," Guy said, though he looked pained.

"Petra doesn't even make top ten on Brook's list of issues, and she might never get closure. You might never get that, either, and on top of disappointing both of you, that could send her around the bend again. You do realize that, right?"

"Trust me, if there's one thing I do understand, it's that," Guy said, and he had a point. He'd had to live with the reality of his missing sibling for all of these years. "But she's not going to agree any other way."

"Is that such a bad thing? Dr. Mobius is not a good guy, remember?"

"You're just going to let a kidnapped man stay kidnapped, Gail?"

I wrinkled my nose because he had a point. People being held captive and ransomed were my own personal hang-up. "Ugh! Why do you have to be right?"

Guy laughed and folded me into a giant hug.

"I'm kicking him in the nuts as soon as we rescue him," I said.

"Fine by me," he said.

I leaned back enough so that I could poke him in the chest. "And if you're going with Brook, I'm going with you. I don't trust her. Not negotiable."

He gave me a genuinely surprised look. "I thought you were going to, anyway?"

"Oh," I said, my shoulders visibly deflating. "Okay, then. Be sensible about it."

He kissed the side of my head. "Always."

But before we could go back in, I grabbed his wrist. "Wait, do you even know where to begin searching for Petra?"

Guy looked at the floor, not meeting my eyes. "I may have looked into some things over the years."

"You don't have, like, one of those TV show conspiracy boards with the strings and everything, do you?"

"No. Nothing that extreme. Just some files, and having some fresh eyes on those might help. Brook hasn't agreed yet. I doubt she will, actually."

I squeezed his wrist. Thankfully, he was pretty much indestructible, as I sometimes had a hard time judging my new strength.

"I'll do it," Brook said the second we walked back into the room. Her eyes were suspiciously wet and I noticed that a couple more pieces of the TV had been shattered. Angélica also looked far more annoyed than she had when we'd left.

I pulled up short. "Seriously?"

"I don't want anything to do with Mobius when we find him. You leave me alone in a room with him, I will kill him." Her voice stayed deathly calm.

If nothing else, statements like that explained why she was currently in prison.

"Got it," Kiki said, looking a little weak-kneed with relief. "You won't have to deal with him. You just have to help us get him back."

"In exchange for looking for Petra," Brook said, glaring at Guy.

"You've got my word on that," he said. He held a hand out to shake and I wanted to roll my eyes at him. Didn't he understand where Brook's powers originated?

Luckily, she only shook his hand. "Then let's do this."

I had a very bad feeling about this.

But that wasn't unusual, really. Not with my life.

# CHAPTER 4

The worst part about hostage situations—that brief, pants-wetting moment of terror at the beginning aside—wasn't the threats or even the pain or listening to the villains lose themselves in the poetry of their own terrible soliloquies. No, years and years of dealing with the villains of Chicago had taught me that there was something far worse: waiting.

It was bad enough as a hostage, hanging out and anticipating that moment Blaze would come flying in, fists up and ready to face any number of weapons to come save me. Granted, I'd had my coping methods, which had been primarily daydreaming about all the TV I'd catch up on in the hospital. On the other side of the equation, waiting for the ransom call to come in, it was ten times worse.

"Gail," Angélica said, and I got the feeling she was laughing at me—because she was; it was one of her favorite things to do. "It's been less than a day. This is . . . what would you say? Peanuts. This is peanuts compared to what we usually deal with."

"I know." I hit the punching bag with a fluttering combination, pulling my punches because I didn't want to destroy Angélica's equipment. Her gym, the Power House, was theoretically equipped for Class Cs, but I'd destroyed a punching bag the day she'd opened and she had yet to forgive me. "It's the lack of information I hate most. Who's doing this? Why? Where's Mobius been? Why is this happening now?"

"Mm," Angélica said.

"And I know—" I hit the bag again, a little harder, and she continued to brace it "—Davenport won't share any info. The only reason either of us know about this at all is because of Guy."

"And Kiki, don't forget."

I sneaked a glance at my trainer and roommate out of the corner of my eye. If I had complicated feelings about Dr. Mobius, my creator, Angélica's own thoughts on Kiki had to be a mess. Kiki had been the one to give her the Mobium, in order to save her life. Angélica still had her original powers, but they interacted strangely with the Mobium, and she didn't use them as much now. I knew it frustrated her, but she never complained. Not to me, anyway. Even though we'd cut ties with Davenport, she still viewed our relationship the way she had while we were there, with the same determination to see me succeed and also to protect me. But how much of that loss did she blame on Kiki? Or did she blame Kiki at all? I'd never been able to tell.

Midafternoon on a Saturday meant the gym was semipacked. Angélica had used some start-up capital to gut an older warehouse not far from our apartment. She'd set up several boxing rings next to speed bags, punching bags, and weight training equipment. She had a room dedicated to treadmills and ellipticals, one I didn't use as often. Now that I could run for ages, I preferred to be outside, sneakers pounding against the pavement and the wind in my hair. But I made plenty of use of the rest of the gym, particularly the boxing rings. Usually with Angélica herself.

I hit the bag, a one-two punch followed by an uppercut, and danced back. "Seriously, though, why now?"

"I have no idea, Gail," Angélica said.

"No theories?"

"They'd be theories and nothing more, and not actually all that satisfying."

I wrinkled my nose at her. "You're being all Mr. Miyagi levels of inscrutable today."

"Am I?"

"I'm just saying, you're maybe taking this mentor thing a little far. Theatrically so."

"Mm," Angélica said, and I threw a wild punch at her forehead.

She dodged easily and laughed. "You're too easy."

"So I've been told."

"Now can we talk about what's really bothering you?" Angélica asked.

I scowled and hit the bag hard enough to make it swing lazily, even with Angélica bracing it. "I'm worried about Guy. I don't like him working with Brook. She's dangerous. And no, before you say anything, I am not jealous that my boyfriend's working with another woman."

"Considering his usual crime-fighting partner is an actual supermodel and that never seems to bother you," Angélica said, "I didn't think you were. Of course, I might change my mind, since jealousy is the first place your brain went. Are you jealous?"

"No," I said, jabbing first at the bag and then at her.

She dodged. "You sound a little jealous. Maybe it's not Brook you're jealous of, but Guy."

The idea was so absurd it made me laugh. "What the hell?"

She tried to sweep my legs out from under me. I blocked and made my counterattack, which drove her back a foot. Twenty seconds later, she had me in an armlock. "Hey, I've heard what prison roommates sometimes get up to. Just saying."

"Oh my god, I hope you're joking." I tapped out and squared off against her again, waiting for the inevitable attack. Angélica believed in turning any situation into a learning opportunity for sparring, even making scrambled eggs in the kitchen at two in the morning. Admittedly, food had proved to be a good motivator in that case.

Right now, though, she didn't strike. Instead, she sighed at me. "What are you doing, Gail?"

"Hopefully kicking your ass."

The snort and the reproachful look really didn't go well together, but Angélica tried. "You're a perfectly capable fighter," she said, folding her arms over her chest and looking down her nose at me. She was only, like, an inch taller than me, so it was an impressive feat to pull off. "You need to be working on something else, and we both know it."

I scowled and stretched. "I really don't feel like repeatedly jumping off a roof right now."

"You landed in a dumpster. That doesn't inspire you to work on your phasing?"

Phasing was difficult and it felt more impossible to control than 'porting, which I actually could not control at all. To phase, I needed to be in motion to start, and it was a matter of altering my momentum to "throw" me farther and faster than I could move regularly. A skilled phaser like Angélica made it seem like 'porting by moving from one side of a large space to another in the blink of an eye. I kicked the toe of my sneaker against the ground in annoyance. "I'll get it eventually."

"Not unless you work on it. Right now would be a good time."

"Work on what?" said a new voice behind me.

I straightened up to my full height—as paltry as it was—and swiveled on my heel. "Nothing important."

Jessica Davenport raised an eyebrow at me. "Your trainer doesn't seem to think it's 'nothing important.'"

"*Thank* you," Angélica said, but I could tell she'd gone stiff, like she was wary.

That made sense. As the daughter of Kurt Davenport, Jessie owned half of Davenport Industries and was therefore one of the richest women in the world. She'd inherited more than money from her father—Kurt Davenport was also the original Raptor. He was dead now, but the mantle had been passed down to the woman picking her way across Angelica's cramped gym.

If there was anybody in the room to be wary of, it would be her.

"No, really, it's nothing. I can work on it later," I said to Jessie. I'd gotten to know her when she'd hunted me down after my escape from Detmer. She'd also rescued me from Cooper—but only after using me as bait to find out what he was up to. Our relationship status on all social media networks remained firmly in the "Complicated" zone. I didn't consider her an enemy, but we weren't exactly friends. "What brings you to Chicago? Miss me that much?"

Jessie actually looked partially amused, for once. "I assure you, any day without you is one I consider that much dimmer."

"Is that Wordsworth?" I asked.

"Not quite." She turned to look at all of the activity around us. "Audra kicked me out of my base for the morning. She said that I was annoying her, so I thought I might see if you were up for a bit of sparring."

I squinted at her. "Your assistant has the power to kick you out?"

"It's never wise to cross the woman who knows

your social security number better than you do. You mind?" She nodded at the nearest ring.

I glanced over my shoulder at Angélica, who'd been weirdly silent. She gave me a shrug.

"Sure, I guess," I said. I kicked off my shoes and hauled myself over the ropes in one easy motion. I'd sparred with Jessie before, the second time she'd dropped by to scope out the Power House. The first time Jessie had dropped by, it had been a shock. After all, Angélica's gym was small-time, and Jessie was the Raptor, one of the scariest people I knew. I still had no idea what her powers were. At least sparring with her would give me another chance to figure it out.

Angélica surprised me by jumping up on the edge of the ring and grabbing my hoodie, tugging me back to the ropes. "Remember, it's just sparring. Pull your punches."

"Yes, Mr. Miyagi."

She cuffed the back of my head and called me a rude word in Portuguese, but she smiled.

Jessie climbed through the ropes on the other side, movements a little slow. When she didn't wrap up her hands, I sighed and began to unwrap my own. I preferred gloves on, but Jessie called the shots.

With anybody else, I might have made a crack about the loser buying the beer. I wasn't nearly that comfortable with the Raptor.

"So what are you avoiding, Ms. Godwin?" Jessie asked.

"You really can just call me Gail, you know. I don't mind."

Jessie only gave me a small ghost of a smile.

"I'm avoiding being having to repeatedly jump off a roof for three hours with nothing to show for it but a lot of bruises," I said, watching her stretch. "It seems the powers I absorb I can only use subconsciously. And maybe that's for the best, really."

"A warrior never turns down an opportunity to better herself."

"I'm an assistant editor," I said. That had been my official job title before my inadvertent hiatus while I'd been in prison, anyway. We hadn't really negotiated the new details.

"Even so." Jessie folded one hand over the other, clasped in front of her, and bowed shortly at the waist.

I returned the bow, and had to duck very quickly as she attacked almost immediately. I heard the whistle of air over my head as her fist missed me, and then I was too busy dodging and blocking to do much but focus on fighting off the next blow. As ever, she fought in vicious spurts. She laid into me with a flurry of kicks and hits that I blocked (for the most part), then swung out when I tried to jab back at her. In a flash, she yanked the hood of my sweat-shirt over my eyes.

"Dammit!"

Her foot snapped into my solar plexus, forcing me back onto the ropes. I didn't bother to shove the hood off my face; my hearing picked her up perfectly as she followed that up with a haymaker. I closed my eyes and sidestepped. I heard her jump back as I tried a roundhouse kick. She landed oddly heavily for a woman who was one of the best martial artists in the world.

When I tried to yank the hood off, it didn't budge.

"What did you do to me?" I asked.

"Evening the odds. No rules in the ring, remember?"

"Stacking the odds, you mean." I grumbled a few obscenities. It wasn't the first time I'd had to fight blind. Hell. The last person to make me do that—Jessie's mother, Rita Detmer—hadn't nearly been this nice about it. I didn't bother trying to fix the hood anymore. It seemed wiser to focus on listening to her.

For a minute or two, I even held my own. But a crackle of static caught me off guard, something slammed into my midsection and zapped hard, and she had me in a headlock.

"Ugh," I said, reaching out blindly to tap out.

When she released whatever sticking formula she'd used to glue my hood over my face and I could see again, I looked up into her grinning face. "Are you ever going to fight fair?"

"If it gets my ass kicked, no. Are you ever going to stop whining about it?"

"Maybe," I said, more than a little grumpy. Losing sucked.

Laughter pealed out from the side of the ring, and I looked over to discover that not only had I lost, but I'd had an even bigger audience than I'd thought. I had no idea when Vicki had arrived. Hopefully she hadn't seen too much of me getting my ass handed to me by a woman twice my age. "Nice form, mentee," Vicki said as I yanked off the whole hoodie. "The hood's a good look for you. Maybe that should be your new uniform."

"I don't want a uniform," I said.

Vicki pouted. She wore her own uniform, the black bodysuit that would have enabled Plain Jane to blend in to any shadow if it weren't for the brightness of the white mask currently hooked to her hip. "You should have one, though. You're too witty not to be on the front lines. I could design you something."

"Get in line," I said, thinking about Raze.

Vicki turned to grin at Jessie. "Raptor."

Jessie nodded back. "Plain Jane."

"Guess Chicago's a happening place today," Vicki said, leaning over and digging her elbows into the top rope. "What brings you into town? Please tell me it's to humiliate Gail."

"I had other business, but that was the primary objective, yes."

I gave Jessie a little bit of a side-eye, wondering how much truth there was to that statement. Ever since our adventure blowing up the Lodi Corp building together, she'd taken a weird interest in me. This wasn't the first sparring match I'd endured that had some kind of lesson attached. I had no idea *why*, though.

"And you?" Jessie asked, looking at Vicki's uniform.

"Oh, I'm here all the time," Vicki said. "Sometimes I use my fame for good. Especially to help my friend. If people find out Plain Jane works out at the Power House, they're gonna flock to this place."

I snorted. Vicki liked Angélica okay, but Angélica seemed to find her bothersome.

"That's surprisingly benevolent of you," Jessie said.

"I know, right?" Vicki's smile could light up billboards—and did, all over the world. "Gonna go again? That was really funny—I could stand to see another round or five."

I was saved not by the bell but by Angélica, who came hurtling out of the office with a look on her face that made all three of us straighten up. "Suit up," Angélica said, looking at me. "Our ransomer just got in touch."

"*Finally.*" I vaulted over the ropes and headed for the locker room, where Angélica kept body armor for situations like this.

"Gail. Catch."

I barely had time to catch the object Jessie threw my way, and blinked in puzzlement at the belt in my hands. It had about fifteen little pouches.

Raptor's famous utility belt.

"Are you sure?" I asked. After all, we were just dropping off a ransom payment, and Jessie likely had thousands of dollars of tech buried in these pouches.

"I've got more," she said, waving at me. "You keep it. You might need it."

I hoped not, but with my luck, she probably had a point. I slung it over my shoulder and loped off, calling a thanks over my shoulder. It was time to meet my maker. Again. And probably save him, too.

# CHAPTER 5

"Is this kidnapper serious?" I asked as I stepped to the edge of the building and looked down at the swirling mass of orange traffic cones and pedestrian traffic below us.

Vicki, who'd taken up residence against a nearby pole and was slouching attractively, mask in place, scoffed. "What exactly is your problem with Union Station? Other than all of the people in a potential supervillain's crosshairs?" The last was clearly an afterthought.

I gestured indignantly at the pavement below. "Traffic!"

"We flew over it," Vicki said.

"That's not the point. It's the principle of the thing."

But Angélica frowned at me. "You don't even drive."

"Principle," I said again, and folded my arms over my chest.

While I'd been at the gym, the ransom notice had come to Davenport in an unmarked envelope, delivered to the Chicago waystation in the Willis Tower. Kiki had texted Angélica a picture of it, likely against orders, so we'd managed to beat the Davenport contingent to the scene. We had time, of course, since the payment wasn't supposed to be dropped for another quarter hour. But I chafed against the overly public location of the drop site and the fact that I'd always hated Union Station.

That's right. The jerk who had Mobius had picked Union Station on a prime train-and-bus-travel day. That spoke either of genius—there was no way we could reliably cover every exit—or sadism because who even wanted to brave the construction around that place, anyway? I placed my bets on it being both, honestly.

"Hey, mentee, chin up," Vicki said. "If it all goes to pot, we'll probably get to see some action. You can show off those new phasing moves Angie's been telling me about."

"Don't call me that," Angélica said without looking away from the street.

Vicki pushed her mask up and smirked. She'd brought me into Davenport that first day. Though she hadn't been slated to receive one for a while, they'd assigned her to be my mentor, and the fact that I'd flipped Davenport the bird and had peaced out didn't absolve Vicki of her duties, as far as she was concerned. Whenever she wasn't doing car commercials in Japan or punching foes in the face, she liked to drop by my apartment and dispense what she considered helpful advice.

I didn't have the heart to tell her that being a supermodel by day and a superhero by night wasn't as relatable an experience as she thought.

"The phasing is . . ." I chewed my lower lip while I thought of a proper term for it. "Not going that well."

"Aw." Vicki's friendly punch probably would have knocked somebody less sturdy off of the roof. "You'll get there."

"Thanks." I rubbed my shoulder.

"They're here," Angélica said, and Vicki and I turned as one. Quietly, we watched the group approach on foot. All of them were dressed in plain clothing, dark jackets and black pants.

"Is it as obvious to you that Brook did not come alone as it is to me?" I asked.

"Yup," Angélica said, and Vicki nodded.

"They're going to scare the kidnapper away before Brook even gets a chance to drop the money off."

Vicki snorted. "Four million dollars? He knows she's totally not alone. This is us jumping through his hoops and he knows it. Or she. Could be a she."

"Yay feminism," Angélica said in a deadpan.

From a distance, I recognized the two bringing up the rear of the group. I hadn't expected Kiki to stay away from anything involving her grandfather, but I'd thought she would be on the rooftop with us, quasi-illegally spying on a Davenport op. But no, there she was in the thick of things, talking to the tactical team. The woman next to her wore a trench coat, but I frowned to see white leggings sticking out underneath it.

"They're making Brook do the drop in uniform?" I asked. She had picked such an odd choice for her Chelsea supervillain attire, opting for blinding pink and white that had seemed much softer than the rest of her. Sometimes I wondered why she hadn't picked yellow and green to match her powers. Maybe she just liked pink. I hadn't exactly asked her about it while we'd been glaring at each other across the cell in Detmer. "Why?"

"The kidnapper asked for Chelsea," Angélica said.

"And we aren't worried she'll send people screaming when they see her?"

"It's been months since we had a Chelsea attack and she didn't cause *too* much damage," Vicki said.

I looked sideways at her. Brook and an assorted pack of minions had once leveled a shopping mall. With me, Vicki, and Angélica still inside. She'd been trying to get to Naomi at the time, as Naomi'd had information that Brook had needed to get revenge on Sam.

Vicki noticed my stare and pushed her shoulders up to her ears in a *what can you do?* motion. "On the supervillain scale, one building is practically do-gooder territory."

"Supervillains are so freaking weird," I said, shaking my head.

Luckily, the crowds outside moved quickly, eager to get inside and away from the cutting wind Lake Michigan threw at the city. Ice covered the sidewalks, which meant most people watched their footing and not the tops of the buildings around them. I saw Brook's head swivel, checking the crowd. She held her cowl in her hands but seemed oddly reluctant to put it on.

"Remember," Angélica said, looking from Vicki to me, "we're here to observe."

"And kick ass as needed," Vicki said.

"But to observe *first*," Angélica said.

Vicki muttered her opinion of that under her breath. Angélica and I could both hear perfectly thanks to the Mobium, but we both chose to ignore her. Down on the ground, Brook pulled on the Chelsea cowl and shed the trench coat. She took the duffel bag Kiki held and flew off.

My stomach twisted. I didn't trust Brook any farther than I could throw her. Actually, I didn't trust Brook as far as I *could* throw her. "I'd have thought they needed a bigger bag for four mil," I said.

Those had been the demands: four million, unmarked, nonsequential bills, no bugs or trackers. Come alone. Union Station at noon. *Or Dr. Mobius dies* had been scrawled in messy handwriting underneath. Our kidnapper wasn't one for pleasantries, but I was okay with that, considering that one time a kidnapper had let Guy know he had me via a song and dance number broadcast all over Chicago's TV stations. It wasn't a memory I cherished. Heavy-weight card stock and drop-site coordinates were something of a relief.

We still had five minutes until she was supposed to make the drop. Now it became a waiting game of hoping that Brook didn't abscond with the money and stab us all in the back.

"What are the odds Brook's in on this, again?" I asked.

Vicki shrugged.

I scanned the sky for Guy, looking for the fluttering half cape that was War Hammer's trademark look. Vicki on her own was more than enough muscle for this operation, but having Guy around would have been nice. His text had said he was on his way, so he should be there soon.

"Two minutes," Angélica said, looking up from her watch. I began counting backward from sixty in my head. Vicki remained obviously bored and loose-limbed between us. I fiddled with the balaclava in my hand and adjusted the belt Jessie had given me. "One minute."

Though they were both playing it cool, I heard the soft relieved breaths my friends made when Brook rounded the corner. The pink-and-white cape fluttered in the breeze, catching the wintry sunlight. She landed beside the post office box the coordinates pointed to, and stuffed the bag inside. I held my breath.

Nothing happened. Nobody on the street seemed to notice the glaringly bright supervillain among them, their heads ducked down against the cold, hurrying about their day. Brook's head swiveled about.

I turned my head to ask if that was it, and that was, of course, when the screaming started.

I had to give most supervillains this: they definitely

know how to make an entrance. A giant fireball exploded in front of Union Station, scorching the pillars of the building's façade. The heat hit like a sucker punch to the jaw, even at over a block away, and the screaming grew louder. Car horns beeped and tires squealed and I finally located the source of the fireball, mostly from the fact that pedestrians were scrambling away, slipping and falling on the icy sidewalks.

A group of supervillains strolled down the middle of the street like they owned the town. The woman in the middle, who wore a spiked and studded black leather vest over a sleeveless red shirt, waved her hand, flipping a car easily.

My stomach dropped. I had never actually seen the woman in person, but I'd seen plenty of pictures and a lot of video of her destroying New York. Tamara Diesel was one of Raptor's most infamous nemeses, and for some reason she was in Chicago and walking straight toward Brook, who'd leapt into the air with her fists clenched.

"Oh, crap," I said, running to the edge of the building. I reached a hand out to grab a ride with Vicki, but she'd already launched herself, bulleting toward the group in the street.

Angélica paused, crouching on the edge. "This is why you need to practice phasing."

"Villains now," I said. "Scold later."

She rolled her eyes at me and jumped. A split second later, I saw her hit the ground almost a block away, already running for the overturned car. Vicki flew at

Tamara Diesel and was knocked back a solid twenty feet. Tamara hadn't come alone. I could see a man in a burned-black duster, no doubt the source of the fireball, a spindly woman I recognized from a previous fight, and a man in a green hoodie and stained khakis. I didn't even want to know what his power was.

They would be too much for Vicki and Angélica, even with the Davenport mooks running around. I needed to get down there.

I looked down at the pavement below and felt briefly dizzy. That was a lot farther than four floors and there was no dumpster full of squishy and disgusting things to break my fall.

On the street, Angélica's head whipped toward me. I didn't need supersight to see the annoyed look on her face.

"I hate everything," I said, and launched myself off of an honest-to-god skyscraper. Phase, I told myself, *phase*, use your momentum—

I fell like a brick. The ground rushing at me wasn't an unfamiliar experience, thanks to all of the supervillain encounters I'd had, but it definitely wasn't a welcome one. My heart in my throat, I plummeted straight for the pavement. Any second now, I'd blink and I'd be on my couch, and getting back to this fight would just be a pain in the butt.

Instead, Guy caught me. I grunted as his chest plate slammed into me. "About time you got here," I said, my voice shaking. "Which is totally Gail-speak for thanks. That could have been . . . bad."

"Sorry I'm late," was all he said. He dropped me on my feet and took off with a little wave.

On the ground, I raced to help Angélica because I could already see one of the villains heading her way. Surprisingly, a white blur joined the fight already breaking out in the middle of the street. Vicki's fire bolts joined with Brook's yellow-and-green rays, aiming at the passel of supervillains wreaking havoc. A bolt of Vicki's fire splashed on the pavement to my left as I tackled Angélica to the ground. Instants later, a woman's hand slapped the air where her head had been. We both rolled to our feet and faced the woman, who was still thirty feet away, her arm contracting back to its normal length.

"You again," Angélica said.

I didn't blame her for the sigh. We'd fought Stretchy McGee, or whoever the hell she was, when Brook had showed up at the mall to kidnap Naomi. Angélica had won then, and the woman, who was gangly even before the weird rubber powers kicked in, definitely looked like the type to hold a grudge.

She whipped both arms out and I yelped, leaping aside. Angélica wasn't fast enough to dodge the hit, but she shook it off, spun on her heel, and launched herself at the woman. "Help the others," she shouted at me as she blocked a counterstrike. "I've got this."

Arguing would only piss her off. I turned to look around. The fireball thrower, I could see now, was the infamous Scorch. He'd kidnapped me over three years before, and I hadn't missed him at all in the meantime. The dude took pyromania to the next level. He shot gusts of flame from his wrists while Guy nimbly dodged each blast. Vicki and Brook seemed to be taking on Tamara Diesel and the man in the stained hoodie. They fought together in almost perfect tandem. It was like watching some kind of beautifully coordinated dance.

I took a step back in awe and my heel hit a patch of ice. I landed flat on my back, knocking the wind temporarily out of my chest. When I looked sideways, I saw a flash of gray out of the corner of my eye. I rolled over, elbow dragging through a frigid puddle, right in time to see a man in a gray hooded jacket reach into the post office box where Brook had dropped the ransom payment. A glimpse of the black bag was all I needed.

"The kidnapper," I shouted before I thought about it. The man, who'd been walking hurriedly with his hood up, broke out into a run. Trusting that my friends had the superfluous supervillain issue under control, I ran after him.

He ducked into the station, probably hoping to lose me in the fleeing crowd. I sped after him, leaping down the stairs four or five at a time and dodging around people. This would have been the perfect time to phase, really. I pushed that hindsight to the back of my mind where it belonged and pumped my legs harder. The kidnapper shoved civilians as he ran by, knocking them into my path. "Sorry, sorry," I said as I hurtled over them like I was at a high-school track meet.

The man spun—I couldn't see his face since he was wearing some kind of mesh mask—and knocked a cart over into my path. I skidded and nearly crashed into it. When I made the leap over it, though, a sharp punch hit me right between the shoulder blades.

It knocked the wind out of me again. I landed in an ungraceful sprawl on the hard ground, wrist and back singing with the sting. Automatically, I rolled to the side and a glob of something steaming and yellow hit the ground where I'd been instants before. The acrid scent of burning sewage hit my nostrils.

I jumped to my feet and found myself facing off against the green-hoodied man. And now that I was close enough, I realized I knew him. I groaned. "Toadicus, what the hell?"

Toadicus flicked his tongue over his rotten yellow teeth. "Do I know you?"

"Never mind," I said, and he shot another glob of goo at me. Some of it hit my mask when I didn't dodge fast enough. Frustrated, I just spun and ran again. The kidnapper had disappeared deeper into Union Station, toward the tracks. I didn't have time to deal with a two-bit frog villain who'd kidnapped me for laughs a couple years before.

Unfortunately, Toadicus's other froglike qualities made him a little difficult to evade. He hopped in front of me. I socked him in the midsection and ducked around him as he grunted and folded forward. My cheek started to burn, so I yanked off my mask.

Toadicus jumped and landed in front of me again

by the entrance to the tracks. I saw it in that weird slow motion that happens when adrenaline becomes overpowering: his throat bulged like a toad's as he readied to hawk another loogie, which would hit me in the face. I didn't have time to duck. I watched him open his mouth.

A blast of yellow fire hit him directly in the chest and knocked him backward. Yellow goo geysered everywhere as he screamed.

"Thanks," I shouted over my shoulder at Vicki.

"I'm here for you, mentee!"

I pointed ahead, still running. "Kidnapper!"

"Dammit." Vicki launched herself into the air, streaking by with a gust of wind. I chased after her. Union Station had several tracks with narrow platforms between them, and there were plenty of escape routes into the train yard. Vicki pulled up short, hovering in the air. "Which way? What's he look like?"

"Gray jacket, hood, jeans!" I whirled in place, sniffing and listening and doing anything I could to track down the man I'd been chasing. Luckily, I caught a whiff. I pointed. "That way!"

Vicki was a fast flyer, but the Mobium made me almost as quick on two feet. We booked it across the tracks; I leapt clean over them from platform to platform. Three platforms in, at the darkest part of the enclosure, I finally spotted the man, sprinting next to one of the passenger trains. People pressed themselves to the windows, watching him go. "Vicki!"

"Got him!" She put on a burst of speed and slammed

into the man, sending him sprawling onto the concrete. As I ran to help out, the man suddenly rolled onto his back and raised his arm. From his sleeve spewed a cloud of thick blue gas that swallowed Vicki temporarily. The smell of apricots spread everywhere.

Vicki dropped to her knees.

And then she began to cough.

# CHAPTER 6

"**N**o!" I shouted.

Vicki's cough rattled like she'd sucked in a truckload of toxic fumes. On her knees, she spun toward me, reaching out. "Stay back," she said, and her voice was so urgent that I stopped without thinking about it.

Unfortunately, this was the opening that the kidnapper needed. While Vicki coughed and I gaped in horrified silence, he scrambled to his feet and jumped onto the tracks. I hesitated, torn between running to my friend and chasing after him.

Vicki collapsed with a dull *thump*.

I sprinted forward. The blue smoke had already dissipated, but all I could see was one of the world's strongest and best superheroes crumpled on the ground in absolute misery. I slid the last few feet on my knees like my old softball days, not caring that it ripped my pants. My brain had gone absolutely numb with shock. "Plain

Jane!" I said, only just remembering not to use her real name. I shook her shoulder, and her head lolled limply to the side. "Oh, no. No, no, no, this isn't happening. Jane, can you hear me? Are you okay?"

There was no way I was yanking off her mask, not in such a public space, but I leaned over to listen. Was she even breathing? I needed to call 911, but the Davenport 911. God, this was the *worst* time to be on the outs with them—

Vicki surged up with a deep gasp, making me jump. "Jane?" I asked.

"I'm fine, I'm fine," she said, sitting up. But when she stumbled to her feet, my breath stuttered in my chest.

She weaved like a drunk.

"Just give me a minute," Vicki said, holding up a hand. "I got it."

"Are you okay?" I asked, even though it was obvious that she wasn't.

"Please." At least her voice seemed back at its normal confidence level. She waved her hand at me. "I got hurt way worse than this fighting Near Death Man. I'm fine. Did he get away?"

"Yeah. I was a little more worried about you."

"That's sweet." She coughed again and it was like my blood had been replaced by ice water. That cough really did not sound good.

"What'd he hit you with?" I asked, grabbing her arm because she'd started to sway.

"Knockout gas, maybe. Whoo. That was a trip. Do you smell apricots?"

Good to know I wasn't the only one. "Yeah. Maybe you should rest," I said, craning my neck to look around. She was still swaying and I'd never even seen Vicki winded, let alone drugged. "Seriously, sit down or something."

"I'm fine," she said, her voice dropping into a threat.

"I'm going to run back and fetch Guy," I said. "He'll help us get out of here."

"Gail, I'm fine, there's no need to—"

"Duck!" Kiki's voice came out of nowhere.

I hit the deck, shoving Vicki away so that she swooped sideways. The glob of yellow goo sailed harmlessly through the air. In an instant, I spotted what I'd missed in my worry: Toadicus hopped full speed down the line of cars, green eyes glowing with anger. I could see Kiki behind him, a frustrated look on her face. Her psychic powers weren't going much help in a battle.

"Why won't you just croak already?" I said, feeling for the belt at my waist. My hand closed around one of Raptor's little throwing blades and I hurled it at his face. He ducked, like I expected, and the minute he righted himself, I slammed my fist into the side of his jaw and knocked him out in one blow. He hit the side of the train with a dull *whump*.

"I had him," Vicki said, coughing.

"Sure, but I need to pull my weight around here, too," I said, and Kiki rushed up to us.

Before she could open her mouth, though, a fireball exploded behind us. I grabbed Kiki and twisted in midair as the concussive force hit. It threw us into the concrete platform, but my back took most of the weight. We grunted as we landed, our heads cracking together. I groaned.

Scorch, whose black duster had definitely seen better millennia, hovered in the air, smirking at Vicki. "You don't see Plain Jane around Chi-Town much these days," he said, his voice gravelly like he'd been chain-smoking since the third grade. "Pity. I almost missed your butt-ugly mask."

I groaned and pushed Kiki off of me. Some super-villains were definitely better with the banter than the others.

Vicki scoffed, but I could hear her voice shake. She pushed herself to her feet and crossed her arms over her chest. "Still prettier than your face, charcoal-breath."

"We need to get out of here," Kiki said, tugging at my shirt.

"I can't leave her, she's hurt."

"She looks fine. Can we—"

Vicki launched herself into the air and wobbled, arms and legs flailing in an uncoordinated mess as she tried to stay aloft. Kiki stared. I stared. Scorch stared.

Vicki's boots hit the platform. At least her flame powers seemed to be working as she shot a bright bolt of fire at Scorch, who flew easily to the side. He returned fire and Vicki dodged backward, actually tumbling off of the platform and onto the tracks. She caught herself three inches above the ground and tried to charge at Scorch.

Her boots dragged across the tracks.

"Oh, that is not good," I said.

Kiki still had her hand fisted in my shirt. "She's losing her power," she breathed. "Oh my god, she's losing her power. What happened? What's wrong with her?"

"No time for that now!" I broke free of Kiki's grip as Scorch sent another beam of fire at Vicki. She stumbled as she tried to evade it. When I tackled her out of the way of the next bolt, she screamed. Her suit was smoking when I jumped off of her. "Ki, get her out of here!"

"I've got it," Vicki said, but I shoved her toward Kiki, who grabbed her arm. I picked up another one of the throwing blades out of my belt and hurled it at Scorch. At least it made him dodge, giving Kiki enough time to bodily drag Vicki to safety.

Scorch began to laugh, and the sound crawled up each vertebra of my spine, eerily cold. "This is a good day. Doesn't this feel like a good day?" he said, a wide grin stretching the shiny burn scars on his cheeks. He looked at me, flicking his fingers dismissively so that a fireball hurtled at my head. Since there was no heart behind the hit, it missed.

I flung another knife at his head in retaliation. He burned it out of existence. A cloud of ash floated to the ground. "I'll deal with you later," Scorch said, and began to fly off.

"Gail!" I whipped around to see Kiki waving at me, frantically. "You can't let him get away!"

Oh, shit. Let loose, Scorch would take the news that

Plain Jane had lost control of her powers to the super-villain community. It might be temporary, it might not, but either way it wasn't news we could afford to let out.

I sprinted hard, watching the tattered hem of Scorch's duster flutter as he flew off, laughing. Instinctively, I pushed off and arced through the air. My shoulder knocked into the back of his knee and I wrapped myself around his boots, incapacitating his legs before he could kick me. Luckily, my dense weight helped: we crashed onto a platform, him cursing the entire time.

I rolled out of the way of a blast of heat and flame. Reaching blindly into the belt, I grabbed a glop of what felt like sticky putty and lobbed it at Scorch's hand, right before he could shoot a jet of fire at me. The putty expanded and exploded over his arm, throwing him back so he thudded hard onto the platform. I dove at him, trying to wrestle him into a choke hold, but the instant my skin came in contact with his, I let out a cry. My hand sizzled.

He destroyed the Raptor's antifire gel with another burst from his palm and tried to knock me aside. I dodged and kicked him in the midsection, making him double over. When he sprang back up, I pepper-sprayed him in the face. His high-pitched screech brought a sick sense of satisfaction. The uncontrolled whip made of pure fire, however, made me yelp. I scrambled back and a fireball engulfed the air right in front of me, the force of the blast slamming into me so hard it carried me backward right into one of the station's support pillars.

The last thing I saw before a black curtain descended over my vision was Scorch's smirk and red eyes as he launched into the sky.

Oh, hell.

It probably said a lot about me that when I opened my eyes I expected a hospital room. That was how I still felt waking up most mornings, even though my Hostage Girl days were long behind me. Back then, I'd spent a lot of time getting the maximum benefits out of a gold standard health insurance plan. Granted, now I had the Mobium, and it was rare to wake up under the harsh fluorescent lights and to the beeping of the pulse monitor, but old habits died hard.

I really didn't expect to wake up in Angélica's gym, though. In the middle of a boxing ring, no less.

"Huh?" I asked, blinking around at me. I was dressed for a workout—if you ignored my torn sweatpants—but everything smelled fried to a crisp and my skin felt like I was recovering from a horrible sunburn.

Jessie Davenport popped into the edge of my vision and my world made even less sense. She raised her eyebrows at me.

"Did you knock me out?" I asked.

"Nope. I put you in there because it seemed like the most comfortable spot in the house." She frowned. "I always forget how heavy you are."

"So does everybody else." Warily, I sat up. "Why am I here? Why are you here?"

"Everybody else is at Davenport and I got the feeling you hate Medical more than I do. I offered to take care of you since it didn't seem like anything serious."

I looked around. "Where's Guy?"

"I've been texting him updates." Jessie held up her phone, and thanks to my keen eyesight, I read six different versions of *still hasn't woken up, breathing normally.* "I see you used the fire gel. Good choice, though it only pisses Scorch off. If I'd known he was a possibility, I'd have given you stronger stuff."

"Uh, yeah." I was too muddled to want to talk tactics with this random superhero who had taken an odd interest in me. I put my hand to my forehead and winced at how grimy it felt. What had even happened? Why was I here? Why did it feel like I'd run a marathon with no sun protection? And why was my stomach churning so much?

Vicki.

Oh god. Vicki.

It all came rushing back to me in a flood. "Vicki," I said out loud. "Is she—"

Jessie shook her head tightly, and my heart leapt into my throat at all the different things that could mean. "She's alive. I'll take you to see her now that you probably won't wind up in Medical," she said.

She broke down the story as she took me to the Loop in a zippy little sports car that cost about three times what I made in a year. By the time we were ushered straight through to the 'porter—Marsh the security guard apparently feared Jessie more than he didn't respect me—I had a general idea how the fight had gone. Guy, Angélica, and Brook had fought Tamara Diesel and her group off, but Scorch had gotten away with the information that Plain Jane's powers were on the fritz. We'd left most of Union Station intact, which was unexpected, but the kidnapper had escaped with the money. Davenport was analyzing surveillance now.

I ran my hand over my face. I'd let the kidnapper get away with the money. I'd let Scorch get away with the information. Two gold stars for Gail Godwin.

"You did better than you think," Jessie said as we walked to Medical together. She kept her hand on my shoulder. "You used your head, you helped get Vicki to safety. Some days that's all you can do."

From the Raptor, successor to the world's very first superhero, that felt like a platitude. I'd failed, pure and simple, and the shame of it sat oppressive on my shoulders. "The blue gas," I said, forcing my thoughts away from that path. "What was it?"

"They're analyzing that, too."

Helpful.

"We do have access to some of the best researchers on the planet here," Jessie said mildly.

"Nobody likes a braggart."

Jessie snorted.

Medical wasn't quite a mess when we arrived, but the receptionists definitely looked strained and pale. They practically stood at attention when Jessie walked in. "Plain Jane?" she asked.

One of the receptionists pointed. They looked like they wouldn't mind if she kept walking and did so in a hurry.

Jessie shoved her hands in her pockets, though. "Has there been any change?"

"Dr. Davenport will know better," the receptionist said. I blinked. I was so used to hearing her called Kiki by everybody that it took me a moment to figure out who they meant.

Jessie finally seemed to take pity on the poor workers, strolling past them. I saw a couple of the nurses shoot me curious looks—since when did I hang out with Jessie?—but I kept my head down as I followed her. My stomach was a roiling pit of nerves. I hoped Vicki was okay. I had no idea what could be strong enough to mess with Plain Jane, who'd once flown through three buildings in a row without altering her speed in the slightest.

Guy and Angélica were sitting in the hallway when we approached. "Gail!" For somebody over six feet, Guy could scramble fast when he wanted to. He scooped me up in a giant hug, surrounding me for a moment in the smell of sweat and aftershave. "You're okay."

"What's a little head trauma here or there?" I asked, hugging him back. I turned to Angélica. "Vicki?"

Angélica shook her head and the knot between my shoulders tightened.

"No hug for me?" Jessie asked, raising an eyebrow at Guy.

He tilted his head. "Did you . . . want one?"

"Not particularly. Anyway, I'm just here to drop off the patient and to check on my niece." She said the last word like she wasn't used to using it, and for all I knew, she wasn't. Eddie and Jessie Davenport had never been big on claiming Kiki as family; I hadn't even known she was a Davenport until I was firmly caught in the middle of the giant conspiracy to save her. The distance between them felt a little hypocritical. Kiki's maternal grandfather, paternal grandmother, and actual father might all be supervillains, but the family matriarch was also the world's first supervillain. Jessie turned her attention from Guy to me. "I trust Gail can keep me updated about Vicki."

"I can?" I asked, and Jessie gave me a look. "Oh. I can. Yeah, I can do that. Sure."

Jessie disappeared into the room that I assumed contained Kiki, Vicki, and the Medical staff before I could thank her for taking care of me. Once she was gone, I grabbed Guy's hand and slid down the wall, tugging him with me so that we sat across from Angélica.

I swallowed. "Is Vicki . . . ?"

"She doesn't seem to be in danger of dying," Angélica said, snapping her gum. She'd apparently recognized the trepidation on my face. "But something's wrong. Kiki and her team have no idea what, though."

I held tighter to Guy's hand. He shifted to place an arm across my shoulders.

"What happened out there?" he asked. "Kiki was able to give us a few details, but she was a little busy."

I filled them in about the supervillain attack as best I could. "But where did they come from?" I asked. The passel of supervillains that had shown up was completely random. I hadn't even known Toadicus and Scorch knew each other, and yet they'd arrived together. "Were they there with the kidnapper? Are they the ones that have Mobius?"

"No idea," Guy said. "But we'll find him, whoever has him."

"And Vicki will be okay," Angélica said.

I raised an eyebrow at her.

"Vicki has to be okay. If she's not, she'll do nothing but whine at me, and I refuse to believe I've done anything so horrible in this life as to deserve that." Angélica's fingers were twisting together, and I imagined she wanted to be back at the Power House, destroying a speed bag or five. "So for all our sakes, she's got to be okay."

"She's going to be okay." Guy nodded at her calmly.

I shifted because his chest plate was poking my shoulder. I missed his Blaze uniform at moments like these. It was a lot more formfitting than the War Hammer armor, which had been bulked up to keep the public from finding out that the bearer was a bit slimmer these days. Blaze's uniform had been soft and familiar. I rested the back of my head against his shoulder. "I screwed up," I said.

"What?"

I stared up at the tiles in the ceiling. "I let the kidnapper get away and I let Scorch get away, and now probably everybody knows something's up with Plain Jane."

"Scorch is a Class B supervillain who can fly, and you're . . . well, you're an assistant editor," Guy said, keeping his voice gentle. "You didn't screw up. Holding your own is more than enough. Nobody's going to hold that against you."

"I have the Mobium. I could have at least stopped one of them. And Vicki was only there because she was watching my back—"

"Stop," Angélica said, glowering at me.

I closed my mouth, but didn't stop the sigh in time.

Angélica's glare only deepened. "The last thing Vicki needs right now is a pity party," she said.

"Angélica, be nice," Guy said.

"No, she's right." I pushed myself to my feet. "I'm being stupid." Even if I'd failed, I knew better: Vicki was my mentor and she saw me as a responsibility and she'd make that choice over and over again. Angélica had made a similar choice once that had led to her death—which thankfully didn't take—and I hated that just as much. But that was part and parcel of the heroing lifestyle, and I had to accept that. "I'm not good company right now. I think I'll go see Jeremy."

"Want me to go with you?" Guy said.

I shook my head. In his current state, Jeremy wasn't exactly a sparkling conversationalist, and I needed some alone time. With the way news traveled in the Davenport Complex, his room would probably be the only quiet spot I could find. "Text me if anything changes?"

"Will do."

I took a deep breath and let go of my boyfriend's hand, walking off. It had been too long since I'd been by to see my ex-boyfriend. No time like the present.

# CHAPTER 7

I left Medical and headed deep into the Davenport Complex, past my old apartment, into the New Powers sector, wincing when something exploded with a muffled thud on the other side of the wall in Pyro. I cut left to avoid Underwater and walked through Electrical, wondering as I always did which bright idiot had put those two next to each other. Tempting fate much? But as long as I avoided Psychic, I was happy. I'd never had any good experiences with psychic powers. Kiki, at least, didn't hold it against me if I flinched away from her when she touched my arm without warning.

I pressed my palm to the panel that stood at chest height outside of Room 307, took a deep breath, and stepped inside. Giving Davenport the finger a couple months before meant I had severely limited access, but Guy had gotten me cleared for at least this much. Inside, it was quiet, the temperature slightly cooler than the hallway. Resting temperature, Kiki had called it the first time she'd brought me to visit Jeremy. The lights were supposed to be dim and soothing, and my eyes adjusted without trouble, but it always made my skin itch. It felt unnatural. Or maybe it was just a reminder that we were deep underground, something I really didn't care to think about.

Jeremy lay on a bed in the middle of the room, eyes closed. He looked exactly the same as he had the last time I'd visited. Just as I knew he would. Nothing ever changed.

As ever, the sight of his face put a falter in my step. After a couple of weeks in the hospital, when it was obvious he wasn't in a hurry to wake up from his coma, they'd transferred Jeremy to the Davenport Complex. The cot he lay on was custom-made for its grounding properties, though it looked like any other hospital bed. Jeremy's face remained slack, his skin pale in the low light. A couple months' growth of beard prickled at his chin. For a man who prided himself on physical upkeep—daily trips to the gym, hours spent grooming in front of a mirror, a better skin-care regimen than my own—that was the most heartbreaking part of it all, seeing him waste away like this. The doctors had no idea when or if he would wake up. They'd assured us that his brain activity seemed normal, but there might be other factors they couldn't understand unless he woke up.

Given that even now I could see tiny little currents of static discharge flicking between his thumbs and forefingers, shockingly bright blue against the dimness, it wasn't hard to guess what those other factors might be.

Jeremy was a cautionary tale. For all I'd struggled with what the Mobium had done to me, Jeremy had been through worse. He'd electrocuted himself to stop Lemuel Cooper, Kiki's sinister boyfriend, from killing her (and the rest of us). And worst of all, Jeremy's heroic act of self-sacrifice had been to stop me from taking his place. It could very easily have been me on the cot and him sitting in the chair I lowered myself into now. It had been such a stupid, boneheaded thing for him to do and it regularly made me want to cry whenever I looked at his empty face.

"You won't believe the day I've had," I told him. Kiki had said that it was possible he could hear whatever we were saying, though I had my doubts. He didn't look peaceful in his coma. He looked like he simply wasn't there. But I gamely charged on. "It hasn't been as bad as Vicki's day, but it's not great. But before I get into it: what is it with bad guys and Union Station? With all the damn construction around there, it's like villains just live to make our lives miserable."

No response, but I hadn't expected one. I touched his hand and the zap from his powers traveled harmlessly up my arm. It was like touching a doorknob while wearing wool socks on carpet. Even though I'd known it was coming, I called him an unflattering name and settled back. Words came tumbling out: I told him about the fight, about Vicki, about waking up and my heart-to-heart with Jessie. He'd probably get a kick out of hearing about her little stunt with my hood during our sparring match earlier, but the only answer when I described it in great detail was the slow and steady beeping of the heart monitor.

"You need to come back," I said, the noise breaking through the false cheer and bringing with it a wearying layer of sadness. "You might have been an asshole a lot of the time, but you're still my friend. And Vicki's friend. And she could use all the friends she can get right now."

After that, I fell silent, sick to my stomach. Just what had happened to Vicki? What had that blue gas done to her? Was it permanent? Could they fix it?

My phone buzzed with a text from Guy: *they're letting us in to see her.*

*See you in five*, I texted back.

I touched Jeremy's hand again, ignoring the shock. "As usual, you're missing all the good stuff," I said, though I didn't know if that was true or not. "Wake up soon."

And I left to go see Vicki.

**V**icki sat on the cot, her uniform stripped to the waist to reveal an obnoxiously orange sports bra underneath. Her mask lay on the pillow. I tried my hardest not to stare at the purple diodes on her temples and chest or the panicked look on her face. Sweat covered her forehead and torso, beading on her upper lip. For somebody that instantly became the center of attention every time she entered a room, she seemed pale and diminished.

Kiki gestured me over to where Angélica and Guy had already clustered. She leaned in, dropping her voice low. "We don't know much yet," she said. I frowned, wondering why I sensed worry when her voice was devoid of all emotion. It must have been from her heartbeat or something. "All I can say is that it's really not good."

"*What* is not good?" Angélica asked, folding her arms over her chest.

Vicki's head snapped up. So much for talking quietly. "My fire's gone," she said in a ragged voice.

She held up her palm. I'd seen her gleefully lance fire over fifty feet, but now the barest flicker of flame, smaller than even the offering of a lighter, formed in the air in front of her palm. "It's just gone," she said, dropping her hand back to the cot. "I can't fly, either."

"It's like nothing I've ever seen." Kiki pushed her fingertips into her forehead. "Her powers have completely vanished, like she's—"

"Normal," Vicki said, and the way she said the word, it might as well have been an obscenity. She drew her feet up onto the edge of the cot, hugging her knees to her chest. There weren't tear tracks on her face, but I could see her eyes shining. I'd never felt quite this hopeless, not without there being railroad tracks and chains involved. I had no idea what I could possibly say to her, and judging from the silence, nobody else knew, either.

"We're still running tests." Kiki stepped over to the computer and typed in a few commands. I understood the charts that popped up but only because I'd seen them displaying my own stats. "This is what Vicki's levels are supposed to be at. Here are her new levels." She hit a button and the numbers shifted drastically. "These readings are Class D."

Class D. No superpowers.

It felt like a metal band wrapped itself around my chest and squeezed tight, choking off the air. Vicki, Plain Jane, the most powerful superhero I knew, had lost all of her powers. A simple hit of that weird blue gas and she was . . . she was just another human. I didn't hear Guy or Angélica breathing, either, as we stared at the screen. The air felt hot and stifling as the horrible reality crashed over us.

"It's temporary, right?" I said, and my voice sounded off to my own ears. I didn't even really like my own powers some days, but all of them gone, just like that . . . "They'll come back. Her powers will come back."

"I have every confidence they will," Kiki said.

I gave her a funny look. "No, you don't," I said before I could stop myself. I didn't know how I knew that, but the thought had pushed its way into my brain.

Kiki tilted her head at me, opening her mouth, but a sound filled the room that made all of us freeze: a sniffle. Vicki dropped her forehead to her knees, and the dam broke. Angélica gave Kiki and me a *cut it out* look and strode across the room, dropping next to

Vicki on the cot and hugging her. Vicki's sobs stayed almost painfully quiet, but I could see her chest and shoulders shaking as Angélica held on.

I stepped over toward them, but Kiki put a hand on my arm. "Just a moment," she said. "At the station, you said you smelled apricots, too?"

"I wasn't close, but yeah, I did." I shook my head as an entire new type of fear coiled in my gut. Vicki had taken a full dose right to the face, and she was losing her powers. Would the gas work on me, just more slowly? I looked over at Vicki, my stomach sinking. My powers were really new, especially compared to hers, but I already couldn't imagine life without them. I swallowed past the horrible constricting lump in my throat. "Guess this means you're going to poke me with something sharp."

"It hurts me more than it hurts you," Kiki said.

I managed a humorless smile. "That's a lie."

"Yes."

"Gail could be losing her powers, too?" Guy asked, reaching for my shoulder.

"She doesn't seem to be exhibiting any of the same symptoms," Kiki said. "But I do need to check. It'll just take a minute."

Guy looked torn between following us and remaining with Vicki, so I gestured for him to stay put and followed Kiki to the other side of the room. We went through the very familiar exam and I tried to pick apart how I felt, if anything seemed unusual. I was a little sluggish, but that could be a result of having just been knocked unconscious. Across the room, Vicki continued to cry.

"Why do you think it's permanent?" I asked Kiki in an undertone.

"I don't." Kiki typed in my blood pressure and pinched the bridge of her nose. "Maybe. Either way, if it is permanent, I'm scared of the implications."

"What implications?"

"Let's worry about you first."

She finished the exam by taking two vials of blood from my arm, and I waved her off before she could put a bandage on my arm. It would heal in less than a couple minutes. "Are you going to test everybody?" I asked.

"I don't think anybody else was close enough, and I don't want to cause unnecessary panic." Kiki swallowed and I looked down at the crease of her elbow, where a little gauze pad had been taped. She met my eye, evenly. "We don't know how widely the gas spreads or how quickly it disperses. Better safe than sorry."

"Okay." My mouth felt like cotton had been stuffed inside, soaking up the moisture. "Where's Brook?"

"They're keeping her in a cell nearby. She's not talking to anybody."

"Can I see her? Maybe she'll talk to me."

Kiki shrugged in a *have at it* way. "Guess that's another prison roommate thing, huh?"

Not particularly, but if they all wanted to think that Brook and I had this deep bond because of the horrific experiences we'd shared at Detmer, maybe it was better to let that misconception spread. If the heroes knew what kind of luxury they were handing over to villains by sending them to Detmer, the entire world order might collapse. Kiki finished putting the last of my data into the computer. Looking at her, I was struck with an intense feeling. Fear. Not entirely for Vicki, either. After all, Davenport had disregarded the kidnapper's requests, letting him get away with four million, and he still had Mobius. He had the money. Was there any reason to keep Mobius alive?

I might have hated the man, but I wasn't a heartless jerk.

"Hey," I said. "We'll get Mobius back. Somehow. I've never known the people in this room to fail."

Kiki gave me a puzzled look. "Thanks, Gail." She unclipped her own badge and pushed it over. "This'll get you in to talk to Brook."

"I'll be back in a few minutes," I told Angélica and Guy, who sat flanking the still-crying Vicki. Tears as a rule didn't make me uncomfortable—I'd seen enough supervillains break down into them over the years—but helplessness threatened to overwhelm me. "I'm going to go get some answers."

Guy gave me a tiny smile. "Good luck."

I stepped out into the corridor and closed the door on the sound of Vicki's sob.

**U**p close, Brook didn't look or smell that great. They hadn't let her change out of her Chelsea gear, which was dirty and scuffed. The downsides of wearing white armor into battle, really. She glanced over when I came into the room, eyes flicking up and down once, and returned her gaze to an obviously enthralling invisible spot on the wall across from her. Her mask remained clutched in her fists.

I leaned against the wall by the door, but I didn't relax. "You look like hell."

"You know what I missed these past few months? Your insightful commentary. Of course I look like hell. They won't even let me have a shower and I haven't slept in three days."

It wasn't hard to guess the source of her exhaustion. I'd had a hard time sleeping when I'd left Detmer myself.

"I miss the beds there, too," I said.

Unexpectedly, she sighed. "It's like sleeping on a damn cloud."

"I dream about the thread count on those sheets," I said. "Some days I'm tempted to become a supervillain just to go back."

"You'd be terrible at it. For somebody so small, you're just brimming with really stupid feelings."

I looked at the cloth twisting in her hands and felt a stab of pity. Brook had agreed to help us find Mobius, and unlike the last time she'd faced Guy or his brother, she hadn't lunged straight for his throat. She'd hurt my friends—repeatedly—but she'd also spent years in a cage while scientists experimented on her. It was hard not to feel *some* kind of empathy, even though I really didn't want to.

"Are you working with the kidnapper?" I asked.

Brook snorted. "Nope."

Her heartbeat never changed, though that wasn't the most accurate lie detector. She could hear mine, too, which was downright inconvenient. If she said something that got under my skin, there'd be no way to hide that.

"Did you contact somebody to work with the kidnapper on your behalf?" I asked.

Her heartbeat sped up a little. Interesting. Brook remained facing forward, expression never changing. "For what it's worth, intentionally? I didn't contact anybody. It's not my fault Davenport sucks."

"What are you talking about?"

"Sending me out there in my Chelsea gear? Who are they trying to kid?"

"What," I said again, "are you talking about?"

Thanks to the reflexes, I caught the mask when she flung it at my face. The follow-up attack I braced for never came, though. Brook had gone back to her staring contest with the wall.

"What the hell was that for?" I asked.

"I thought Mobium was supposed to make you smarter. Look it over, dumbass."

I muttered a few choice insults under my breath and

turned the cowl over in my hand, feeling the rigid fabric that made up the hawkish mask. After thirty seconds of probing, I found the anomaly: a bump under the cloth, where the mask was rigid. I scratched at it with a finger-nail until a little tracker was revealed to the light.

"What the hell? Who's tracking you?"

"Three guesses and the first two aren't the super-villains who showed up out of the blue today," Brook said, rolling her eyes.

"Tamara Diesel is tracking you? What? Why?"

Brook bounced her head back into the wall a couple of times, looking to the ceiling as though she were praying for patience. "Because I owe her."

"For what?" I asked. Vicki'd had a point when she'd said that Brook was in the supervillain minor leagues. Tamara Diesel was top tier. She fought heroes like Raptor.

"You really think I escaped from years of being Lodi's little lab-rat freak and immediately gained my own minions and buddied up to a bunch of supervil-lains? I was in a cage. I barely knew what year it was, let alone how to gather allies." Brook gave me a sour look. "Tamara's people found me. I had something they wanted."

"What was that?"

"I can fly and I can hit things really hard," Brook said, her voice now dripping sarcasm. "What do you think they wanted? God, keep up. Tamara Diesel wants you to do something, you do it. In return, she helps you out. That's just the way it works."

That . . . made a horrifying amount of sense, actually. Supervillains either seemed far too organized or not organized at all. Knowing there was some kind of supervillain mafia don—and that it was Tamara Diesel herself—put everything into perspective. It also made me wonder, not for the first time, if the Villain Handbook was a real thing or not. I decided I didn't want to know.

"So how come Davenport didn't find the tracker?" I asked.

"It's only active when I'm wearing the mask."

"And you didn't think to mention that hey, just maybe, if you put the mask on, supervillains might happen to show up wherever you are and blow shit up?"

Brook scowled. "I had my reasons."

"Helpful. Why not go with her today? It would have been easy to turn on us."

"Not as easy as you think. Showing up somewhere with Plain Jane and War Hammer is a pretty big sign I've switched teams. Not willingly, but who ever cares what *I* want to do, anyway? Tamara Diesel? Not exactly the forgiving type."

I listened to her heartbeat speed up. "I'm sure Tamara could be talked around. You can fly and all."

"Jealous?"

I was, and she could probably tell, but I only continued to stare at her, waiting. There was something else, something big that I was missing about Brook's motivations, and it bothered me that I didn't know how to begin pinpointing what it was. So I settled for the blatant stare that Angélica had always used on me.

Apparently I'd learned well, because Brook sighed.

"My chances of finding her are better if I stick with Davenport," she said.

"Finding . . . oh. Petra."

"So I'm going to stay here," Brook said. "I'll help them fight their stupid do-gooder battles. The sooner I get this over with, the sooner little Bookman can help me find Petra."

Little Bookman was such a weird nickname for Guy, but Brook *had* known him in high school, so I didn't say anything. It was also kinder not to share my current hypothesis about Petra's fate. "Oh," I said.

"Judge all you want, I don't care."

"Actually, I think that's weirdly noble." I'd never had a best friend until Angélica, and when she'd died temporarily, I'd wanted to avenge her. Granted, that was where things got complicated because the person I'd thought had killed her happened to be the same one in the room with me now. I studied her and tried not to think about all of the similarities between us. "Thanks for telling me."

"Just because I'm helping you out now doesn't mean I won't change my mind if a better offer comes along."

"I guess I appreciate the honesty. Though, really, if you want allies in your search for Petra Bookman . . . warning them that bad guys are going to attack? That's a prudent thing to do."

Brook's shoulder jerked in an approximation of

a shrug. "I didn't think any of them were actually a match for Plain Jane, but apparently I was wrong, so whoops."

"That wasn't Tamara's group." I pushed myself to my feet and brushed off my sweatpants. I kept the tracker clenched between my thumb and my palm. I'd give it to Jessie, since she and Audra adored weird little gadgets. "That was whoever has Mobius. Of course, nobody around here has any idea who it actually is, still."

"You know I don't actually care, don't you?"

"Charming. Let me know if you need anything. I'm kind of persona non grata here, but . . ."

"Whatever." Brook dismissed me with a flick of her fingers.

"As always, a pleasure talking to you," I said. Just as I held Kiki's badge to the door, the door opened to reveal the badge's owner. Immediately I straightened up.

"You need to come with me," she said. She looked past me, to Brook. "Both of you."

# CHAPTER 8

During my very brief stint living in the Davenport Complex, I'd heard about the Nucleus, but I'd never seen it. The central hub of Davenport, where all of the mission operators—if heroes needed them; most preferred to go solo—worked. Every gathered piece of data for hero and villain alike was filtered through the Nucleus. All I knew about it was that it was supposed to be impressive. And that it had once housed a chart listing my odds of surviving the next supervillain encounter, until Guy had found out about it and had destroyed it in a fit of rage. He didn't lose his temper often, but when he did, it was a sight to behold.

I hadn't realized that the Nucleus was essentially NASA's mission control, but with more colorful outfits around the water cooler.

Flanked by guards, we followed Kiki down several hallways I'd never traversed before. I could sense

Brook's wariness matching my own. Kiki pressed her hand to a scanner and a door slid open, leading us even farther underground. The lighting switched abruptly from the high-key blinding whiteness of most Davenport hallways to a moody, atmospheric glow. A muted purple carpet took the place of the linoleum. Runway lights led the way downward until the room opened into a gigantic and cavernous chamber, the center of which was taken over by neat rows of desks and computers. The walls—which for some reason were bare rock—were covered with monitors that listed the city and time underneath. At the desks, people in short-sleeved button-up shirts either typed away frantically or napped into their coffee. Several chairs along the outer walls contained a mixture of Davenport personnel and, if I had to guess from the gaudily bright costumes, superheroes currently on call.

I spotted a blond man across the room, and stopped walking abruptly.

"It's fine." Jessie Davenport appeared at my elbow and I almost looked around for the puff of smoke that usually preceded magic tricks. "Eddie's got other things to worry about. He won't bother you."

"Good," I said. Eddie Davenport was handsome in a too-perfect way, his suit stylishly cut, his hair professionally coiffed. He stood among a group of other executives near the front of the room. The last time I'd faced him, it had been really hard not to punch him in the nose.

"And before you ask, I cleared you both." Jessie

looked at Brook, who was eyeing her suspiciously. "But stick close to Kiki, anyway." She nodded and did that vanishing trick again in the split second I looked over at Kiki. I jumped.

"Spooky," Brook said in a dry voice. "What's going on, Red?"

"It's Kiki," Kiki said. "And you'll see."

There was definitely an undercurrent of tension running through the techs working the computers from the way their eyes darted to the very obvious manner in which they weren't looking toward Eddie Davenport and the other executives. I glanced around, spotted a clock that read DOOMSDAY, and was relieved to see there wasn't anything displayed on it.

Guy and Angélica joined us a minute later. "Where's Vicki?" I asked.

"I gave her a sedative," Kiki said.

It took a bit to wrap my mind about that. There was no way a sedative could ever take Plain Jane down.

Eddie Davenport broke off from the group of executives and stepped to the podium. "There's a situation," he said, which I supposed was probably a common opening to briefings in the Nucleus. He clicked something in his hand and helmet-cam footage began to play on the screen over his head. I recognized the area outside of Union Station before it got too blurry and shaky to comprehend. Even though I knew it was coming, the exploding fireball in front of the pillars made me jump for a second time. The screen filled with Tamara Diesel and her cohorts. Smaller monitors below showed individual mug shots belonging to Tamara, Scorch, Toadicus, and Stretchy McGee.

"Earlier today, four known assailants launched a full-scale assault on an ongoing operation," Eddie said. "As far as we can determine, they were present to retrieve an asset of Davenport's, and may not have known about our operation at all."

I looked at Brook, whose face remained impassive.

He clicked the pointer again. This time an old photo of Dr. Mobius filled the screen. Brook flinched. I scowled.

"For those of you not up to speed on this morning's mission—we were attempting to ransom Dr. Christoph Mobius. Until we were contacted with a valid ransom demand, we believed Dr. Mobius to be deceased. Unfortunately, we encountered a wrinkle. This is a transmission received half an hour ago. We believe it's from the person who kidnapped Mobius."

Another click. Another video began to play.

A nondescript form in a gray hooded jacket that I recognized from the train station sat down in front of the camera. A mesh mask covered his or her face, blocking all features.

When he—I assumed he was male, anyway—began speaking, his voice was modulated. "Greetings, potential buyer," he said. "Today I'm offering a deal on a very unique product. Allow me to provide a demonstration."

A star-shaped transition wiped across the screen and changed the shot from his mask to another, far more familiar mask. My heart stopped for precisely three beats. The Plain Jane mask was distorted by the nearness of the camera, but I could still pick up details behind it: the darkened roof of the overhang from the train yard behind her, an out-of-focus shot of me far behind, the top of the train.

Blue exploded everywhere on the screen. I realized that the camera must have been on the kidnapper's cuff, next to the dispenser. Thanks to high-definition, I could see that it wasn't a gas, but a fine blue powder that dissolved almost immediately in the air. My stomach roiled as, once again, I watched Vicki suffer and struggle. Another star wipe changed the shot from the jerky and bouncy kidnapper's camera to an overhead camera that showed everything happening below in crystal clear detail. Including, I realized hazily, my face without a mask. I'd tossed it away when Toadicus's putrid goo had started to burn my skin.

I hadn't noticed a camera at the time, but reality shoved its way into my brain like a spike now: the kidnapper had set this up.

It had been a trap.

Angélica sucked in a breath as she obviously came to the same conclusion. Around the room, I could hear techs and other costumed heroes shifting uncomfortably as they watched. The second time Vicki hit the ground, Eddie hit the PAUSE button and silence blanketed the room.

"Plain Jane is on-site and we're hard at work analyzing what happened to her," he said, and I found his face only marginally more pleasant than watching a still image of my good friend getting hurt. "The rest of the video goes on to offer this new product to the highest bidder, due to Davenport having reneged on a previous deal with him."

Technically, they had. The ransom note had said to come alone.

"We believe that this message has been sent to several key players," Eddie went on. "And thanks to an error on the part of a colleague—" his eyes found mine across the room and my hands closed into fists "—knowledge of Plain Jane's predicament is no doubt widespread among the villain and hero community by now."

Angélica muttered a very unflattering word under her breath in Portuguese. Guy's hand closed around my shoulder. I glared harder at Eddie. He couldn't resist the opportunity to be a dick, could he?

"Given Plain Jane's influence on the local and international superpowered communities," Eddie said, "expect there to be a rise in villain activity. A special team will be organized to track down information and hopefully subdue this scientist before he or she can release this compound into the world."

I swallowed, hard. This sounded like a nightmare. And judging from the unease and the way everybody in the room couldn't sit still, I wasn't the only one seeing the dangers.

"As of this moment," Eddie said, "everybody is on call. Remain vigilant. We don't know how permanent the effects of this compound are, but we're not willing to risk it."

He clicked again and mercifully the image of Vicki lying on the ground vanished. "One note before I begin handing out assignments," Eddie said. "We're still on the lookout for Dr. Mobius. We have reason to suspect his kidnapper might have been somebody close to him. Anybody who has any personal information about Dr. Mobius should speak with me or their superiors about it. Dismissed."

The room lights came up again and I immediately turned toward Kiki. "What isn't he telling us?" I asked. There had to be a reason Eddie hadn't played the entire video. If anybody would know, Kiki would.

"There was another ransom demand." Kiki took a deep breath. "Whoever has him, they're trying to sell Mobius to the highest bidder. He invented it."

"What?"

"This blue powder that's causing all the trouble? My grandfather created it."

Angélica put a hand on her shoulder. "Sins of the father," she said in a quiet voice. "Remember they're not yours."

Kiki looked down and nodded, but I could see her chin trembling and I could feel the guilt rolling off of her in waves. "Either way," she said, swiping her hand surreptitiously across her cheeks, "we all need to be careful. That ransom demand was sent to all of the interested parties. Anybody who knows anything about my grandfather will now have a target on their back."

"Oh, good," I said. "I was worried that we didn't have enough trouble in our lives."

As if it could read my thoughts, my phone buzzed. I pulled it out of my pocket and sighed when I saw a scrambled number that could only be Raze. Speak of the devil.

*you'll fight TAMARA DIESEL BUT NOT ME????? What gives?!?*

Raze also included way more emojis than I would expect from a self-respecting villain.

"Trouble?" Guy asked.

"After a fashion. It's Raze," I said. "She's mad that I fought other villains."

Brook raised her eyebrows. Thankfully, any sarcastic comments about our time in Detmer were apparently buried under the gravity of the situation.

*It wasn't planned!* I texted back. *And wait, how did you know??*

*please like davenport has that many heroes that short.*

"Eddie wants to keep us all on-site," Kiki said.

Brook rolled her eyes. "Damn, and here I was looking forward to some beach time."

"Gail, you and Angélica, too."

*Don't be a jerk*, I texted back to Raze. I looked at Kiki. "Knowing Eddie, he probably thinks I'm in league with Mobius."

"Probably."

My phone buzzed again. I wasn't sure how Raze was able to convey rage through the vibration of a phone, but I wouldn't have put it beyond her. *how else can I convince you to FIGHT ME???* she texted.

I didn't dignify that with a response, shoving the phone back into my pocket. "Please tell me I don't have to share a room with Brook again."

Brook flipped me off.

"My old apartment's technically on-site," Guy said. He'd moved back to Chicago when he took up the War Hammer mantle, but he was rich enough to keep several places. He looked over at Angélica. "You can stay there, too. Sam's room is open."

"I've got a place to stay, actually," Angélica said, and Guy raised his eyebrows.

"Can we get this conversation with Eddie over sooner rather than later? My day's already gone down the toilet. I'd like it to turn around and that's not possible until *after* I talk to Eddie the turd," I said.

Kiki opened her mouth like she might protest. At the last second, she seemed to reconsider. "I need to get back to Vicki," she said. "Stay available, Gail, in case I spot anything on your results. Try not to lose your phone."

"Yes, ma'am."

Since it looked like Eddie would be busy talking to the other executives, the rest of us followed her out. Angélica split off to escort Brook back to her cell, so I walked with Guy toward his on-site apartment. "It's really convenient, if you think about it," I said.

"What is?"

"Everybody who knows anything about Mobius is already on-site for Eddie to boss around," I said. "Apparently we've all got a giant target on our backs, which isn't great. But at least none of us are Class D—" technically, Vicki didn't know all that much about Mobius, so she didn't count "—so we can all take care of ourselves."

"If a normal person knew anything about Lodi Corp or Mobius, Davenport would've dragged them in already, so nothing to worry about there," Guy said.

"Yeah, that would be—" A thought hit, and I snapped my head up. "Oh, shit."

"What?" Guy asked, immediately on alert.

I felt my entire body go cold. "Naomi."

**"I** should have put it together sooner," I said, wanting to thump my forehead with my hand. The last time I'd tried, Guy had grabbed said hand. He was still holding it, actually, as we rode the 'L' toward Naomi's cramped apartment in Bucktown. We could have flown there faster, but Eddie's current rules for Davenport personnel meant not drawing any attention. We were already technically breaking the rules by sneaking out in the first place, so it was better not to push our luck.

Outside of Davenport, it was a different world. The media, sensing an easy target, had gone into a feeding frenzy. Pictures of Vicki lying on the ground, grainy and blurry because it was surveillance footage, were all over the Domino and the news feeds. Had the kidnapper released them, or had the media simply found them?

I would have honestly put my money on the latter.

For one day, at least, it appeared as though *Where Is Blaze?* had been replaced by *What's Wrong with Plain Jane?*

Not all of this mattered as much as the truth that had been staring me in the face the entire time, a truth I hadn't even put together. It *couldn't* be a coincidence that Mobius had resurfaced at the same time Naomi had mysteriously found an old journal and files on him. I should have dragged her to see Kiki the instant she'd brought her suspicions up to me. Instead, I'd completely forgotten about her research.

"You've had other things on your mind," Guy said, drawing my attention back to the train car. We'd changed into civilian clothing, and he had his backpack with the War Hammer uniform inside slung across one shoulder. "Go easy on yourself. Mobius is kind of a sore subject."

"There's oblivious and there's missing the really, really, really blindingly obvious. She's involved in this somehow."

"Is she, though? Naomi was always going to look into Lodi, especially after they caused so much trouble. She's curious. It really could be a coincidence."

"It's Naomi," I said, which I felt encapsulated my entire point. If there was trouble in my life recently, Naomi Gunn was somehow at the center of it. That was just an undeniable truth, like Shark-Man's biggest battles inevitably winding up on the Golden Gate Bridge.

"You're not being very fair to her," Guy said.

"I'm totally being fair. Also pragmatic and realistic."

Guy shook his head, his lips curving up a little in a small smile.

We disembarked and I looked around automatically, the same way every Chicago resident did, for any supervillain activity. They preferred transit lines because they were always guaranteed an audience. Luck appeared to be on our side: we were able to cross the street and hurry the couple of blocks to Naomi's place.

Even better, I could hear her moving around inside. I pounded on her front door.

"You know," she said when she yanked it open, her toothbrush hanging out of her mouth, "you can knock like a normal person. Really. No reason to scare me out of my damn mind."

I brushed past her. "Where did you get that information about Mobius?"

Naomi pulled her toothbrush free. "Sure, no, come in. Make yourself at home. It's not like I could have company or anything."

"I can hear that you don't." I gave her an exaggerated eye-roll. I wasn't entirely uncouth.

Guy stepped in a little more awkwardly and smiled politely. "Hi," he said, giving her a hug. "How's tricks?"

I ignored the formalities and strolled into the main area of her loft. Her TV was tuned to one of the twenty-four-hour news channels, but it was muted. I looked away from Vicki's crumpled form on-screen as Naomi stuck her toothbrush in the kitchen sink and rinsed it off. "What's going on with Vicki?" she asked, reaching for her ever-present notebook.

"Classified. Where did you get that information about Lodi and Mobius? I hardly believe you dug that up from the local library."

"Would you look at that?" Naomi pulled a pen out of her ponytail. "That information is suddenly classified."

"It's important," I said.

"Mm-hmm." Naomi held up the pen, poised over the notebook. Her tilted eyebrow relayed the message easily enough: no information would be shared without a little quid pro quo action. I gave her an annoyed look.

It was Guy, of course, who came to the rescue.

"Naomi," he said, stepping forward. "Vicki's in trouble. If you have information that can help us figure out what happened to her . . ."

"Trouble how?" Naomi looked from him to me.

I glanced at Guy. He inclined his head the barest centimeter.

"Her powers vanished. She got hit with something and, poof, no powers. I may have gotten exposed, too. Kiki's running tests." I shoved my hands into my pockets and bunched my shoulders up around my ears. "It's something to do with Mobius."

"How do you know?"

"Because it was Mobius's kidnapper that did it to her. Or Mobius himself. We can't tell. He might be in on it."

Naomi held her hands up in a time-out gesture, eyes wide. "Mobius is alive? Wait—kidnapper?"

Guy sighed. "Why don't I explain while you take us to wherever it is you found the information?"

"How about you explain and I decide if I'll take you to wherever it is I found the information?"

Guy folded his arms over his chest. "Or, I invite you to come have dinner with Gail and me next week and you tell me now?"

"Deal," Naomi said quickly, and I didn't blame her. It was almost too bad Guy had become a superhero. If he hadn't, he'd no doubt have a five-star restaurant I wouldn't be able to afford to eat at. Naomi tucked her notebook into her back pocket and crossed over to the refrigerator, rummaging around in the vegetable drawer until she pulled out a file folder.

I raised my eyebrow at that.

"I live on takeout. People don't think to look there until the very end, and by that time, hopefully I've already stopped them. What's going on with Dr. Mobius? How do you know he's alive?"

"A ransom video of him showed up a few days ago. Apparently he's not as dead as we thought, which will make the scientific community happy." Dr. Lemuel Cooper had been willing to kill to get his hands on the supposedly deceased Dr. Mobius's notebooks. I gestured at Guy, who was much better at summarizing situations—much less likely to get sidetracked—than I was.

As was his habit, he broke it down, going over the

timeline of Mobius's ransom video, everything that had happened at Union Station, Vicki's lack of powers, and finally the video that the kidnapper had put out, offering the power-negating powder to the highest bidder. Naomi scribbled the entire time he wrote, and I helped myself to the open bag of chips and a carton of leftover tikka masala from her fridge.

When Guy was finally done, and I'd polished off the carton, Naomi put her pen down and stared at the countertop in front of her. Something was bothering her. I could tell from the way her heart rate had picked up, but she hadn't scolded me for eating her food, either.

Sure enough, my suspicions were confirmed when she finally looked up.

"I think all of this may be my fault," she said.

I couldn't help it: I turned to look at Guy with my best *told you so* face.

# CHAPTER 9

We took Naomi's car, which was two shaky steps up from a junker and so short on legroom that Guy had to be folded up like an accordion in the front seat. Even I felt a little cramped, but beggars couldn't be choosers at this point, and if Naomi was right, we needed to move quickly.

"I know I wasn't supposed to be looking into Lodi," she said as she drove us toward Evanston, "but it's frustrating. I really don't think Davenport was doing *any* research, and they should have been because here's this company actively trying to create superheroes instead of manage them. Don't they realize how significant that is?"

"I think it's more a matter of not wanting people within Davenport to get the same idea," Guy said, shifting awkwardly in the front seat.

Naomi switched lanes with all the grace of a typical Chicago driver, which is to say: like an asshole. A car behind us laid on its horn as she cut it off. "That's a ridiculous mentality that will only breed more companies like Lodi," she said.

"Maybe, but it also prevents Davenport from becoming Lodi itself," Guy said.

"If you say so." Naomi didn't seem too impressed. "Davenport is still such a monopoly that if companies like Lodi did spring up, they'd be able to swat them down like the mighty hand of a superhero god that they think they are. At any rate, that's too philosophical for now. I was fascinated because Lodi was there one day, and it was gone afterward. It felt too tidy, you know? No loose ends at all? Come on."

"So you started digging," I said, narrowing my eyes at her.

"Mm-hmm. I found some files that led me to more files that led me of course to more files because if there's one thing that's universal, it's bureaucracy and paperwork. And there was a lot there about Mobius. More even than I showed you, Gail. He was an asset to Lodi. They kept him prisoner for years, working on various inventions that I can't find anything about in the files. But I do know he had an assistant, and from what I can tell, the 'assistant' was more of a taskmaster, keeping an eye on both Mobius and any test subjects they had."

"Wait," I said. "Subjects? As in plural?"

"I think they died and were disappeared in true Chi-Town fashion." Naomi tapped her fingers in agitation against the steering wheel.

Seeing as Cooper, one of Lodi's scientists, had been more than eager enough to dissolve me in acid, I wasn't actually surprised. "I see," I said, the words sticking in my throat. "So the assistant—"

"I'm just saying: if somebody's kidnapped Mobius and knows a lot about his work, it's probably this guy."

"Does he have a name?" Guy asked.

"No. I've been doing as much digging as I can, but he obfuscates his name as much as he possibly can. I can give you everything I know about him later, which isn't much. At any rate, back to the matter at hand, I was able to find a file in the records on Mobius that referenced some land that I'm pretty sure Davenport doesn't know about, that Lodi owns." Naomi waved a frustrated hand and cut a third driver off. I felt proud of Chicago when I heard what the driver shouted at her in response. "I checked it out."

"By yourself?" I asked.

Naomi snorted. "Nothing's managed to kill me yet."

"Not for lack of trying," I said.

Her grin popped up bright on her face. "You're cute when you worry. Anyway, like I was saying, I checked it out. Didn't find anybody, but I did find *something*. And now that I'm thinking about it, our esteemed doctor and his evil assistant—or whoever the kidnapper is, if it's not that guy—may have been holed up there and I may have been the fox that startled the pheasant out of the grass."

"What do you mean?"

"You'll see what I mean when we get there."

*There* proved to be an old office building in a strip mall with the windows boarded up, far enough from any major roads that it had been completely neglected by time. Naomi parked in the parking lot and we extricated ourselves from the car as we looked around. It didn't really look like the site of mad scientist shenanigans, but given that Dr. Mobius had once held me captive in a house in the suburbs, I knew better than to be fooled. I left my senses open as I followed Guy and Naomi into the building, slipping through a board that we pried up from the edge.

At one point, the interior had probably been something boring like an accounting firm or one of those EZ Cash Loan scams that tries to look professional and instead preys on people. A few desks remained from its previous life, battered and covered in scratches, gnaw-marks, and droppings from vermin. An overpowering smell of mold hit my nostrils, inspiring a sneeze or five as I stepped in.

"Lodi sure knows how to keep it classy," I said, looking around at the mildewed carpet and rot-stains on the walls.

Guy grinned. "This place doesn't feel like a horror movie at all, no."

"Right? I like the ambience. This way," Naomi said, heading toward what had probably been the manager's office, where part of the ceiling looked like it had caved in. I could see the winter sky through a giant hole.

Halfway into the little office, a smell hit me.

"He was here," I said, lifting my head and looking around. "Mobius. He came through here at some point."

It made my knees weak. Seeing his angry face on the video was one thing, but scent was the strongest sense tied to memory, and for another awful moment I was back in that house in the suburbs, too weak to fight while Mobius changed my life irrevocably. I turned my head now until I could pinpoint the source of the smell: a crumpled pile of flannel in the corner of the office.

I picked it up and sighed. He'd always dressed like a lumberjack.

"You definitely stumbled onto something," I said to Naomi, setting the flannel shirt down on the back of the broken-down office chair. The room had been pretty well looted, but a desk remained. Daylight filtered in through cracks in the boarded-up windows, catching on the dust motes we'd disturbed.

"The files were on the desk," Naomi said, opening and shutting drawers when she found nothing inside. "Just out in the open . . . like somebody had been reading them and maybe I'd interrupted."

"Something about this place feels off," Guy said, looking around.

"What do you mean?" I asked.

"The dimensions don't line up." Guy folded his arms over his chest and squinted at the interior wall of the office. "I'd have to look at the blueprints to be sure, but this wall feels out of place."

He stepped over and began prodding the wall around the faded remains of an inspirational office poster.

"You think there's a secret room back there?" Naomi asked, looking eager. I didn't blame her, though her face did go wary a split second later. "Wait, if there's a secret room, somebody could have been watching me the whole time! Why wouldn't they just knock me out? Or worse, kill me?"

"If you had the journo face on," I said, "they were probably too scared to."

Naomi stuck her tongue out at me.

"No idea," Guy said, ignoring my aside. "But you were definitely lucky, if they were watching you."

"I'm not sure luck has anything to do with it. I may have accidentally set everything in motion by coming here. The timing's way too suspect," Naomi said. Guy continued to run his hands over the wall, not even straining to reach the ceiling (tall people suck). "I find these files out in the open and you confirm that Mobius has been here, and then almost the same day, this guy decides to ransom Mobius? Did I somehow cause this?"

"Wouldn't be the first time," I said.

"You love me, and you know it," Naomi said.

Guy made a frustrated noise. "I can't find the catch," he said. "Step back."

When he was satisfied that we were far enough away, he took a deep breath and began to push against the wall. I watched the muscles in his back and shoulders strain under the pressure. The entire building seemed to groan; I looked worriedly at the ceiling as dust and debris began to fall. "Uh, Guy . . ."

"Just a sec," he said, voice ragged. The walls began to creak. Tiny fissures spread out from the corners and the edges of the door. Wary now, I grabbed Naomi's shoulder, getting ready to shove her underneath the desk or shield her if Guy brought the ceiling down. My body could take a few hundred pounds of concrete. Probably.

Luckily, Guy took a step back. "What—" I started to say, but he startled me by drawing back and slamming his fist into the wall as hard as he possibly could. There was a loud clang, almost like an explosion, and his fist and arm went through the wall, all the way to his shoulder.

"Got it," Guy said, pulling his arm out. "Help me out?"

The punch had shattered the drywall, making it easy to peel away. It revealed a metal wall behind it, now bearing a nice puncture from Guy's fist. Without a word, we each took a side of the puncture and pulled. The metal groaned but eventually gave way, widening into a hole large enough for me to poke my head through.

It took a few seconds for my eyes to adjust to the darkness. The lair below was open and dim, lit by a strange indigo glow. "Yup," I said, pulling my head out of the hole, "someone had a secret lair under here. God, I hate secret lairs."

"You and me both," Guy said, though Naomi looked absolutely delighted, poking her head through to get a good look. Guy scratched the back of his head. "I don't suppose you saw a way in?"

"Staircase," I said. I pointed. "Behind the wall right there. I'm assuming there's a secret catch somewhere, but the door's wood if you want to skip the rigama-role."

"Excellent," Guy said, and kicked the wall. More dust pattered to the ground, and the door flew off its hinges. I heard it bouncing down the stairs. "I'll go first, if you don't mind."

"Yeah, sure, ignore chivalry," I said, and Guy smiled at me.

Naomi followed on his heels, phone camera click-ing away, so I brought up the rear, keeping my senses open for any signs of danger or booby traps. The lair wasn't large, but it was decidedly out of place in the middle of an abandoned business park. I looked for any sign that it belonged to Lodi, but unlike Daven-port, they weren't really all that big into splashing their name everywhere.

I wrinkled my nose. The lair was so typical. Un-derground, moodily lit, filled with scientific apparatus crowding the desks that I never had a hope in hell of understanding, equations written on chalkboards. The sight of a mussed cot and the shackles in the corner turned my stomach.

A second cot in the opposite corner didn't contain shackles at all.

Naomi clicked away like a fiend. "Mobius was defi-nitely here, right?"

"Trust me, he was here. The place reeks." I could smell him most strongly on the sheets of the cot with the shackles. A fireplace in the corner showed evidence of papers that had been burned, likely in a hurry. Destroying the trail. I bent to run my fingers through the ashes. "Looks like they left in a hurry. You definitely upset something with your snooping, Naomi."

Guy looked apologetic. "I need to call this in," he said.

"What? No! There's so much here, there's no reason to tell Davenport yet," Naomi said. "This isn't their find."

"Supervillains are going to be looking for this place, too," I said.

"Why?"

I stared at her. "Everybody and their brother is looking for the person who took Plain Jane's powers away. This place is a solid clue. Most of them are dumb as a box of rocks, but some supervillains would be smart enough to track this place down. Until this guy is found and all of the depowering agent is secured, anybody that knows anything about Mobius is going to be stuck at Davenport. That means you and me."

"Like hell I will," she said.

Guy raised his eyebrows at me as he stepped away to make the call.

"Sorry," I said when Naomi whirled on me in indignation.

"I thought you hated Davenport."

"I do, but this is huge." I continued to comb through

ashes. Luckily, the fire hadn't destroyed every scrap of paper. "To give you some perspective: Tamara Diesel is involved. She fights Raptor, and that's way over my usual level."

Naomi snorted. "You're Hostage Girl. You don't have a usual level."

"I *was* Hostage Girl. Now I'm an office worker with superpowers who ended up in a fight against Scorch today." My stomach rumbled, a reminder that I hadn't eaten the five-course meal I needed to recover from that. I picked up a half-piece of paper, rolled my eyes at the indecipherable formula on it, and set it aside for the Davenport techs to comb over later. "Scorch kicked my ass, for the record."

"You seem fine now, though," Naomi said.

"Blame the Mobium." A second scrap caught my eye because it had red pen marks scribbled all over it. As Naomi poked through a filing cabinet, I held the paper up to the light, recognizing Dr. Mobius's handwriting from his notebook. Only one word proved legible. "Demobilizer," I read aloud. "What do you suppose that means?"

"Demobilize means to remove somebody from military service," Naomi said.

I snorted under my breath. "Nerd."

"You asked. Whatever it means, it's mentioned in some of these files, too." Naomi pulled out a little wooden box and tried to wedge her fingernails underneath the lid. "Hey, can you get this open? I want to know what's inside."

She tossed the box. Right as she let it go, her fingers must have brushed against a secret latch, for the lid slid right open. I saw a telltale flash of very familiar blue that made me shout, but it was already too late. The box arced through the air.

"No!" In a burst of speed, Guy jumped right between us and batted the box away. Blue powder exploded where he'd hit the box—right into his face.

# CHAPTER 10

**U**nlike Vicki, they put Guy in quarantine.

Unlike Vicki, they didn't let me anywhere near him. No matter how hard I tried or how many Davenport techs I threatened to deck, even while Guy repeatedly said, "Gail—Gail, it's *fine*," trying to get me to stop. Davenport's crew descended on the lair, hauling the weak and dizzy Guy one way and me another, and panic scrambled in my chest like a living creature.

"Hit her with reusabital or something," one of the techs grunted as four of them struggled to pull me away.

They did. It made me dizzy for half a second. Apparently they weren't up to date on my file or the fact that repeated exposure to the knockout drug had made me immune. I lunged forward, ready to race for Guy and the stretcher until Naomi choked out, "You're going to get us killed, *stop*. He's fine."

But he wasn't fine.

After they dragged us back to New York, I couldn't see him at all. In fact, I couldn't see anybody: they dumped me in a cell not unlike the one where they'd put Brook. This time I didn't have Kiki's credentials to get me in and out. It was for my own good, the tech had claimed when they'd shoved me inside.

And for my own good, I'd made some sizable dents in the wall. In addition to bruising my fists, it did absolutely nothing to quell the tidal wave of panic and fear building inside of me. Whenever I closed my eyes, I could see that moment, the blue powder exploding, Guy's horrified face as he fell to his knees and coughed, just like Vicki had. I saw the pitiful little flame of Vicki's last power vanishing, only now it was happening to Guy, who'd always been strong and unstoppable and almost immovable.

And they wouldn't let me see him.

I punched the wall until I ran out of energy. Hunger, a constant companion, gnawed and churned away at my stomach, so I sank to the floor, inadvertently mimicking the same pose I'd found Brook in earlier right next door. I'd done absolutely nothing criminal—well, okay, a little breaking and entering, technically, but was it really criminal when it was land owned by a corporation that had once been about to murder me?—and I was being treated like the actual supervillain next door. This was ridiculous. This was why I hated Davenport.

To make matters worse, the root cause of my loathing for Davenport showed up in my doorway. And he had the audacity to be holding a very full tray of food, the absolute bastard.

"You," Eddie Davenport said, "are a goddamned menace."

"Fuck you, too," I said. "Why am I in here? I haven't done anything wrong."

"I explicitly ordered you and your buddies to stay on the premises." Eddie's too-handsome face twisted into a scowl. "We're dealing with one of the biggest crises this community has ever seen, and you can't even obey a simple order. And now yet another one of my top heroes is currently out of commission. That's two cities that are missing their headlining heroes, Miss Godwin, and you just happened to be present for both of those events."

Yeah, because I had the luck of a one-leaf clover. I raised my chin, folded my arms across my chest, and tried not to let him know how damn good the food smelled. My stomach didn't seem to be falling in line with that agenda, though, for it gurgled. "You can't pin that on me. I had nothing to do with it."

"You disobeyed orders."

"Hey, genius, I don't work for you. I don't work for any of you. In fact, I'm pretty sure I explicitly told you to do something illegal to a farm animal, and the ironic thing is that by keeping me in this cell, you are going to eventually interfere with my actual job. I don't have to follow your orders," I said. As best I could tell, it was the early hours of the morning on Sunday, so I actually had a little time before my coworkers would miss me—not that they really would—but I felt my point stood. "I want to see Guy."

"He's in quarantine right now." Eddie set the tray on the room's desk. "Medical informs me that you'll begin to suffer if you go much longer without nourishment. Consider this a gift from the company you *don't* work for."

"You mean the company holding me hostage, and believe me, that's not something I say lightly."

"Why did you go against my orders? I told you to remain on-site."

"Because Naomi knew something that could help Vicki." Duh.

"And you had to drag one of my headliners into it?"

"It's not like we knew there was Demobilizer there. It looked abandoned. It was an accident, and it's the last thing I could have wanted to happen. I wish it had hit me instead."

"I do, too. Except that it did."

The temperature in the cell immediately plunged into arctic territory. I'd been exposed? I was going to lose my powers? I hadn't breathed in any of the powder, I didn't think. After Guy had fallen over, coughing, he'd waved at me to stay back. But if I *had* been exposed . . . "What? I'm infected?" My voice wavered and cracked.

"That's the interesting thing, Miss Godwin." Eddie pulled his phone out and showed me the screen. "This is what Medical found when they tested your blood.

Apparently some of the toxins got into your bloodstream at Union Station."

"But I don't feel any different." I didn't have any flashy powers that would be obvious to lose like Guy and Vicki did, but I still felt normal if a bit hungry. The food Eddie had brought was outright taunting me now.

"That's because you appear to be immune to this Demobilizer powder." Eddie glared daggers at me, like this was somehow my fault. In his version of the narrative, it likely was.

"The Mobium," I said, breathing the word. It had caused so much trouble in my life, but it had also saved me so many times. "Did . . . did I adapt to that? Like I did with the pepper spray and the knockout drugs? The Mobium can fight off something that powerful?"

"We're still running tests." Eddie pinched the bridge of his nose and breathed through his teeth. He really didn't want to tell me whatever he was about to. "The current hypothesis is that it's possibly a companion to the Mobium, which makes sense given that the two appear to have the same inventor."

"God, I hate that guy," I said without thinking.

Eddie looked like he very much wanted to agree. "We've got nothing conclusive, but for right now it looks like you're immune. So congratulations on that, Miss Godwin."

"Congratulations? *Congratu*—Guy and Vicki don't have powers right now, and I'm supposed to be happy that I'm immune to whatever it was that knocked them flat?" I snatched a roll off the tray and considered flinging it at his head. The sick feeling in my stomach grew. Guy had to be going crazy. He'd had his powers for a decade, ever since the explosion had granted them to him and his siblings. What must he be going through right now? What did that even feel like? "Excuse me if I'm not exactly thrilled about this news."

"Trust me, I would much rather it were you than them. Your return to Class D status would solve a lot of my problems," Eddie said.

Prick.

"You're trouble," he went on, "and an amazingly large pain in the ass for somebody of your stature. I should have let you rot in Detmer."

"Bullshit prison sentences do appear to be your specialty," I said.

Eddie breathed through his teeth again. "Here's what is going to happen," he said. "I am facing one of the biggest crises this community has ever seen, so you hopefully can understand that I am too busy to run herd on some problem-causing Class C who can't follow a simple directive. But we find ourselves at an impasse because, right now, you are one of three people immune to the very chemical agent I can't safely send any of my troops to face. Which means I am conscripting you to fight in the name of Davenport."

"I already have a job," I said, my own jaw clenched.

"Right, yes, that little assistant editor job you play at. When are you going to grow up and see that your place is here? You've got superpowers now."

"It's still my choice," I said.

HOW TO SAVE THE WORLD 129

"I'm sorry," Eddie said, his voice patently insincere in a way that made me want to drive my fist into his nose, "my mistake. Did you not want to help Mr. Bookman and Ms. Burroughs? Would you prefer they languish forever without their powers? Medical is hopeful that if we can secure Dr. Mobius, he might have a solution."

"You think Mobius is going to have an antidote?" I asked, scoffing.

"You'll find we have ways to persuade him to make one, if an antidote is indeed possible." Eddie tucked his phone away into his suit pocket and brushed off his sleeves. "Until then, try to consider the job voluntary. It'll make it so much easier on all of us."

"Why me?" I asked. "Angélica worked for you for years."

"She has powers outside of the Mobium. Are you really asking her to give those up?"

Dammit, he had a point.

"Fine," I said. "I'll help you out, but only for Vicki and Guy's sake."

"I'm glad we've reached something of an agreement. Enjoy your dinner. We won't take it out of your paycheck." He strolled to the door and waved his badge at the scanner. At the last second he turned. "An orderly will be by with updates on Mr. Bookman's condition, and I'm sure they'll let you in to see him in the morning if your attitude has improved significantly."

"Gee, thanks," I said, though the words tasted like poison on my tongue. "For the record, you're a dick."

"Stay classy, Miss Godwin."

And with that, the door shut behind him. I considered throwing the crushed roll in my hand at it, but that would only be a waste of food. With a scowl, I ripped into it with my teeth. It felt horrible to idly sit and eat when I knew my friends were going through something so awful as losing their powers, but my body needed the fuel. I worked my way methodically through the dishes Eddie had left behind, cleaning each one off in turn, barely tasting anything. So the Demobilizer didn't do anything to the Mobium. Were they related? Would the Mobium cancel it out somehow and give the powers back?

If anybody could figure this out, it would definitely be Kiki and her team. On one of my rare visits to her actual office, I'd seen her diplomas on the wall. She must have been a genius to get through as many of them as quickly as she had. Vicki and Guy meant a lot to her. They were her friends. She could figure this out.

When the door opened, I'd finished most of the food and was reaching for the final plate. I tensed, spoiling for a fight, even though it was probably one of the orderlies. It wasn't.

"Great," I said, closing my eyes. "Yet another Davenport. Just what my day needed."

Jessie took the insult well, all things considered, and tossed something at me: my jacket. "Huh?" I asked.

"I convinced my brother to let me spring you," she said. "The beds in this compound are shit. Come on."

I didn't need to be told twice. I didn't quite understand why Jessie had taken such a liking to me, but anything was better than staying in a cell. I'd had enough of that to last a lifetime. "I want to see Guy."

"Medical's not letting anybody in. They've got him sedated—it wouldn't do you any good."

But I'd be able to *see* him. It would tell me something. What it was, I had no idea, but I didn't exactly care. I needed to see him.

"We'll come back first thing in the morning," Jessie said. "Promise."

It was on the tip of my tongue to retort that a promise from a Davenport meant nothing to me, but all things considered, Jessie had done her own fair share of watching out for me. Maybe I should wait to look this gift horse in the mouth until I was a little less exhausted and worried about my friends.

"Where are we going?" I asked, following her out of the cell.

"The Nest."

"The what? Oh, god, please tell me that's not what you call your base."

Jessie had the decency to look at least a little uncomfortable. "It was Audra's idea," she said. "I wanted no part in it. But what Audra wants, Audra gets."

I didn't sleep well, which went without saying.

Part of the problem was that when Jessie said I could sleep at her base, she literally meant in her base. Not in a guest bedroom or anything: in the base itself.

We traveled by 'porter to Chicago and she set me up on a cot right next to one of her many, many tactical vehicles in the parking bay. Apparently Jessie babied her cars more than anybody I'd ever met, because the atmosphere control was phenomenal, not too warm or too hot. But it was still an eerie place to be expected to sleep. And I didn't enjoy the fact that I was in Chicago and Guy was in New York. Sure, it was one 'port away, but it was still too far.

Sometimes the Mobium allowed me to drop off to sleep no matter what was on my mind, especially when I was healing from something like being hit on the head. Today I wasn't nearly so lucky. In the echoing garage, I tossed and turned on my cot, eventually kicking the blankets down to my feet and staring at the ceiling. Every time I wondered what it would be like for Guy when he finally woke up, a sick feeling washed over me.

There had to be some way to fix this. We'd find Mobius, and he could reverse everything. He'd know why the Demobilizer hadn't worked on me. This had to have a happy ending. I refused to accept anything less.

At some point, I must have drifted off to sleep because I was woken by something buzzing. Not my phone, I realized, groping blindly for it in the dark. The buzzing seemed to be matched to the computer consoles along the wall glowing a bright red.

"What the . . . ?"

Jessie trotted in, already in the black bodysuit she

wore beneath her armor. "Go back to sleep," she told me as she pulled said armor on. "Just a minor villain. I'll deal with it."

I sat up. "Want backup?"

"Nah. I can handle this."

"If they have the Demobilizer—"

"Not a problem for me." She snapped a gas mask onto the lower part of her mask. "Raptor's always prepared. Remember that."

"Uh, sure," I said. She took one of the motorcycles, roaring off into the night and leaving me on the cot with the blankets bunched around my socks. I sighed and lay back down. It made sense that the Raptor might take over any calls against supervillains. After all, Guy-as-War-Hammer was Chicago's main hero, and he was currently under sedation and without his powers.

Eventually curiosity got the better of me. I rolled off the cot and crossed to the computers, hoping she had some kind of guest log-in. To my surprise, G._GODWIN was listed on the possible log-ins. Seeing no password prompt, I warily placed my palm on the scanner.

It let me right into the system.

"Weird," I said, shaking my head. Maybe she'd done me a favor and had set up FreeCell or Solitaire or something in case I wouldn't be able to sleep. Instead, I found a full and robust lineup of programs available to me, most of which I didn't recognize. Shrugging, I tabbed over to the internet and browsed the Domino's site. I'd tried to look into the situation on my phone, but the Nest had, like, a light-speed-fast connection, so this was way better. In less than a minute, I had several dozen different sites up across the monitors.

I settled in to read, keeping an eye on the live feed from the Raptorcycle. There'd been a shortcut to it on the home screen, so I didn't feel like I was snooping inappropriately.

Besides, not many people got a chance to watch Raptor kick ass up close and personal. I had before, but I much preferred it this way, when the target wasn't me. She was much, much scarier on the other side of a fight.

**U**nfortunately, there was only so much web browsing that my tired brain could withstand. After my thirty-third article about Plain Jane, my eyes began to drift closed. I logged out, climbed back onto the cot, and almost slept through Jessie returning. She stumbled tiredly back to what I assumed was a much more appropriate room for sleeping than a cot out among the cars. She still wasn't awake when I woke, so I explored until I found a fridge and cooked myself a full breakfast. There was no way I was going back to Davenport Tower without Jessie—not without Eddie throwing me in a cell—so I forced myself to wait and texted Guy instead.

To my surprise, he texted back right away. *Where are you?*

I hit the CALL button instead. It went to voice mail.

*Can't talk. In a briefing. Should pay attention, but don't care.*

Why did they have him in a briefing? Shouldn't they be running extensive tests and seeing if there was some way to reverse the effects of the Demobilizer?

*Are you ok???* I texted. *I'm in Chi-Town, btw. You wouldn't believe me if I said exactly where.*

*I never have a hard time believing you when you say things like that.*

He had a point. He texted a few more times, confirming that Vicki was with him and they were in the Nucleus. Angélica had apparently been looking for me, so I made sure to text her that I was staying with Jessie. But that wasn't what concerned me.

No, I was bothered by the fact that Guy seemed to be dodging my questions whenever I asked how he was. He demurred answering, usually turning the conversation around to me—Was I eating enough? Was it true that I'd told Eddie to fuck off?—and that set off alarms in my brain.

I needed to get to New York. I needed to see him.

"No," Jessie said when she finally strolled in, wearing an oversized Columbia U hoodie and toweling her hair dry. "Not right now."

"But—"

"We go to Davenport and my brother's going to come up with some kind of suicide mission for you. I'd prefer to keep you out of sight for now."

I blinked at that. "Why do you care?"

Jessie shrugged.

"No, seriously," I said.

"My niece likes you and your little pack of trouble-makers, so we'll go with that. Did you leave me any food or am I going to have to call in delivery?"

"It's on the stove," I said, feeling grumpy. Why did she care so much, anyway? Yes, I was friends with Kiki, even though our relationship was a little strange—murdering a man together kind of cements a bond whether or not you want it to—but this was just bizarre.

"I don't understand anything that's happening," I said. "Which, to be fair, is not that unusual. Whatever. I assume there's somewhere I can take a shower?"

"I left you some hot water and everything," Jessie said, smirking.

After my shower, wearing borrowed clothing, I made my way to the main gym area of the Nest, where I took my frustration out on a punching bag and went for a long run on the treadmill. I didn't wear myself out, even though I wanted to.

"You're not good at being idle, huh?" Jessie asked, wandering by as she crunched into an apple.

"Not when I'm being kept in the dark." I'd had years of forced idleness to suffer through, though I was usually chained and gagged during these periods. Really, some days I wondered if I should be concerned by how much supervillains had shaped my psyche. Right now I wanted to hit something substantial. No, scratch that: I wanted to see Guy. And Vicki, too. But mostly Guy. I stepped off the treadmill and took a few deep breaths.

"I guess I just don't get why you won't sneak me in to see Guy or tell me what's going on with him."

"Not much to get. My brother's an asshole, and I refuse to let you be his next casualty."

"What's the deal with you two, anyway? Do you, like, hate each other?"

"Dad wanted him to follow in his footsteps. Eddie went to law school." Jessie crossed her arms over her chest. "And I became the Raptor. Which Dad never wanted."

"Why not?"

"Because that meant I had to fight Fearless."

Okay, that was a tangled web. Fearless was Rita Detmer, the world's first supervillain. She also happened to be Jessie's mother. "But Eddie would've had to if he'd become Raptor," I said.

"Welcome to the mind of Kurt Davenport." Jessie finished off her apple and tossed the core into the trash without looking. "Eddie resents me for not letting Raptor die like the rest of the Feared Five, and I resent Eddie for being kind of a dick."

So I wasn't the only one who felt that way. I patted at the side of my neck with a gym towel. Raptor and Fearless were famous for their grand, city-block-leveling fights. "What was it like?" I asked. "Having to fight your mom?"

"It sucks. I don't recommend it."

I snorted. My own mother was still somewhere in Muncie, Indiana, probably. We hadn't spoken since I'd set out before my eighteenth birthday. Was that worse or better than her being a supervillain hell-bent on killing me? I couldn't decide. At least the indifference hadn't ever been life-threatening.

"But that's the problem. Whoever is Raptor automatically gets the honor of fighting Fearless. It's just the way things go. Whoever's in this suit next will discover that for themselves," Jessie said.

"That's a lot of responsibility," I said. For as fit and terrifying as she was, Jessie was also over fifty with two kids. One of them would probably be the next Raptor, which was quite a legacy. And a heavy burden to bear, really. So I gestured at her with my water bottle. "You take over and become Raptor, then you have to learn how to, what, save the world or something?"

"Let's hope you never have to."

"Have to what?"

"Save the world," Jessie said.

I raised my eyebrows. "Are you saying if it's my responsibility to save the world, we're all doomed?"

"No." Surprisingly, she smiled. "I was talking about the cost. But that's a little heavy for right now. You might want to grab another shower."

"What? Why?"

"I have a feeling you're going somewhere soon."

# CHAPTER 11

*I have an idea.* After Jessie's vague pronouncement, Guy's text didn't surprise me. Really, nothing about Jessie Davenport should have surprised me at this point. Maybe that was her superpower. Maybe she was just really good at precognition. It would explain so much. I rubbed my ear with a towel, trying to get rid of a troublesome bit of water stuck inside it. Another text from Guy arrived: *How do you feel about being Nancy Drew?*

*Does that make you a Hardy Boy?* I texted back.

*Only if I can be Frank. Can you sneak away from wherever you are and meet me somewhere? Would pick you up, but . . .* He ended the text with a shrug emoji.

"Hey, Jessie," I said, poking my head out of the bathroom. "What are my chances of sneaking out of here?"

"If you manage it, you'll be the first," she called back. "But I'm willing to let you walk out the front door if you wear concealed armor."

*I can get away,* I texted back to Guy. *Where do you want to meet?*

The address he texted back made me raise my eyebrows. *Seriously?* I texted at him.

*You have supervillain friends, right? They like you?*

I snorted. He really overestimated how personable people found me. But now that he mentioned it . . .

I sent off a text message before I could convince myself it was the worst idea ever. *I'll meet you there,* I texted Guy, and I went to bug my weird jailer to see if I could borrow her car. Preferably the one with the flamethrowers, as where I planned it go, I might need them.

She only gave me a *you have got to be kidding me* look.

"Why not?" I asked.

"I've seen you drive, remember? I'll give you a ride."

"Oh, fine."

Guy had texted me the address to a bar in Wicker Park. The bar itself didn't seem all that impressive: nautical-themed, with a little steering wheel for a boat over the door, the paint outside peeling and shabby. Just a typical Chicago bar, not really built to draw the eye. Unless you knew this bar's secret: that it was a gathering place for the evil-inclined. I'd only been inside once, but I'd been less than impressed. That may or may not have had something to do with the fact that there was an entire wall dedicated to supervillains taking selfies with an unconscious me.

Jessie pulled up beside it. Overhead, the shingle sign read MIND THE BOOM in faded red lettering, and I wondered if supervillains ever really had any self-respect, drinking at a bar with the most pun-filled name I'd ever seen.

I climbed out of the passenger seat. "Do I have a curfew, Mom?" I asked.

Jessie rolled her eyes. "Do your best not to end up in an inordinate amount of trouble."

"So a moderate amount is okay, then?"

"Let's go with *expected* rather than *okay*. Text me when you're done."

God, what a weirdo. I crossed the street toward the bar—Jessie had to know what it was; I doubted there was a single supervillain secret that she wasn't privy to—and looked around. Luckily, Guy towered over everybody and was more redheaded than a tequila sunrise, so he was incredibly easy to pick out of a crowd. I would just have to be careful. He would probably be depressed and I would need to be supportive and . . .

"Gail!"

I turned and barely had time to brace myself before I was scooped up in a giant bear hug. Guy spun me around, hugging me tightly and crushing me against his chest. Or mostly crushing me. His hug had none of his usual strength, but that wasn't the weirdest part of it.

No, the weird thing was the way he absolutely beamed at me as he set me down.

"Um," I said, since the wires between my brain and the rest of me seemed to have decayed. Guy's smile was positively infectious. I peered up at him and was tempted to poke his chest to make sure he was still flesh and bone. "Are you a robot?"

"Nope. Hi." He kissed me a great deal more enthusiastically than usual. Guy wasn't by any means reserved with affection, but in public he tended to get a bit shy. "How are you? You look rested. Where even were you?"

"The Nest."

A line appeared between his eyebrows. "What?"

"I think I've been adopted. Anyway, that's not important. Are you okay? Is this, um, is this happiness some really strange form of denial? Because I'm here for you, like, whatever you need."

"That's really sweet, but I'm fine."

I peered up at his face, not really convinced. This had to be some really strong denial. Like, crazily strong. Either that or Davenport had put him on some seriously heavy-duty antidepressants. Physically, he looked healthy, and he didn't smell or feel any different. His hair was a little messy, like he'd been running his hands through it, but his eyes were bright and clear and green and almost twinkling.

"Gail," he said, as my face must have shown all of the skepticism going through my brain, "I'm *fine*. Look, pinch me. You'll see that I'm not a robot and that I'm perfectly okay."

"You're happy about this?"

"I feel great. You have no idea."

"You're happy without your powers."

"Ecstatic."

"But . . . *why*?"

"Because I'm free." Guy said it so simply that I nearly took a step back in shock. "For once in my life, I don't have to fly somewhere and save the day, because I can't. It's such an amazing feeling. No guilt. This is wonderful."

"Wow," I said. I hadn't quite thought of it that way, but: "Wait, does it really wear on you that much? How come you never said anything?"

His shoulders went up to his ears. "What would it have done?" he asked. "The powers and responsibilities are going to be there whether I wish they are or not. It never seemed worth it to waste my energy. Of course, maybe this is all temporary, but whatever, I'm going to enjoy it." He grinned. "You look good."

"Now I know you're lying. I barely got any sleep."

"Should've gone with a sedative." He played with the ends of my hair and swooped forward, stealing another kiss. "I tell you, it does wonders."

"I'll take your word for it."

A throat cleared behind us. "That's gross, just so you know," a familiar voice said.

I turned, stepping out of Guy's arms—we were in public and right in front of a supervillain bar, to boot—and quickly adjusted my shirt. "Oh, good. You got my text. Hi."

Raze gave me the most unimpressed look in her arsenal. She wore some kind of acid-washed jean jacket and a sideways ponytail—though she had her casual visor over her eyes, which were much larger than the average human's—and seemed to believe it was still the 1980s. "This doesn't look like a battle," she said.

"What's she doing here?" Guy asked, looking between us in confusion.

Raze scoffed at him. "What's *he* doing here?"

"Actually, I have no idea what the answer to either of those questions is. I assume Guy here has a plan. Raze, this is my boyfriend, Guy. Guy, this is Raze, my biggest enemy."

They shook hands, eyeing each other warily. Belatedly, I realized that these were two people who probably should never have been introduced. But there wasn't much I could do about that now.

"We're looking into anybody who knows anything about the drug that's taking powers away," Guy told Raze.

She made the sign of the cross backward. "I heard about that. Keep it away from me."

"It's actually not that bad once you—okay," Guy said, shrinking a little under the weight of Raze's glare. I didn't blame him. The too-large eyes made any glare automatically twice as ferocious. "The good news is we're trying to get our hands on the rest of it so it doesn't affect anybody else."

"You didn't get hit, did you?" Raze said to me, looking accusingly at Guy.

"I'm fine," I said, since it would've taken too long to explain that I technically had. And if Raze found out I was immune, there wasn't anything really stopping her from trying to draw my blood and reverse-engineer a cure. Given that most of her experiments had the solitary goal of causing as much pain as possible, I didn't actually have a lot of faith in her inventions. "A friend of mine did get hit, though. And we need to find out either who's doing this or get to a cure."

"Which is why we're here?" Raze glanced at the sign over the door of the bar next to us. "This place isn't really where the big movers and shakers go, you know? I mean, this is my watering hole."

I knew that much. I'd once gone into Mind the Boom and had told the barkeep that I wanted to take over Raze's territory. Raze hadn't held it against me when she'd gotten out of prison, either. Instead, she'd been flattered that I'd thought of her. Some days, I wasn't sure Raze was looking for an enemy. But she also didn't seem to have the word *friend* in her vocabulary, so we made do with our strange little relationship. She twisted her fingers through her ponytail and tilted her head to the side, waiting for me to answer.

"It's a pretty long shot that anybody in there will know anything," I said. "And are we sure about this? I mean, supervillain bar. We know my history with them."

Guy squeezed my hand. "Mind the Boom's supposed to be neutral territory, or so I've heard."

"Where did you hear that?" I asked, eyes wide.

He jerked a shoulder. "I may have met a couple villains for drinks here to negotiate terms of handing over hostages."

Raze was now studying him, either like he was an

idiot or like she was trying to figure out which mask he wore. Honestly, it was obvious: he was over six feet tall, green-eyed, and hanging out with Hostage Girl. But then, nobody had seen Blaze for months, so maybe it wasn't as obvious as I thought.

"Wait a second," I said, blinking several times. "Your plan is really to wait for bad guys to show? That's it?"

"Neutral territory," Guy said.

"Yesterday villains wanted Br—Chelsea back, so they tried to blow up Union Station. For a minor slight against them," I said, giving him a look. "This is about a drug that takes out superpowers. Do you think neutral territory is really going to matter?"

Raze snorted as she shivered and pulled her jacket tighter around her frame. I really wished she would wear warmer clothing. It was November. "I hope the villains get the drug. Better than Davenport getting it."

Guy and I gave her baffled looks.

She rolled her eyes. "Do-gooders, ugh. I'm cold. I'm going inside."

I followed close on her heels. "What do you mean by that?" I asked as we stepped inside.

"I mean you do good." She flicked her fingers at me.

"No, not that. What do you mean you don't want Davenport to have it?"

"Oh, yes," Raze said, "let's give the all-encompassing evil eye corporation the ability to decide who does and doesn't get to keep their powers. That sounds *smart*."

Come to think of it, she had a point. I rolled the idea over in my brain as I followed her into the bar. If the Demobilizer was as effective as it appeared to be, Davenport having ample access to it—and possibly being able to replicate it—was beyond game changing. Instead of sending people to Detmer, they could simply remove their powers and send them back into the world. They already wielded too much influence and domination over the superhero community. If they had the ability to nullify powers at will, what sort of offenses would they deem the Demobilizer appropriate for? I'd already stared down the barrel of their justice system and had been sent to prison for a crime I hadn't committed. If they'd had the Demobilizer then, would I even have powers now? The thought was a sobering one as I took a seat at the bar between Raze and Guy.

The nautical decorations—fake fishermen's nets, some weathered buoys, cheesy plastic trout caught in the netting—hadn't gotten any better in the months since I'd been there last. In addition, the bar seemed really empty for Sunday around lunchtime. It had been mostly empty the last time I'd visited, too, so maybe having supervillain clientele wasn't all that lucrative. They probably tried to pay by holding the bartender at death-ray-point. Or maybe there was an honor code among villains that they treated their watering hole with respect. After all, the bar had far fewer scorch marks than I would expect from an evildoer gathering place.

Guy shook his head at Raze, leaning around me to make his point. "Tamara Diesel and her lot would only use it to destroy heroes and then they would take over the world," he said.

"So they shouldn't have it, either," Raze said, looking bored as she pulled out a butterfly knife and began to flip it around. Guy reached for it and I grabbed his wrist in case he didn't remember he wasn't impervious to sharp blades anymore. "Maybe nobody should have it."

"This is the very definition of a Pandora's box," I said, my brow wrinkling.

"Probably," Raze said. She flipped the blade over. I pretended that it coming within millimeters of my skin was an accident. She perked up. "Actually, I changed my mind. *I* should have it."

"No," Guy and I said.

Raze sighed like we were being unreasonable. "No, really, I should. My IQ is through the roof. I'd make all the best choices about who gets powers and who doesn't based on how much I like them. This is brilliant. It's a fair system unless I don't like you."

"Not happening," I said.

Raze shook her head regretfully. "I need a better nemesis. You're a depressing stick in the mud, Girl."

Guy looked at me sideways. I'd explained Raze's logic to him time and again, but she needed to be experienced to be believed. "I keep telling you the same thing," I said to her.

But Raze shook her head. "I have invested far too much into this enemy-ship to let it go now. Oh, hey, Sal."

Since I hadn't heard the bartender and I usually heard everything, I jerked hard enough to hit my elbow on the bar, narrowly missing the flick of Raze's butterfly knife just above said elbow. I thought I saw

Sal the bartender pause momentarily in the doorway to the back room, her gaze on us, but it could have been an illusion through the sudden tears of pain. I blinked those away and shook out my elbow. I'd hit my funny bone perfectly. It was a talent, really.

"Hostage Girl," Sal said, flicking up her eye patch so that her bionic eye swept over me in a scan. "You're looking a little less like a fugitive this time." The bionic eye scanned Guy, who looked a bit awkward folded over onto the bar stool. "Who's this? Another villain?"

"Not exactly," Guy said.

"Uh-huh." Sal turned and gave Raze a high five. "Don't usually see you on Sundays."

"Her idea." Raze jerked the blade at me. "She's looking into that power-sucking stuff."

"Uh-huh. What's your poison?" Sal asked her, and I worried that it was literal.

"Lemon juice. Five shots, straight, neat. Sour as you can get it." Raze looked at me. "And I'm not sharing with either of you do-gooders. You can get your own sour squeeze."

Sal looked from Raze to me, face switching to decided amusement. A line of scarring traced the skin around her eye patch. I figured it had to do with the reason she had a bionic eye in the first place. "You want to know about the power-draining juice, too? And you thought you'd just ask around here? Are you some kind of junior gumshoe?"

"My friend got hit," I said. I didn't look at Guy. "Two of them did. One's more upset about it than the other."

Sal rested both hands on the bar top and regarded me. Only me, though. Raze and Guy she ignored. It was unnerving having that one eye focused on me. "You're also friends with Chelsea."

I blinked at that. "What? Not exactly." Belatedly, I realized I should have denied any connection to Brook a great deal more vehemently. From the way Guy went tense next to me, he seemed to agree. "Wait, how do you know that?"

"I run Mind the Boom," Sal said, giving me a look that pointed out how much she disliked me for making her state the obvious. "She was spotted for the first time in months at Union Station. And so, Hostage Girl, were you."

Damn Toadicus, I thought. Next time I saw him I was kicking him extra hard in the gizzard or whatever frog parts he really had. If he hadn't messed up my mask, I wouldn't be in this much trouble.

"Dangerous people are looking for Chelsea," Sal said. "I don't want them finding her at my bar."

"It's not like I brought her with me. She's not here," I said.

"I can see that. Is that going to change?"

I squinted at her. "Why do you want to know?"

"It's not important. Just know that if she ever shows her face here, your drink gets replaced with arsenic."

"I think I'd be able to tell if it was arsenic," I said.

Sal raised an eyebrow. "Would you?" She set a drink in front of me: an Irish car bomb. I'd ordered one the last time I'd been in the bar, so it was a little scary that she had that kind of memory.

"Uh." Guy held his hands up in a time-out. "How about we not threaten to poison the clientele?"

Sal didn't look at him. She set a shot glass full of lemon juice in front of Raze, who happily sucked away at it. "Who's the stiff?" she asked me.

I bristled. "My boyfriend."

"He's too tall for you." Sal refilled Raze's glass. Raze downed that, made a face, and waved her hand in a *keep 'em coming* gesture. Sal shrugged to herself and poured another shot of straight lemon juice.

I exchanged a look with Guy. This was just bizarre. "Do you . . . have some kind of problem with me?" Guy asked.

Sal straightened abruptly. "No," she said. "Raze, I'm cutting you off."

"But that's only three!"

"And last time you had more than that, I had to peel you off the ceiling. You're done." She looked over my shoulder. "Looks like your one o'clock appointment is here, Hostage Girl."

"What are you . . . ?" I trailed off, my insides going cold. I hadn't heard a thing, which could only mean that something very, very bad was going on behind me and things were probably about to go to hell in a handbasket.

Sure enough, I turned, and standing there in the main part of the bar, right next to the wall full of Hostage Girl selfies, was Tamara Diesel.

For a second, I could have heard a pin drop.

And then Tamara strode forward so quickly that I didn't have time to react, and grabbed me by the throat. "Hostage Girl," she said. "Just who I was looking for."

Oh, crap.

# CHAPTER 12

Tamara Diesel, unsurprisingly, was even *more* terrifying up close.

For example, being a block away from her in the fight at Union Station hadn't impressed upon me how cold, flinty, and ruthless the woman's eyes truly were. Or the fact that the metal spikes on her leather vest happened to be splattered with something that smelled suspiciously like human blood. The left half of her head was shaved—save for a very short star-shaped patch of hair—the other half in cornrows that followed the contours of her scalp. She had a scar bisecting her lip and a sneer that put Angélica's to shame.

Fear made my heart actively stutter as her hand tightened around my throat. This close, I could smell her chapstick. I put up a hand to stop Guy from leaping at her, just in case he'd forgotten that he was a great deal squishier than usual.

"Uh," I said as Raze looked over with interest. "I don't think we've formally met."

Her teeth were very white when she sneered. "You know who I am."

"I'm out." Sal tossed her dishrag down and raised her hands in the air. "You want to fight, I'll give you the name of my insurance company. Good luck paying the premiums."

I wondered if they still sold Hostage Girl insurance. It was a strange and almost absurd thing to think when a woman literally had a hand around my neck, but the thought did go through my mind. Thankfully, she wasn't cutting off my oxygen or trying to hold me up by the neck. I had no desire to find out up close just how strong Tamara really was.

"I'm not here to fight," Tamara said, looking me up and down.

"I hope you don't feel the same way about being sassed," I said. "Because with me that's pretty much what you get."

One corner of her mouth tilted downward. Tamara Diesel didn't have a sense of humor? That was almost worse than that time she'd decided five boroughs in New York City was two too many. At least she wasn't actively choking me, but her hand was around my throat and that was a problem. Also, why did she have to be six inches taller than me? Would it kill them to send me a supervillain that I could meet at eye-level?

"Either way, it appears you've got me," I said, trying

to change the subject before Tamara started squeezing. "Literally. What exactly do you want?"

"I need a moment of your time," she said, studying my face. Abruptly, she let me go and I put a hand to my throat, massaging the skin there. I tried to remember if "has a grip like a hydraulic press" was listed among the known superpowers for her because *wow*. "Over here. My companions will keep your friends company."

On cue, Toadicus and Stretchy McGee stepped into Mind the Boom. I looked around for Scorch, but apparently my fire-nemesis was nowhere to be found. Tamara jerked her head at them and they stepped over to flank Guy and Raze.

My hands closed into fists. Reassuringly, Guy touched my elbow. "Looks like I've got a new drinking buddy," he said, jerking his head at Stretchy. "Go on. I'll get acquainted with my new pal. We'll learn each other's life stories, we'll laugh, we'll joke. It'll be fun."

Apparently losing his powers made him a little more of a smart-ass. It was a good look on him, actually.

Raze scoffed. "I have no intentions of bonding with this—" she looked Toadicus up and down "—reptile."

She said it like she clearly didn't feel he was worthy of such a title. I didn't bother to point out the error.

"Try not to shoot anyone," I said, since I didn't feel like starting something I wasn't sure we could finish. I grabbed my Irish car bomb, useless by this point because it was meant to be chugged, and pushed myself to my feet. It wasn't easy, especially since my knees had mysteriously turned to goo, but I kept my spine straight and walked across the warped wooden flooring to have a one-on-one meeting with a top-ranked villain.

Tamara pulled a chair back for herself. It scraped extra loudly in the stillness and tension of the bar. "Hostage Girl," she said, inclining her head as she sat.

I took a seat across from her, staying on the edge of my chair and trying to ignore the panic jack-rabbiting through my veins. "Ms. Diesel. Or is it Mrs.? Is there, like, a Mr. or another Mrs. Diesel?"

Again, her lips curved downward. This conversation really was not going to go well.

"Ms., it is. I got it," I said. "I can work with that."

She pulled out a ridiculously oversized gun and placed it on the table between us. The gun was massive. It looked like it could blow a few fist-shaped holes in me. A frigid drop of sweat slid from my hairline and into my body armor, which I knew from personal experience had the ability to withstand a bullet or three. But would it hold up against this monster of a gun? And why did somebody as powerful as Tamara need a gun, anyway? "I can't say I was expecting to see you out in public. Somebody with a better survival instinct might have stayed indoors and out of trouble."

I lifted my glass and took a sip. It tasted particularly foul, but I smacked my lips. "I got thirsty."

"In a supervillain bar."

"I like the ambience. Reminds me of a Jimmy Buffett song." I plucked at the shirt I'd borrowed from Jessie. "My other shirt's at the cleaners, but it's Hawaiian print."

Guy's snort as he tried not to laugh was almost deafening in the quiet.

"At least he thinks I'm funny," I said, since Tamara's face never lost its stony countenance.

"I want to know everything you know about the Demobilizer."

"It's blue," I said. The fact that she knew its name meant she'd apparently been a recipient of the kidnapper's video. I wondered if her email had the word *villain* in the domain. "It kind of smells like apricots."

There was a pause. She expected me to go on, evidently. "That's it?"

"That's everything I really definitively know," I said, since self-preservation instincts were apparently for chumps. "The rest is all conjecture."

"You think you're cute."

"I'm less than five-two and ninety percent of my friends are, like, a foot taller than me. By those standards, I'm adorable."

Tamara Diesel moved fast, I'll hand her that. In a blink she had me by the collar. My shirt wasn't sturdy enough to bear my weight, so I heard a ripping noise. Jessie was going to be annoyed about that. "I don't find you cute," Tamara said. "I think you're an idiot."

"I like you, too," I said.

"Tell me about the Demobilizer." She shook me a little.

"It's an invention of a really vain man who insists on putting some form of his name on everything he creates," I said. "I'm not a scientist. I couldn't tell you how it works, except that it's probably bad news and the last person who should have it is you."

I braced myself for a hit that never came. Tamara breathed out through her nose. "You were right," she said over my shoulder at Stretchy. "She does know something. Use the beanpole. Sounds like she could use some motivation."

"Wait, what?" I blinked and in an instant Stretchy had an arm wrapped around Guy, circling him twice. He struggled, but his superstrength had been sapped by the Demobilizer.

"Guy!" I tried to rip away from Tamara, but she was too strong.

"I'm fine," he said. "Kind of tickles, actually."

He was lying: his face was rapidly turning red, and frustration was evident in his eyes. But he smiled.

"Start talking or I squeeze harder," Stretchy said, and Guy grunted.

"Let him go." Anger made its way up through my chest, nudging aside the fear. I might be scared out of my mind for Guy, who was so incredibly breakable now that it almost made me feel light-headed, but I'd been in his shoes over and over again for four years. And I hated bullies. I slid my fingers under my shirt at my waist, hoping that Tamara Diesel wasn't paying close attention. We were so screwed. "Let him go or you'll regret it."

"Tell the lady what she wants to know," Stretchy said. Toadicus smirked. I looked over my shoulder at Tamara, who still had a grip on my shirt. Silence stretched over the bar until—

*Clang.*

All five of us jumped. Raze, who'd slammed her third and final shot glass onto the bar top, didn't notice. She let out a ladylike burp. "Sal, I could use another one of those," she called toward the back room.

"You can drink at a time like this?" I asked.

"They're threatening you, not me. Sal!"

"Enough." Tamara nodded at Toadicus, who grabbed Raze around the middle, moving to pick her up.

He yanked back a bloody hand and screamed.

No point in waiting for a better distraction. I slapped the side of Tamara's neck, aiming for speed rather than strength. The taser patch I'd slammed into the corner of her jaw sprang to life with a fizzle of static and a bright blue flash. I launched myself right as it went off, sliding for home toward Guy and Stretchy. My knee drove right into Stretchy McGee's scapula. Nothing crunched because the woman was probably made of rubber, but she still screamed.

Tamara stormed toward me, homicide written on every feature. As Guy struggled to free himself from Stretchy McGee, I scrambled upright. Unfortunately, I'd forgotten the telekinesis: Tamara raised her hand, fingers spread, and the invisible force hit like a battering ram. It slammed under my sternum, the force of it scooping me up and backward. My shoulder blades hit the bar so hard that my head recoiled back and agony sang up my spine, knocking the breath from my lungs.

I cried out and tried to push against the force, but it was like I was surrounded by invisible steel arms that threatened to choke me. Tamara stood in the center of the bar with her hand still extended, the irises in her eyes glowing so brightly that I could see them clearly even in the dim lighting. No wonder she regularly made the top ten lists for scary-ass villains. The look on her face was going to give me nightmares for a month.

From the way Guy gasped, I apparently wasn't the only one to think so. At least on the other side of the bar, Raze seemed to hold her own. She kicked a downed Toadicus in the stomach repeatedly. "Keep! Your! Froggy! Hands!" Each word was accompanied by a kick and a grunt. "Off! Of! Me! You stupid reptile!"

Guy and I were considerably more screwed. I couldn't move, and even though I'd damaged Stretchy a little, she was still standing.

Tamara's eyes never left mine as she peeled the taser patch from her skin. There wasn't even a rash left behind, which told me all the other goodies Jessie had given me would be equally useless. Not that I could even use them. Tamara had me completely immobile, which felt truly strange. Usually when I couldn't move, ropes or chained were involved. The lack of anything visible around my body sent cold fear coursing through me in little choppy waves. We were truly outmatched, and Tamara hadn't even broken a sweat. My heart began to pound, and I fought the urge to actually whimper as she stalked up to me.

She dropped one hand so that the telekinetic hold fell away. Before I could even react, though, she had me by the neck again. She tried to lift me, a line appearing between her eyebrows when she realized how heavy I was. In the end, she settled for tightening her grip, which really wasn't much better. My hands began to shake.

"You're a pain in the ass," she said, "but you're worth more to me alive than dead. How about you cease these pathetic little attempts at rebellion and I let your boyfriend live?"

"That doesn't sound like something I'd do," I said.

People make fun of short people, but they don't realize that when you're closer to the ground, it's simply easier to get at the kneecaps and the groin. I went for the former now, kicking sharply at her left kneecap.

She didn't even do me the courtesy of flinching. "Are you done?" she asked.

"Probably not," I said, wheezing a little.

"You know something. And even better, there's somebody who knows more about the Demobilizer than you do," she said, narrowing her eyes at me.

"There is?"

"Chelsea was there. If I'm not mistaken, she was delivering a ransom payment."

"I don't know anybody named Chelsea."

Tamara jerked me closer to her. I stared at her nose. "I think you do. She mentioned a twerp that foiled a few of her plans before she got herself captured by Davenport."

"Twerp? Really? That's hurtful."

"Bring her to me. She owes me."

"I told you—"

"If she helps me find the Demobilizer, I'll consider her debt forgiven."

Guy made a soft noise behind me and I tried to remember if he knew that Brook was in debt with Tamara Diesel. Sometimes I had a hard time recalling who knew which piece of information at any given point in the day. Eddie Davenport and his bizarre insistence on keeping my friends apart had struck again.

"You want her to know that, you tell her yourself," I said.

"Linda," Tamara said.

Linda must have been Stretchy's real name, for her arm tightened around Guy and he grunted in pain. I struggled, but Tamara Diesel didn't even flinch. If anything, her grip doubled. How she wasn't crushing my larynx, I had no idea. I tried to pry her fingers free and get to Guy, who was going from red to white. "Leave him out of it! I mean that."

"What are you going to do about it?" She scoffed and I had to admit that it was a good question. I was outclassed on every level: every villain in the bar—including the one I'd brought with me—was stronger than me, I couldn't depend on Raze in a fight, and even with the doomed Toadicus down, both Linda and Tamara could kill Guy without breaking a sweat. I'd been in some bad situations during my Hostage Girl days—and the person who usually saved me then was the reason I couldn't effectively fight back now.

I opened my mouth. I didn't exactly know what was

going to come out, other than something sarcastic. But as my luck would have it, Raze ceased kicking Toadicus and walked over to the bar, stopping me before I could speak. "Sal!" she called. "Seriously, it's not fair to cut me off so early. I want—"

"Shut up," Tamara said, her voice rising to a roar. She turned, hand up to knock Raze back with her weird telekinetic powers.

Raze turned and shot her in the face.

I saw the little flash of her green-and-gold pain gun and instinctively flinched, years of being the target of the same gun working out in my favor. I was close enough to hear the crackle of the bolt striking Tamara's cheekbone. She jerked back, her grip loosening, and I dove out of her grasp. I didn't bother with grace. Instead, I scuttled back like a crab, desperate to put as much distance between me and the scary supervillain as possible.

Tamara wiped at her cheek and swung toward Raze, homicide in her eyes. "You little—"

Raze's rocket boots kicked on, propelling her out of range of Tamara's swipe. Telekinetic force buffeted against the walls, rattling the window blinds. Raze darted about like a persistent frog dressed in outdated clothes. "Do you know how hard it is getting her to return a fight? Do you, huh? Do you?"

With Tamara distracted, I bolted for Linda. She still had Guy trapped in the stretched-out rope of her arm, which was coiled around him like an anaconda. I lunged for them. Right as I did, Guy stomped hard on her instep and brought the back of his head smashing into her face. They both reeled a little.

I punched her hard in the midsection. It was like driving my fist into rubbery foam: way too much give. "Eugh," I said.

Either way, it was enough for Guy to break free, shoving Linda away so that she rolled behind a stool. His eyes went wide and he tackled me to the ground. A second later, gunshots echoed, sounding like explosions and making the ground beneath us reverberate. Wood splintered and flew as I gawked at a hole in the wall right where my head had been.

Common sense kicked in. I shoved Guy behind the bar, ignoring his yelp of surprise, and rolled after him. "Is it just me," I said, "or is using a gun cheating?"

"Definitely cheating. Effective cheating." Guy shoved his hair out of his eyes. The bar wouldn't protect either of us for long, but we remained crouched there for a second. Over our heads, Tamara continued to ventilate the walls of Mind the Boom.

Raze dropped down on my other side, looking grumpy. She clicked her tongue, and pulled out a fist-sized green sphere from her jean jacket. "Should've let me have another lemon shot," she said, like Sal was somehow at fault for all of this. She tossed the green thing carelessly over her shoulder, so that it arced over the bar top and into the main seating area.

A second later, the walls shuddered. The air turned vaguely cyan for a moment.

Tamara blasted a bottle of vodka off the shelf in retaliation.

One of Linda's creepy too-long arms snaked over the side of the bar. I shoved Guy out of the way, grabbed a jar of olives, and smashed it down on her fingers. A hiss of pain erupted from the other side of the bar as Linda drew her hand back. Juice dripped everywhere.

"Tamara wants you alive, I think," Guy said. "So we've got that going for us."

"The part where we're literally in a shootout with supervillains in a supervillain bar, not so much."

"Well," Guy said, his smile pulling to one side, "you can't have everything, I guess."

Inexplicably, even with terror making it difficult to see straight and expensive alcohol exploding all around us, I wanted to laugh. "I love you," I said.

His eyes lit up. "Ditto."

Raze rolled her eyes at us, breaking the moment. Whatever. It was romantic. "You might not have everything," she said, "but you do have me."

And with that said, she began to pull a frightening amount of weaponry out of her jacket and boots, disregarding the laws of physics. Guns, tasers, shock sticks, little green grenades, vials, pressurized needles, all of it formed a pile while Tamara continued to unload into the walls. It felt like a tantrum by this point. Raze turned to us with a wicked grin. "Take your pick."

I reached for one of her ray guns. Raze's frigid fingers latched around my wrist and jerked me back. "This does *not* make me a do-gooder," she said. "I am doing this in the hope that you will show up for a real hero-villain fight someday, and you can't do that if you're dead."

"Razor X, you are the baddest villain I know," I said.

Raze preened and pulled a different gun out of the pile. "Take this one, it's got better reverb."

"Thank you," I said, and Raze wrinkled her nose at the courtesy.

Angélica had not actually trained me on much weaponry that wasn't a bo staff or nunchucks, but it wasn't like I had much of a choice now. We were pinned down, Guy didn't have his usual fortitude, strength, or ability to heal, and Tamara wasn't leaving without me. So I took a deep breath, looked over the ray gun to make sure there wasn't a safety (there was, which startled me), and readied myself. I peeked over the counter and fired off two quick zaps. They missed Linda by half an inch and destroyed a potted plant in the corner. I dropped back down and winced. I hoped Sal wasn't too attached to that fern.

Rather than choosing a weapon of his own, Guy looked around, craning his neck.

"What are you looking for?" I asked as Raze laid down a blast of purple fire.

He pointed.

It took me a second to realize he wasn't pointing at an outdated Supervillain of the Month calendar, but at the little red box next to it. "The fire alarm, really?"

"You think Davenport won't pay attention if the fire alarm goes off in a known supervillain bar?"

"That is a really good point."

"Think you can cover me?"

"I think Raze has us covered," I said, since she was grinning and chucking every weapon in her arsenal at Tamara and Linda. They weren't firing back as often, but they were still making their presence known with the occasional shattered bottle of fancy tequila.

"Wish me luck," Guy said, swooping in and stealing a kiss.

"Ew," Raze called over an explosion from one of her cyan-grenades.

Guy crawled across the area behind the bar on his belly, wincing occasionally at the shattered glass. I doubled my efforts to try and hit Linda with the ray gun, letting Raze deal with Tamara. She was the one who'd pissed her off, after all. And I really didn't want to add Tamara Diesel to my personal list of enemies, though I figured she'd already seen to that. Dammit, I was actually trying to stay out of the Davenport world and live something of a normal life. Getting into a gunfight with supervillains over a substance that could change the entire superhero community was the core definition of not doing that. No wonder Jessie had said I should never want to save the world. It was kind of a pain in the ass.

Guy finally reached the fire alarm. I nudged Raze, jerking my chin at the fire alarm and then back at the unseen Linda and Tamara.

But Raze frowned. "Really? You'd do that to Sal?"

"Raze. We've already destroyed half of her bar."

Raze looked around at all of the holes in the wall, the wood splinters and glass on the floor, and nodded. "You may have a point. Very well. The loud one is mine—you take the slinky one."

"I thought all of you supervillains knew each other's names," I said, squinting at her. Guy gave us a *hurry up and do it already* look.

Raze, unexpectedly, began to tear up, which was always weird to see with her overlarge eyes.

"What?" I asked, impatient now. "What is it?"

"You—you called me a *super*villain."

"Raze."

She snapped to attention. "Right, yes. Protect the overgrown ginger. Got it."

When I signaled, Guy surged up to yank the fire alarm, and Raze and I rose up to lay down a blanket of cover fire for him. I heard a very un-villain-like yelp as Linda dove to safety, but Tamara didn't even flinch. She continued to shoot not at us, but at Guy. I saw her hit the wall next to him in slow motion, then an inch closer, and then—

Raze's blast hit her in the wrist and the shot went wide, missing Guy completely and hitting a black box on the wall I hadn't noticed. Sparks exploded outward and foul-smelling smoke began to spew. An instant later, Guy's fingers closed around the lever of the fire alarm. Loud, piercing shrills broke out, so deafening that all of us clapped our hands over our ears.

Another scatter of sparks shot into the air, and Mind the Boom flickered and changed.

The weathered booths meant to look like drift-wood suddenly became dark and scarred, broken in half time and again and clearly fixed haphazardly. The stool legs were all bent crookedly, the metal dinged up and rusty, the fabric covered in duct tape. Scorch marks covered the walls at almost regular intervals. A gigantic hole clearly caused by a fireball had been boarded over with obviously new wood. Every piece of nautical décor vanished. The photographs on the Hostage Girl wall remained the same, but the corkboard beneath them had warped like it had been too close to the aforementioned fireball. Apparently I wasn't the only one shocked: all of us stood up and looked around, gaping.

It looked like a place you'd expect dangerous super-villains to hang out, actually.

There was a loud *thwack* and all of us jolted in surprise. A blink, and I was looking at the regular Mind the Boom, with its cheesy nautical aesthetic. Sal, looking well and truly grumpy, stood next to the black box that Tamara had hit, holding the broom she'd just whacked it with. "Are you *done*?" Sal asked in a tone that dripped with acid.

"No." Tamara turned and fired off a single shot.

Raze whimpered.

"No!" I dove at her as she crumpled. Out of the corner of my eye, I saw Sal and Guy duck out of the way, but I focused on Raze, who'd curled up, one hand clutched around her shoulder. She hissed out a variety of swearing that didn't sound like any language I knew.

"Raze—Raze, are you okay?"

Sal was suddenly there, pushing me away and yanking off her over-shirt to help stop the blood flow. She had a cluster of raised horizontal scars on her shoulder, but that was probably par for the course for a supervillain barkeep. "Focus on getting the morons out of my bar," she said without looking at me.

Raze let out a little mewl of pain.

I tossed Guy a ray gun and turned, anger boiling in my midsection. There wasn't really any way I could damage Tamara, but in that moment, I wanted to. Raze was *my* enemy, not hers. The only one allowed to fight her was me.

And god, I really needed to stop spending so much time with Raze if that was my logic.

I sprang up onto my feet and aimed, this time at Tamara. She barely flinched when the ray bolt tagged her shoulder, but it did turn her vindictive smile toward me. Until her cell phone rang.

She answered it, ignoring the fact that I hit her knee and her side. She fired off another bullet in my direction that splintered the bar in front of me. I yelped and dodged out of the way of the debris.

Sal's annoyed hiss was plenty loud in the following silence. "Would you *please* convince her to stop destroying my bar?"

"She got a phone call. That might convince her to—" I heard the front door opening and closing and risked a peek over the top of the bar. Tamara and Linda were nowhere to be seen, though Toadicus remained in a crumpled green heap. I rose to my feet, half expecting this to be some kind of trap. But no, apart from us, the bar was empty. "Huh. She's gone."

"Good," Sal said.

I dropped back to my knees. "Raze, are you okay?"

"No," my best enemy forever said, giving me a malevolent look. "I got shot."

"It's not life-threatening," Sal said.

"Speak for yourself. It *hurts*." Raze writhed in place and I felt my stomach twist.

"Gail." Guy had his phone out. "I think I know why they left. Kiki just texted. The kidnapper's offering up Mobius right now."

"Where?" I asked, stomach dropping.

Guy swallowed hard. "Wrigley Field."

# CHAPTER 13

"If there's somewhere you need to be that's not my bar, by all means help yourself," Sal said.

I looked at Guy. I could feel myself torn in two: I needed to be at Wrigley Field and I wanted to run so far away that it wasn't even funny. But I couldn't deny that I was immune to the effects of the Demobilizer, and with Guy and Vicki off the roster and Sam still in the wind, they were down several of their heavy hitters. But Raze . . .

Sal rolled her eyes. "I can take care of her. Please go away. Feel free to never return."

"You should go," Guy said.

I looked down. Raze was still bleeding and obviously in pain. But I couldn't leave her, not when it was my fault that she'd been in this fight at all. I took a deep breath. "I'll come see you in the hospital and we can set up our fight time."

Raze immediately stopped wriggling. "Really?"

"Promise."

"I'm holding you to that. Go deal with that annoying do-gooder shit. Take any gun you like. Though, really, you need to get your own weapons at some point. I expect you to bring your A-game to our showdown."

"Of course." I held up the one she'd given me and nodded my thanks as I put the safety back on. I could practically hear Sal's relieved sigh as we left.

Outside, Guy tensed, holding his arms out like he was about to take flight. For the first time, I saw his expression flicker. "Right. I think you're on your own for this one. Stay safe, okay?"

"How the hell am I supposed to get to Wrigley in time?" Flight. Flight would be such a handy power to have right now.

Guy looked around. When his gaze stopped on a nearby rack of the bright purple rent-a-bikes on the corner, I began shaking my head preemptively. "No way."

"If you phase—"

"Phasing winds up with me in dumpsters and you saw what happened last time. I nearly became a Gail-shaped pancake on the concrete."

"You're going horizontally, not vertically. You'll be fine. And you really don't have much time."

He had a point, as much as I hated to admit it. Guy moved like he was about to wrench the bike out of the rack with strength alone, but at the last second seemed to remember he was powerless. He pulled his wallet out and swiped his credit card through the reader. "Make sure you return it within six hours, or else they're going to double-charge me," he said with a small smile.

I gave him a sarcastic laugh. He came from one of the richest families in Chicago.

"Feels weird, you going and me not. I'll stay here and let the Davenport rep know what's happening," Guy said.

"Thanks." I had to stand up on tiptoes and grab his face to bring him down to my level, but there was no way I was going off to face a fight of this nature without a kiss. Unfortunately, I didn't have time to linger; after a few seconds, I pulled back and wrinkled my nose at him. "I'll do my best to survive this."

"I like this plan. Good luck!"

He waved me off as I grabbed the bike and started to pedal. Why had Mobius's kidnapper selected Wrigley Field? Was he just as much of a showoff as your average garden-variety supervillain? It just *figured*. Hell, half of them picked the Bean so they could see themselves in the mirror the entire time.

Focus, I told myself, pedaling harder. If I was going to get there in time, I had to utilize a skill I could only access subconsciously. This was why I stayed out of the superpower world. Nothing about my life was intentional, really. I'd been given superpowers against my will, been kidnapped against my will, stayed at my job despite misgivings. The fact that the Demobilizer didn't affect me was just another thing I couldn't control.

But maybe I *could* control one thing. So I took everything Angélica had tried to teach me and I pedaled as hard as I could. Trying to build up as much speed as possible, I attempted to phase.

I threw myself face-first over the handlebars and landed in a heap on the concrete. Fifty feet in front of the bike. So. Partial success at least.

"Ow," I said to the sky overhead. Perhaps an icy November day wasn't the best time to ride a bike and learn to use one's superpowers at the same time. At least I'd been partially successful. Scrambling to my feet, I jogged back to the bike, picked it up, and started to ride again. I pedaled as hard as before, concentrated, and did everything I could to bring the bike with me.

I jumped forward a block. Reflexes kept me from skidding across a patch of ice, though I clipped a newspaper vending machine with my elbow. I tried again, nearly giving myself a headache as I put all of my focus into my task. This time I jumped three blocks. Then five. A mile. By the time I neared the right neighborhood, I had it down, stretching every bit of speed and momentum I possibly could into the phasing.

Of course, I overshot Wrigley Field by half a mile.

I skidded to a slushy stop, looked around at the intersection, and grunted. Quickly, I checked my phone. There were four missed calls from Angélica.

"Where are you?" she asked immediately when I called her back.

"On my way to Wrigley Field."

"How did you—oh, you must be with Guy."

"I was. Speaking of, you should know Tamara Diesel's probably at Wrigley Field."

"How is that a 'speaking of'—I don't even want to know actually. Yeah, she's been spotted. When can you get here?"

"Which entrance are you at?"

"I'm over on Addison."

"Got it. Give me a minute." I hung up on her annoyed follow-up question, which she would no doubt scold me for. I jumped over two blocks and pedaled the rest of the way. At least Angélica was easy to spot: she might not have been dressed up in superhero armor, but she had a bright red jacket that looked far too light for the Chicago weather. I skidded to a stop beside her.

She gaped at me. "Where did you even—"

"I phased here," I said, yanking my hair free of its messy ponytail and attempting to shove it all back into some semblance of control. "So instead of yelling at me, you should pat yourself on the back for being an awesome teacher."

She relented with a shrug. "I do that every day. Here."

She held up her phone, which showed a feed from inside Wrigley Field, the ivied walls prominent in the distance. A tarp covered the field for the off-season, but at home plate I could see two figures. One, wearing a ski mask to hide his features, stood over the other one, who was slumped forward on his knees. A sign hung around his chest, but the image wasn't clear enough for me to make out the words. I could, however, see his face almost perfectly.

My stomach pitched.

"That's definitely Mobius," I said, keeping my voice steady as I handed the phone back. "What's the sign say? 'I'm a major tool'?"

"Your typical grandstanding. Some nonsense about how the entire stadium is rigged with Demobilizer, and if anybody attacks, the kidnapper's got a dead man's switch."

"What about gas masks?" I asked.

Angélica's smile was made of sharp edges. "Nobody knows if they'll be effective. Given that there are about ten different supervillains outside of this stadium, nobody else seems to be willing to risk it."

"So, what? Davenport's sending us in?" I said, folding my arms over my chest.

"Not us. You."

I swiveled on my heels and raised my eyebrows. I'd heard it perfectly, I knew that, but: "Excuse me?"

"You saw Brook's reaction to Mobius—she won't be rational about him. Mobius knows you have the Mobium, but he doesn't know about me. Davenport would prefer to keep me as the ace up its sleeve."

I looked at her red sleeve and barely refrained from asking if she was supposed to be the ace of hearts or diamonds. That kind of wondering made me realize I was a little closer to panicking than I had thought.

"They're expecting me to just walk out to the middle of Wrigley Field and say, 'Hey, you, give me the scientist'? This is a terrible plan. But then it seems to be a day for them, so why am I not surprised?"

Angélica handed me an earwig. She grabbed my arm, stilling my hand before I could pop the little earpiece in. "I know it's not great," she said, stepping close and lowering her voice. "And I know you hate him and you have every right to, after what he did to you. But Mobius means a lot to Kiki and she's important to both of us, remember."

Right. Kiki Davenport, niece of the worst man on the planet, granddaughter of the second worst. The walking example of *you can't choose your family.*

"I got it," I said. "I was always going to do it. I'm whining because—"

"You're scared. I get it. But I'm here to back you up if you need it. I'll be right in your ear the whole time." Angélica let go of my arm so I could slip the earpiece in. "Where'd you disappear to last night? There was a rumor Eddie had thrown you in a cell."

"He tried. Jessie sprang me, and I slept in her base."

Angélica raised her eyebrows.

"Yeah, I don't know why she's taken such a liking to me lately, either," I said. "But let's go fix this problem so we can get the world back to normal and I can go back to work and pretend I'm a regular human again."

"By all means." Angélica jerked her head and I followed her into Wrigley Field.

This was going to go so well. I could already tell.

**S**ome of the same Detmer guards from the assault at Union Station had set up shop in the tunnels underneath Wrigley Field, which I imagined very few people but stadium workers ever saw. A dank smell about the place made my nose itch, but that wasn't the worst part of gathering in the little underground room.

No, that would be the handcuffed figure in the corner.

"You brought her? Are you sure that's wise?" I asked, blinking several times at Brook, who of course glared at me. Whatever connection we'd forged yesterday was now completely gone.

"She's immune," the team leader said.

I looked at Angélica and it struck me that Davenport—who was regularly responsible for preventing the end of the world—was pinning its hopes on a prisoner and two people that had turned their backs on the organization. At least we were well-supplied: each of the guards was kitted up with a fancy communication system and state-of-the-art armor. They offered me a set, but I lifted my shirt to show off the armor I already had.

"The payment," the team leader said, handing me a shiny briefcase. "You will secure the samples of the Demobilizer and the scientist—"

"Yeah, yeah. Give him the money, get the stuff. Deal with it when shit inevitably explodes."

The team leader gave me a look that said he was very used to dealing with superheroes and that he did not particularly enjoy his job. I hoped he had a good 401k.

"It's not rocket science," I said as Angélica looked away innocently. "Can I see a map?"

"Why do you need to see a map?"

I stared at him. "In case I need to run away."

He scowled and pulled up a set of blueprints on his tablet, passing that over to me. "At least try to secure the money if you do choose to run."

"No promises."

"You won't need the map," another guard said. "You'll have us to guide you."

I'd already memorized it. "Yeah," I said. "Because that never goes wrong. Anything else I need to know?"

There was, of course: they ran like a military operation, which meant a full briefing. While Mobius and his captor stood over our heads somewhere on the field and supervillains circled around. Clearly they didn't understand the meaning of urgent. I listened as Angélica stood behind my left shoulder, giving them a look that was as unimpressed as I felt. When they finally released me to walk through the tunnels, she stayed with me, keeping her head down.

"Doesn't the kidnapper have cameras watching?" I asked, very belatedly.

"It's likely. He'll just think I'm a civilian."

"Yeah, until you punch through some concrete or something," I said, snorting.

"I'll try to avoid that. Dead giveaway and all." Angélica put a hand on my arm, stopping me. She put her hand over my wrist, which had the little microphone for the guys in the bunker room to listen in. "If it comes down to a choice, take Mobius."

"And let the villains get the Demobilizer?"

"Davenport feels like it's more important, but . . . Mobius is smart. He could theoretically make an antidote. If it's possible."

"And it's what Kiki would want?" I asked, raising my eyebrow at her.

She shrugged, which in itself was an answer.

"Okay," I said. "Keep an eye on me out there."

"Definitely." She hit my shoulder, lightly, and I stopped at the end of the tunnel where the players emerged. This time I really was going to meet my maker.

God, I hated him so much.

The kidnapper spun toward me as I stepped out onto Wrigley Field, home of my ex's favorite team. If he were awake, Jeremy would be so annoyed to be missing out on an opportunity like this. The tarp crinkled under my feet as I stood there, far too exposed. The stands were empty, giving the place a ghost-town atmosphere. In the distance, hovering in the gray sky, I could see the blacks and very-dark-grays of the flying villains, all of whom appeared to be keeping a healthy distance. I couldn't say I blamed them. I kept my left hand high in the air, showing that I was theoretically not a threat, and held the shiny briefcase in my right hand. The kidnapper's eyes went almost comically wide as he took me in.

I could smell the sharp tang of fear-sweat on him.

"Davenport sent me," I said, feeling stupid. The least they could have done was give me a better script. "I'm just here to pay for the asshole and the stupid antipower juice and leave. I don't want any trouble."

Mobius's head snapped up, his hair flying in the icy wind. He was shivering, which annoyed me. I really didn't want to feel bad for the guy.

"You," he said, his eyes narrowed.

"Hi. Do me a favor and shut up." I looked at the kidnapper, taking in the details. He had kind of a weedy build and, like the supervillains I'd faced earlier, a good few inches on me. Unlike his captive, he wore a parka against the brutality of the Chicago winter. So, he wasn't very empathetic, but was smart enough to dress for the cold. Must be a Chicago native. "I'm supposed to talk to you, not him. You give me the stuff, I give you this, yes?"

He gestured with one hand. Apparently talking was not actually going to happen here.

"Yeah, no, stuff first," I said.

He crossed his arms over his chest.

"If you want to play the stubbornness game, that's perfectly fine with me, but trust me, buddy, I'm the best friend you're going to make today."

"Gail, maybe ease back on the sarcasm a little?" Angélica said in my earpiece.

I cocked my head at the kidnapper. "I mean that.

There are a lot of supervillains circling this place and I guarantee you I've met most of them, and apart from a really inappropriate sense of theatrics, they all share one thing: they're not good news. So you give me the stuff and the scientist, and you take this money and everything goes smoothly. Yes?"

I could hear his pounding heart over the wind. Whoever this guy was, he clearly wasn't used to dealing with this level of whatever the hell was happening. His hand quivered as he nodded and reached into his parka. Finally, a man who could see sense.

"You know, this woman is one of my finest creations," Mobius said out of nowhere.

I'd been in enough of these standoffs to know that even though I didn't have a script, this was definitely going off of it. "Shut up," I said out of the side of my mouth, like he was going to hear me but the kidnapper mysteriously wouldn't.

"Elwin, I'm sure you find this fascinating," Mobius said, though he was glaring. "All of those tests you ran on your subject, all those tweaks you made to my formula, all of your failures . . . they were perfected for this woman right here. Does it hurt you, I wonder, to see the culmination of your shortcomings? Oh, I dearly hope it does, as you always were an idiot."

The kidnapper—his name was Elwin? Really?— turned to look at me, his eyes wider.

"My finest creation," Mobius said, raising his head a little. Proudly. Granted, he looked a little jaundiced and his face was even more Halloween-mask-like than

I remembered, but at least he had the energy to still take credit for things he shouldn't. The sign hanging around his neck fluttered against his chest in the breeze. "Gail Godwin."

"Great, thanks, announce to the supervillains flying around exactly where I got my powers. I appreciate that, Mobius. Elwin—"

"Don't say my name!" The kidnapper's hands shook as he put both hands back on his gun. It swung wildly. "Don't do it! I just—I just want to get enough money to leave the country. I just want *away* from all of this—"

"Don't believe him," Mobius said.

"As usual," I said, "you're not helping."

He made a humming noise under his breath. "You look healthier than I expected. Has the metabolism settled yet? I predicted six months, but—"

"Shut up!" Elwin said. "Shut up, shut up. Bring the money over here. I want to make sure it's there, and then all of it, it's yours. You can have it."

I stepped over cautiously, ignoring Angélica in my earpiece telling me to keep my movements slow. The briefcase was locked to my thumbprint, but the team leader had showed me how to transfer it over. Elwin had come prepared with his own black duffel bag. I was sure Davenport had more tricks up their sleeve, but I was only a courier and a bodyguard at this point and I didn't give a damn. That was Elwin's problem. And Elwin's problems weren't mine.

Until third base blew up.

And then it became my problem.

**CHAPTER 14**

**M**y instructions from Angélica had been simple: get Mobius, whatever the cost. So when the earth shook and dirt and pieces of grass and tarp flew, I dropped the briefcase and phased forward, snatching Dr. Mobius up over my shoulder. He was frail, like a bag of bones, and I imagined that the impact caused more than a few bruises. Good.

Elwin yelped and fell backward, landing on his ass and scrabbling away from third base. He raised his hand—

"No!" I said, skidding to a stop.

Too late. He hit the trigger and blue powder erupted from both dugouts and several rows in the bleachers, turning the stadium air Cubs-blue for a second. It was like some weird, possibly deadly promotional tool. The Detmer guards emerged through the oddly festive explosion in gas masks with matte black goggles and helmets. They rushed toward Elwin, who tried to scramble to his feet and run. I stood there and gaped as he was neatly clotheslined and cable-tied, all in under ten seconds.

Angélica appeared at my elbow, having phased over. "You got him," she said. "Good."

"For you, maybe. I don't think he's showered in weeks." Which, coincidentally, was how long he'd kept me unconscious and unable to shower, too. It didn't smell any better on him than it had on me.

"Unhand me, you foolish child," Mobius said.

"Ugh, I really didn't miss you." I scanned the sky for signs of whoever had blown up third base, but Angélica's body language was relaxed. "Wait, did *we* do that?"

"Yes. They wanted the kidnapper to blow his Demobilizer trap."

I frowned. "Leaving us open to attack from every supervillain gathered around here?"

Angélica merely turned and pointed. I had to blink into the sun to see them, but several brightly colored heroes hovered over Wrigley Field, the sunlight catching on their capes and costumes. In an instant, my brain put it together: they'd used me as a distraction, blew third base so Elwin would set the trap off, and now they were waiting for a full-on brawl.

"I'm getting out of here," I said, since I'd already been in one shoot-out that day and I had no desire to repeat that.

"Not yet. We still have to get him to the waystation." Angélica phased over to grab the briefcase and what I assumed were the samples that Elwin was trying to sell. The Detmer guards had yanked his ski mask off, revealing a thin man in his thirties or forties. I jogged by a lot of them, the kvetching Mobius still over my shoulder. The guards had strength in numbers, but once the supervillains arrived—

"Wait a second," I said, stopping before I got to the tunnel where the players always emerged. I did a quick head count. "Is that all of them? All of the guards?"

"I think so, yes," Angélica said.

"If they're all here, then who's watching—"

A blur of color shot by me out of the tunnel. Brook flew so fast that I could barely track her. I worried she'd go after the limp Mobius on my shoulder, but instead she flew up about twenty feet in the air and looked around. She took in the jewel-colored heroes to one side, the gathering villains on the other, and for a second I wondered if she was going to fly straight for the villains.

Instead, she looked toward the ground and something worse happened: her face contorted into a mask of rage so terrifying that all of the saliva in my mouth dried up. She flew straight at Elwin, snatched him up, and bulleted out of there, into the stands and out of sight.

Everybody stared in shock for a second. Behind me, I heard a whooping sound. The back of my neck prickled with heat as a fireball barely missed me, smashing against the tarp and leaving a melted hole. I whipped around and sprinted for the dugout and safety. I hadn't seen Scorch among the villains in the sky, but I could recognize his handiwork when I saw it. And now was not a good time for a reunion. Not when there was a sinking feeling in my gut.

"Brook's going to kill him," I said when Angélica dropped into the dugout next to me.

"What?"

"You heard what Mobius said. Elwin's the one that experimented on her. She's going to kill him."

"Oh, shit."

"Take this." I transferred Mobius to her—let her deal with his body odor—and got ready to follow Brook and Elwin.

Angélica surprised me by pushing the briefcase into my hands. "If they get me, I'd rather they don't get everything," she said, and took off running with the doctor over her shoulder. I debated crossing the open field, but there was no guarantee I'd be fast enough, not with all of the bolts being thrown around by heroes and villains alike. If one of the supervillains were to get the Demobilizer away from me . . .

Up through the bleachers, it was.

I called up the blueprints in my mind and jumped, hauling myself onto the roof of the dugout. Another jump, this one a little wilder, landed me in the stands. I'd been to a couple of games with Jeremy, but this was different. The stadium was far too clean now, no overly salty smell of stale popcorn on the air, no over-played sports anthems on the loudspeaker. While the air lit up with bursts of color from the battling heroes and villains, I ran as hard as I could for the external hallways behind the bleachers. I tried to listen for any sign of Brook and Elwin, but that was a little difficult with the brawl taking place over the field. It was worse than when the Cardinals came to town.

Finally, I caught the sound of sobbing and ran in that direction, so desperate to get there that I phased into a wall more than once. When I finally reached them, I peeked around the corner first. Brook had dropped Elwin in the walkway by the nosebleed seats. The concession stand behind them looked like even more of a ghost town than the stadium itself. Brook stood over the fallen scientist, her chest heaving. The look on her face would be etched into my nightmares for years. Yellow and green swirled out of her open palm, hovering millimeters in front of Elwin's nose while he cowered away. Tears dripped down his face.

Before I turned the corner, I set the briefcase down and slid it back a little. No need to bring temptation in with me.

"You know, we talk a lot about villains," Brook said as I approached. She wasn't looking at me, as her eyes were fixed on Elwin, but she knew I was there. My heart was certainly hammering loudly enough to give me away. "Heroes. Villains. But we never really talk about *monsters*, do we?"

"He'll see justice for his crimes. Don't kill him."

She lifted her gaze from him now, her head tilted. "Do you know what he did to me?"

"No," I said. But I had an idea, having been on Mobius's table myself. "I can't say I do. But you should let him live. Davenport can deal with him."

"Why do you care?"

Elwin was looking at me, too, his face tear-streaked and ruddy. He didn't look very much like a monster, but that didn't mean anything to me. Sometimes the worst villains had the most pleasant smiles. "Please don't let her kill me," he whispered.

I didn't say anything because I couldn't promise him anything. Brook was much more powerful than I was. One blast from her stinging powers would probably burn him to a crisp. By all rights, he had to be the worst kind of human: I hated Dr. Mobius for what he'd done to me, but I'd seen the way this man had kept Mobius in his lair, and now he was gaming the superhero world for his own gain. It would be easier if he was dead.

But I'd already helped kill a man, and it wasn't something I wanted to repeat or to see happen to Brook. Cooper had been strong and unstoppable. He would have killed several people I loved. This man looked like a quivering wreck, black cable tie digging into his wrists and striping the skin around it red and white. He flinched away from the stinging yellow-and-green globules swirling around Brook's raised palm.

"I don't really care that much," I said, keeping my hands high in the air. I'd never been good at hostage negotiation, as I'd been busy being the hostage. "But Davenport's gonna care if you kill this man."

"So?" Brook snorted. "They don't have a hold on me. I could leave right now."

"And get your ass kicked by Tamara Diesel? Trust me, we met earlier and she's not happy with you." No way was I telling her about Tamara's offer to hand over information about the Demobilizer for clemency. "And even then, even if you go back, do you really want to be under that woman's thumb? I don't think she'll help you look for Petra, not like Guy will."

Brook's hand wavered. Just a flicker, but I could hear the way her heart skipped erratically. "I'll find her on my own. I kill him, the world's down one scumbag. I don't see a downside."

"Davenport won't overlook something like that. You can't find Petra from inside Detmer. You don't have those kind of connections."

Brook snarled. "Stop trying to be my conscience, Gail! Just let me do this!"

"If I stand back and let you do that, I'm just as responsible."

"Then let me absolve you." Brook whipped around and sent the beam she'd been torturing Elwin with at me.

It hit me in the chest; I looked down, almost detached from my body. This was the first time I'd really gotten to watch her power at work without being afraid. The pain ray was actually composed of tiny globules of acidic yellow and eye-searing neon green, all of which popped and spattered uselessly against the front of my shirt. Even though it only felt pleasantly warm and a little tickly, it remained a little scary. Like my skin might start bubbling with pain at any second.

"Are you done?" I asked.

Brook shut off the beam and narrowed her eyes at me, no doubt remembering only now that I was immune to her powers. She snarled, her already slippery grasp on her rage clearly losing purchase altogether. But it made her drop her grip on Elwin and sprint at me, which was all I needed.

I phased out of the way at the last second, grunting as my shoulder smacked the cinder-block wall hard enough to send pain stinging across my upper arm. When I dodged out of the way of Brook's pile driver of a punch, my vision went temporarily blurry and my stomach growled.

How long had it been since I'd eaten?

Unfortunately, the adrenaline, my own sluggishness, and this realization all teamed up to slow me down. Brook's punch hit me right in the jaw and sent me reeling backward with little cartoon birdies flying over my head. I shook off the dizziness in time to see her turn and fly back toward Elwin, who'd been trying to scramble away. I lunged and managed to wrap my arms around her calves, struggling to hold on. If she caught him, she would kill him, and I couldn't let that happen. The world blurred again as I tried to keep my grip.

Brook kicked out, the blow glancing off my shoulder. I toppled to the ground, landing hard on my left knee. My mouth opened so I could shout for her to stop.

I never got the chance. From the distance, a thundering *boom* rattled the walls. Everything heaved and quaked around us, and for a second, I was right back on the floor of a mall, watching the world collapse around me. I blinked and I was back out of my memories and in Wrigley Field once more. Right. There was a supersized battle of good and evil happening over home plate. This, I thought, this was why we were on the sixth or seventh version of Wrigley Field, each more goat-cursed than the last. Supervillains loved to destroy the place and superheroes didn't mind helping them out. At least it was the off-season, I thought as the walls shivered and the floor heaved like the deck of a storm-wracked ship. Plenty of time to rebuild before we went through the long process of losing the pennant yet again.

"We've got to get out of here," I said. "Just let Davenport deal with him, Br—"

The walls shook again, harder this time. Plaster rained down on me in a dirty shower. From behind me, I heard something skitter: the briefcase with the Demobilizer slid across the floor. Brook's eyes snapped to it.

It didn't take a genius to see where this was going.

"No!" I said, and the stadium shook harder than ever, pitching me to the side, farther away from the briefcase and from Brook.

Unfortunately, she could fly. She took a running step and bounded up, easily plucking the briefcase from the ground. When she turned to go after the scrambling Elwin, though, the ceiling rained down giant chunks of concrete. They shattered in the space between Brook and Elwin.

I gathered up my rapidly waning strength and let the adrenaline push me, kicking off the wall and shooting across the corridor. By some miracle, I reached Elwin right as a piece of cinder block the size of a basketball fell and clipped Brook's thigh. She drew up short in surprise. I grabbed Elwin by the closest handhold and yanked. We were up on the third level overlooking Clark Street, where there wasn't a soft landing to be found. Too bad. I jumped with the last of my remaining strength and, holding on to Elwin, tried to phase us both down to safety.

Luckily, I hit the ground first and nothing snapped, which meant I hadn't broken his ankle. We landed in a heap in the middle of traffic and I scrambled to my feet.

The car that hit me luckily wasn't going that fast, and it missed Elwin completely. But I was getting a little tired of falling on concrete. I rolled and lay in the street, coughing and dizzy.

The driver shoved his door open. "What do you think this is, some kind of joke? Get out of the street!"

I wearily shot him the bird as I pushed myself to my feet. Elwin lay in an uncoordinated sprawl. Scanning the sky for Brook and ignoring the annoyed honking of the driver, I tugged him to his feet.

The car honked again.

"Hey, jackass, you hit *me*," I said. Elwin blinked into the sunlight as I pulled him along, head wobbling unsteadily on his neck. I needed to put as much space as

possible between us and the doomed Wrigley Field—
looked like the taxpayers were paying for version eight
this winter—and Brook. I didn't see her, which meant
we weren't out of the woods yet on the whole murdering Elwin thing, and her having the briefcase full of
Demobilizer was bad news. Just about summed up my
usual luck, really.

"Where are we going?" Elwin asked as I yanked
him onto the sidewalk.

"Away. Any more than that is need-to-know."

"What are you doing? Are you g-going to hand me
over to her?"

"Not if I can help it." I gritted my teeth. That hadn't
been my first time getting hit by a car, but it was never
pleasant. My ears rang, my vision kept wavering, and
it felt like my skull had shrunk a size or three and was
pinching my brain between my ears. The fact that Elwin's voice was the tiniest bit nasally didn't help over-
much.

"You should let me go," Elwin said. "She'll kill me
if you take me wherever you're planning to go and—"

"Not happening. I'm taking you to the authorities,"
I said. "Duh."

"But—"

"Brook doesn't do things without reason. She's
crazy, but it's a crazy that makes sense." I stopped. If
Brook was making sense, did that make me the crazy
one? I shook my head, which was a bad idea since I'd
just been hit by a car. Black started to close in on my
vision; I willed it away and focused on walking. "If she

wants to kill you, she's got reason, and right now, my head hurts so much that I'm not seeing much incentive to stop her. So you might want to stop talking."

I continued to jerk him along, grateful he was still zip-tied and therefore not as much of a problem as he could have been. We drew odd looks from people who hadn't seen the supervillains and immediately abandoned the area, but this was Chicago. Not many people were going to react to a five-foot-tall woman dragging a handcuffed man behind her, really.

The ground rumbled. I turned and there it was, a block away—Wrigley Field imploding in a cloud of concrete dust and brightly colored sparks. Which hero was that again? It didn't matter, not when my heart was in my throat. I grabbed for my phone. Angélica had escaped, she had to have.

A crack split my phone's screen neatly in half. I'd apparently landed on it either jumping down or being hit by the car. When my fist twitched in anger, the phone practically disintegrated.

"Huh," I said, shoving both halves back in my pocket. "Figures. New plan."

"Where are we going?"

"Walk," I said. The Addison 'L' stop right by the stadium would be a mess thanks to the implosion. I could flag down one of the heroes that was no doubt on their way to assist in the epic battle still taking place in the sky over the stadium, but that might draw unsavory notice, too. So my best bet was to walk to the Belmont stop and hope the Red Line wasn't stopped due to this disaster. I needed to get to the waystation and hand Elwin over. Angélica was probably wondering where I was, and I really didn't look forward to telling anybody at Davenport that I'd lost one of their villains *and* the Demobilizer at the same time. I looked sideways at Elwin. "You got a phone?"

He shook his head, nose running in the cold.

I had to bite my tongue over an aggravated gripe about his uselessness as I pushed him forward. "Walk a little faster."

The bars along Clark Street were emptying of patrons enjoying their Sunday afternoon beer, scurrying to get away. As much as I worried that this was adding more targets to the street, it did make it easier for Elwin and me to blend into the crowd. Of course, if he decided to rabbit, he had a better chance of getting away. He made it less than a block before he realized that himself and broke into a run. I snatched the back of his hood, stomach grumbling, and said, "Uh-uh."

He scowled. Did I find him unpleasant because of what he'd done to Brook, or was he hideous to me because I hated hostage takers? I was too hungry, tired, and battered to pick apart the gossamer strings of my opinion, so I kept my grip on his parka and hurried on with the crowd until a tingling sensation crept from the top of my shoulders to just under my ears. We were being watched. I could only hope it was a friend, but with my luck, I highly doubted it.

My instincts were spot-on. Linda of the stretchy

gross superpowers nearly made me yelp when she stepped into our path. "Hostage Girl," she said.

Instinctively, I stepped between her and Elwin, switching my grip to the front of his parka. It probably looked ridiculous to onlookers thanks to the fact that they were both gangly and I was compact, but I hoped my ferocious glare made up for some of it. "Can we not?"

She jerked her head at a pub called O'Hara's across the street. "You're late."

"Yeah, hard pass. I'm not going anywhere with you."

Her lips stretched far too wide for her face, which was well and truly creepy. When she tilted her head, it went a few degrees too far. "I'd look, if I were you."

"Your powers are really creepy, just FYI," I said, and like an idiot, I looked over.

A flash of red through the front window made my insides shrivel.

"After you," Linda said, smirking.

I took a deep breath that did nothing to stop the blood rushing to my temples or the thrumming of my own heartbeat in my ears.

"What's going on?" Elwin asked, sounding mystified. He squinted at Linda. "Who are you? I'm not going in there—"

"We don't have a choice," I said, though I knew there *was* a choice. I could fight Linda easily enough and get away, get Elwin to safety, but I had a feeling that the alternative wasn't acceptable. I swallowed past the terror clogging my throat and strengthened my grip on the front of his parka. And with Linda smiling at me with her teeth gruesomely stretched out into fangs, I crossed the street and stepped into the front door of O'Hara's, to face off against Tamara Diesel in a bar for the second time that day.

# CHAPTER 15

**G**uy's eyes widened when I stepped through the door. I could see myself in the mirrored wall over his head, and it wasn't a pretty sight. Between the plaster dust on my hair and clothes and the fact that I looked like I'd been hit with a car, I was a little bit of a mess. But that had nothing on Guy, whose face was stained by a trickle of blood leaking from a cut above his temple. A gag had been stuffed in his mouth and his arms were bound behind his back.

It was precisely the opposite of every situation we'd shared for four years. Guy was the damsel in distress, and I was the only thing that could save him.

"Nice of you to join us," Tamara Diesel said, her feet propped up on a table.

I turned my head her direction, never taking my eyes off of Guy. Rage and terror made a dangerous cocktail in my veins. I could feel my hands shaking, but I didn't know if it was fatigue, fear, or fury. "Let him go."

"Oh, I will. But I think you understand how this works a little better than most, no?"

I was done with the games. "Let him go," I said again.

Elwin blinked at the dark interior of O'Hara's. "Who is that?" he asked in a loud whisper.

"Dr. Lucas," Tamara Diesel said, and I felt Elwin jerk because I still had a death grip on him. "How are you doing? Ingenious trap, setting off the Demobilizer at Wrigley Field. Unfortunately, it doesn't seem to have worked."

Elwin Lucas made a distressed noise. "I appreciate the compliments, whoever you are, but the fact that it failed so spectacularly does prove that it wasn't as ingenious as you claim."

"My apologies, I'm being rude. Tamara Diesel." She swung her feet off of the table and offered her hand to Elwin.

Before she stepped forward, I moved between them. Behind me, Linda snickered. "Let him go," I said.

"Ah, no." Tamara folded her arms over her chest. She was smug and she had every right to be: I'd walked in there willingly, but now that I was standing in the bar, I could see that it had been a stupid idea. I could have—done what? Called for backup when I didn't even have a phone and my earwig had vanished? Overpowered Linda to use as leverage? Tamara Diesel didn't seem to have much of a conscience, and given her reaction to Toadicus getting his ass handed to him by Raze, she considered her henchmen expendable in the long run. I hoped they at least had dental.

And if her henchmen barely rated a second look, she would kill Guy without blinking. She'd seen my reaction to him being in danger in the bar earlier, so it wasn't hard to connect the dots. When had they nabbed him? Right after I'd left?

I looked at him now. He must have seen that I had no idea how to get us out of this. The resignation on his face, etched deep with pain, meant that he'd already drawn the same conclusions I had. There were only two ways this could go. One was unacceptable to me and went against everything I stood for, and the other led to all of our deaths.

Tamara Diesel's smile told me she'd read my mind. Hopefully not literally. "So you understand," she said.

"Understand?" Elwin asked. "I'm afraid I don't. Could somebody explain?"

"This is a one-for-one trade, isn't it?" I said.

Tamara raised her eyebrows at me. "Look at that, you *can* be smart."

"It won't work out for you," I said.

She narrowed her eyes. The mark on her cheek that Raze had blasted there still looked red and swollen. "Why? Because the good guys always win?" she asked, her tone mocking.

"Statistically, yes," I said, though the odds hadn't favored me all day. So far every encounter I'd had had ended in disaster.

But trading Elwin for Guy, even if he was the monster that Brook had claimed, went against every fiber of my being. Guy would never stand for it. Granted, he didn't have much of a say at the moment since he was gagged and cuffed, but if he could talk, he'd be telling me not to make the deal. It wouldn't matter to him that he was sweating and blood flowed down onto the collar of his shirt. An alarming amount of blood, actually.

Nausea roiled through my midsection.

"Here's the deal," Tamara said. "You give me the scientist, I let you and the boyfriend go."

"Why?" I asked. "You're clearly at an advantage here, and you know it. So why be nice at all? Don't tell me it's out of the goodness of your heart."

Guy's eyes widened. I could read the message easily: *stop helping the villain, Gail!* He had a point. A single drop of blood dripped off of his jaw, and my free hand tensed into a fist.

Tamara tilted her head, squinting a little at me as though she agreed with Guy. "I'm only after the scientist, as you've proven singularly useless and annoying otherwise."

"Stop quoting my Twitter bio," I said. "I'm going to think you secretly like me or something."

Oh, right, I remembered a second later, Tamara Diesel lacked a sense of humor, and she was holding my boyfriend hostage. Maybe not the best time to sass her.

Her eyes narrowed and her lips twisted up to one

side. "My patience is running thin. If it runs out entirely, you'll find that this deal will have evaporated."

"I really feel I must object," Elwin said, shuffling forward a little bit.

I shoved him back to his previous spot without looking at him. "I'm not handing this man over to you."

"Very well. Sounds like an easy fix." Tamara flicked out a simple pocket knife. The light from overhead glinted along the wickedly sharp edge of the blade, and I felt distinctly light-headed. Even twenty-four hours ago, the knife would have been a joke to Guy. It would have bounced right off of his skin.

Now Tamara strode up to him, grabbed his hair, and savagely twisted his head back, exposing his neck.

"Stop!" I let go of Elwin and took a step forward. "Don't."

Guy shook his head furiously, trying to speak through the gag.

"You can't have it both ways," Tamara said. "It's either the scientist or your boyfriend. It's not that difficult."

"I know it's not." But it was. Sickness rolled through me like a wave. For four years, I had been the one in the chair, the one being threatened, and I had no idea how Guy had ever tolerated it because it was tearing me apart now. I could see the blade perfectly even in the smoky light of the bar. And I knew how easily it would slide into Guy's skin.

In one fell swoop, Tamara Diesel had forced me into making what was an impossible choice. Anybody else might have seen it as easy: they needed Elwin; there was reason to keep him alive. Guy was expendable and would be killed. But Guy wouldn't thank me for saving his life if it meant putting somebody else in danger. And the thought of willingly handing another living soul over to be held captive made me want to throw up.

But I *couldn't* watch her kill Guy.

"Well?" Tamara asked.

I dropped my gaze to the floor and gritted my teeth so hard that my neck ached. "How do I know you won't kill Dr. Lucas?"

Tamara didn't even bother to say, *You don't*, like most villains would have. She merely shrugged. That was fair.

I looked at Guy, who was straining against his bonds, sweat dotting his temples and his neck, his gaze desperate. He shook his head at me, imploring me not to do it. My mouth had gone absolutely dry.

"Don't do this," Elwin said, whimpering a little. It ignited some vindictive spark inside me. *You like this?* I wanted to ask. *This is what you did to Brook and Mobius.* Like Guy, he'd gone pale, and I could smell a new coat of fear-sweat on him. With Davenport, he'd have rights—and probably be exploited, knowing Eddie. With the villains? There would still be exploitation, but it'd probably come with a lot more pain.

Tamara brought her fist down on top of a table, hard. The resulting *crack* echoed through the bar, making me jump hard. "Decide!" she said, her voice rising to a roar. "Now! Or I kill all three of you."

I didn't look at Guy. One finger at a time, I uncurled my hand from the front of Elwin's parka. I heard a gleeful laugh from behind us and one of Linda's too-long arms flicked out, wrapping around the scientist.

Tamara smiled coldly. "I knew you'd see things my way," she said, and raised the knife.

"No!" I said, but she only held up her free hand and cut away the ropes tying Guy to the chair. He surged to his feet and promptly reeled, any remaining color draining out of his face. With the last of my energy, I darted across the bar to keep him from falling flat on his face. I shoved my shoulder under his arm, taking as much of his weight as I could, and glared at Tamara. "This isn't over."

She flicked her fingers. "Begone."

A telekinetic force struck me in the stomach, knocking the breath clean out of my lungs and sending me flying backward. Guy fell next to me, grunting in pain as we tumbled into bar stools. Guy shoved himself to his feet, murder in his eyes as he prepared to storm ahead and save Elwin. He made it a step before he fell forward with another grunt.

"Guy!"

I scrambled to help him. Tamara glanced over her shoulder, looking bored. "I told you to leave," she said.

"We're going, we're going." Even though Guy lacked strength, he still struggled as I grabbed the back of his jacket and pulled him out of the bar. Luckily, O'Hara's had a back door.

We made it to the alley, the stink of the dumpster

nearly overwhelming me, before Guy turned his head toward me. "You shouldn't have done that," Guy said. "You shouldn't have—"

"I never had a choice." I hadn't run the minute I'd spotted Linda in the street, after all. "She was either going to take the scientist or she was going to kill us, and this way we get to live. We have to get out of here. Fast."

Guy's mouth firmed into a white line. I didn't know if it was pain or the anger at me. Neither option helped the guilt trying to tear me apart from the inside. "Why?" he asked. "She's obviously done with us."

"Elwin knows I'm immune to the Demobilizer and if he blabs: big trouble."

Guy swore.

"It's never easy, yeah," I said. "How are—can you walk?"

"For a little bit, yeah. My head's ringing." He sounded mystified, which wasn't surprising. It had been years since a simple head wound could knock him sideways. I grabbed his hand so I'd be close in case he collapsed, and we moved out of the back alleyway as quickly as we could. "Are you okay? You look like you fought with a cement truck."

"You're not far off. Your phone . . . ?"

"They destroyed it. Yours?" he said.

"Got hit by a car."

Guy's eyes widened in alarm. "You or the phone?"

"Both."

"Gail."

"I'm fine. Mostly. We need to keep walking."

Of course, *fine* was debatable, but I'd suffered worse. At least my ankles were okay; I'd once limped a long way on a horrible sprain because Brook had thrown me off of the third floor and I'd woken up blocks away with no memory of it. I was more concerned now because my pain was second nature to me, but every hissed breath Guy pulled between his teeth scared me. He was an awful shade of bone-white, so wan that the bags under his eyes looked like bruises.

"You need an ambulance or something," I said.

"It looks worse than it feels." But he said it through gritted teeth.

"I could try to 'port us," I said, though it was useless. Phasing was one thing; teleporting took years of study, so it wasn't like I could blink and make it happen, as nice as that would be right now.

Guy shook his head, the tendons in his neck standing out. "When's the last time you ate?"

I laughed, though things didn't feel very humorous at the moment. "Point."

"Was that man—the one who—was he the kidnapper?"

"Davenport sent me in to spring Elwin's trap and get Mobius back. Which is pretty much the *only* thing that hasn't gone wrong today. Tamara Diesel has the kidnapper, Brook has the Demobilizer, and Davenport has Mobius."

I hadn't thought it wasn't possible for Guy to go paler, but I was wrong. "Brook has the Demobilizer?"

"It's been a really bad day."

Guy's face contorted into a grimace. "And I haven't helped much."

"Hey, it's okay. I've caused more than my fair share of trouble for you. It evens us out somewhat."

We made it up the block trying to put as much space as we possibly could between O'Hara's and ourselves. Guy needed medical attention. My own problems weren't nearly as pressing. Some food, some rest, and I'd be okay. Guy, though, was still bleeding heavily. Head wounds bleed a lot, but this was ridiculous.

I could feel my strength diminishing with every step. At the end of the block, I glanced over my shoulder and flinched.

"What is it?" Guy asked.

"Stretchy McGee. I don't think she saw us."

But the commotion behind us in the crowd told a different story. I was more than a little familiar with the aggravated squawks of people being shoved out of the way in a chase. Elwin sure hadn't wasted any time blabbing my secret to Tamara and Linda, had he? Did he think it would serve as leverage? Now we were both in trouble.

"She definitely saw us," Guy said, as he no doubt heard the same thing I did. We tried hobbling faster, but Guy was beginning to swoon dangerously.

"Yep."

"Can you fight?"

"I'm out of gas. I can hold her off long enough for you to get away."

"Gail, no—"

"You don't have any powers and you are *bleeding*," I said, panic making my voice go higher in pitch. "Guy, you're not indestructible. If she hurts you . . ." Abruptly, so fast that I nearly knocked him over, I ducked under his arm and turned to face off against Linda. She'd probably stretch and slither her way right past me, but I had to do something. I looked over my shoulder. "Guy. Go."

He grabbed my arm. "Don't give yourself up. I mean that."

"I'll do my best."

He turned to stagger away as I whipped my head back around, ready to fight off Linda. And she didn't disappoint. She came at me the way she'd attacked Angélica, her elongated arms reaching to try and snare me before I could hit her. I blocked the first strike as best I could, though my limbs responded sluggishly, like I was trying to fight in the bottom of a pool. She threw her hand forward across the ten feet of space between us, trying to slap me with an open palm. I batted it away and ducked under another grab, dropping to my knee when some of my energy gave out. Her boot caught me right in the solar plexus. It bounced off of the Raptor armor, but it was enough to knock me backward.

I scrambled back to my feet in time to duck under the clotheslining stretch she made with one arm. I blocked her other arm, but the hand only kept going, the arm elongating until it whipped around my other side, firmly anchoring itself around my middle.

*Gross.*

The force of Linda's shove made me stumble. But Guy had gotten away, I thought as I panted and tried to break free. He could get back to headquarters, hopefully without bleeding out, and tell them that Tamara Diesel and her ilk had me. Maybe they would send somebody to rescue me.

I felt a hand nudge at the small of my back as my head dropped forward. With the last bit of my energy, I raised my head—just in time to see a blast of purple fire spread across the front of Linda's tank top. She crumpled to the pavement.

I looked over in confusion. Guy was holding the gun Raze had given me earlier, its tip smoking.

"You were armed the whole time," he said when I just gave him a baffled look. "Why didn't you use this? I know you think guns are cheating, but so are villains."

"I . . ." I stared at the gun. I'd completely forgotten it was tucked in my waistband.

Just like I'd forgotten the little pouch of goodies at my hip, too.

"I really need something to eat," I said, and took the gun from Guy.

He nodded tightly. "Let's get out of here."

# CHAPTER 16

Before we reached Davenport, they bundled Guy onto a stretcher, even though he insisted he could walk. I followed behind him on foot, limping into Medical, and Kiki jerked her head at the chair. I collapsed onto it and leaned forward, resting my forehead in my hands.

A silver-wrapped package was shoved in front of my face and I wanted to cry. "Can't I just eat a whole chicken or something?" I asked.

"Let's trade taste for efficiency for now." The voice belonged not to Kiki but to Angélica. Who I hadn't even noticed, which told me I was more out of it than I thought. She only continued to hold out the nutrition bar at me, expression unchanging.

With a sigh, I took it. Inside was a lumpy brown horrible imitation of food. There was an official name for these nutritional bars, but mostly we called them crap-cakes. So called because they tasted like crap. Probably worse, actually.

I chewed, even though my jaw hurt. When I'd swallowed, Angélica handed over a bottle of water.

"Forcing crap-cakes and water down my throat, it's just like the old days," I said, my voice weak.

She gave me a small smile. Across the room, Kiki examined the wound on Guy's forehead.

"Feel up to walking me through what happened?" Angélica asked.

"The short version is Tamara Diesel has Elwin Lucas and Brook has the Demobilizer, and it'll be a while before I go to a bar in Chicago again." I chugged water, stopping when it hit my stomach only to be met with an overpowering wave of nausea. I breathed through my nose. Originally, I'd been told that if I didn't keep an equilibrium with feeding myself in order to heal, I would make myself deathly ill. That turned out not to be true, but the moments waiting for the healing to complete were deeply unpleasant.

"Wow," Angélica said, raising her eyebrows. "You're going to need to tell me more than that, though."

I nodded and closed my eyes for a second. "Give me a minute?"

"Dizzy?"

"Sick."

"You mind if I . . . ?" She gestured at me vaguely and I shook my head. Angélica had been my trainer at Davenport and now we were roommates. Any reservations about being touched or having any sense of modesty around each other had long flown out the window. She put two fingers over my pulse point and listened intently. Then she placed a hand on my midriff. "Deep breath."

I obeyed, trying not to wince.

"What caused this, specifically?"

"I tried to phase and ran out of energy, which meant I took the brunt of a fall off the top level. Getting hit by a car after I landed didn't help."

"No, I can imagine it didn't." Angélica probed gently at my sides and front, her frown deepening. She stepped over to a drawer—I glanced at Guy, who was being handed a glass of orange juice—and returned. I groaned at the second crap-cake.

"Your body will thank me," Angélica said.

"My body hates everything on this planet, including you. There won't be any thanking anytime soon."

Angélica held out the crap-cake and stared.

Twenty-three seconds later, I gave in with a sigh. It tasted even worse than the first one.

"Where's Mobius?" I asked. "Please tell me somewhere damp and dank and preferably cold. I need at least one thing to go right for me today."

Angélica rolled her eyes. "Down the hall. We think you may have dislocated his hip."

I felt a spurt of annoyance that puzzled me, as I wasn't particularly annoyed myself. It was callous and rude, but Dr. Mobius had to be in his eighties. I'd rescued him. No reason to be annoyed.

"I got him back alive," I said. "Pretty much the only

thing I did right today, if you think about it. You'll be waiting awhile if you expect me to apologize for his hip."

Angélica's lips pursed, but she didn't push. Instead, she held up Raze's gun, which had mercifully stopped smoking. "What's this?"

"Gift from a friend," I said, turning toward Guy. He sipped juice as Kiki ran some kind of scanning wand over his torso, and it made my entire body ache to see him hurting like that. At least it looked like the pain-killers were starting to kick in.

Angélica set the gun down. "R&D'll want to see it."

"I'd rather they didn't."

Angélica's look told me exactly how ridiculous I was being. "Fine," I said. "But I need a phone. I need to text somebody."

"What happened to yours?"

I pulled the pieces of it out of my pocket.

"Of course," Angélica said with a sigh. "Just use mine. And take me through everything from the beginning."

By the time I'd finished breaking down my awful day for Angélica, Raze answered my text and assured me that though she might need a couple of days, she would be in fighting form for our epic showdown. Guy's forehead had been stitched, yellow smeared all around the wound. He needed rest and fluids, Kiki said, but she didn't think he'd been permanently damaged by either Tamara's attacks or my manhandling.

"Unlike my grandfather," she said, turned away from me.

"I didn't have to save Mobius, you know," I said.

"What?" Guy said. All three of them were looking at me strangely, which was a bit unfair. They knew how much everything about Dr. Mobius messed with my head.

"Never mind," I said. Guy seemed content with that; he closed his eyes and leaned back, holding an ice pack to his head. Angélica had her eyes narrowed and Kiki tilted her head at me. "Other than the hip, is he okay?"

"Eddie and all of his lawyers are talking to him now," Kiki said, her voice tight. "They want to know if he can fix Guy's and Vicki's powers."

Guy's smile was strained at the edges. "Focus on Vicki," he said. "I'm fine like this."

Both Angélica and Vicki turned surprised expressions his way, and I supposed they had a point. He looked wrecked in a way I hadn't seen since Brook—acting as Chelsea—had nearly killed him. She'd used Naomi's research to commission a device that would force Guy into his vulnerable state and the resulting mess had not been pretty. His injury today was a sight better, but it was still vaguely wrong to see him hurt when one time I'd seen him bring a knife down on his own hand. The knife had broken. Guy's hand had been unmarked.

"I mean it," he said. He grimaced. "Headache aside, that is. Where's Vicki?"

Kiki paused significantly at the computer. "Where else? With Jeremy. Again."

"Maybe while she's there, she can shake him awake. He's missing all the fun stuff," I said.

Again, all three of them turned to look at me. What I'd said wasn't that sarcastic or awful, so I frowned back. But I still felt a spurt of puzzlement nonetheless.

Angélica opened her mouth, but Kiki touched her arm. "Let's give these two a minute," she said, nodding at Guy and at me.

Angélica's squint at me as she left the room was decidedly suspicious.

"Vicki's with Jeremy?" Guy asked, leaning back against the wall. I could feel my strength returning, though my midsection burned with fire. I crawled onto the cot next to him.

"Yeah," I said, picking up his hand and lacing my fingers through it. I needed to take advantage of Medical's showers and get some new clothes, as every movement sent little wafts of plaster and concrete dust floating into the air. "How is Vicki doing? Is she okay with it like you?"

"Not exactly. Vicki actually likes having powers."

I swiveled to look at him in surprise. "And you don't?"

He was silent for a long moment. Then he shook his head. "I mean, there are upsides, of course. I can fly and not everybody can say that."

"Yeah," I said with a little more rancor than I meant to.

He squeezed my hand, one side of his mouth curling up just the slightest bit. "I'm aware that I'm privileged, Gail."

"In more ways than one, rich boy."

The lip curl became a full-blown smile. "Your disdain for my wealth will never fail to amuse me, Miss Public Transportation."

"Hey, not all of us can fly."

"Neither of us can now. I never had a choice, you know. Not where my powers are concerned."

He'd been a teenager when an explosion had blown up the cement factory he'd been exploring with his siblings, granting all of them powers. Though it had taken him a while to join Davenport, he'd been flying around as a hero the whole time. Had he ever tried to be normal? I wondered now. Of course, given that I had only been trying to be a normal human for three months and I was already the Raptor's special project and helping Davenport out with hostage situations in my spare time, I couldn't exactly judge. Maybe it had been the same way for Guy. He'd never complained. I knew parts of the lifestyle bothered him—the villains' relentless pursuit of me, for one thing—but I'd always gotten a sense of contentment from him.

"On either side," he said, going on. "Dad wanted Sam to follow him in business, but Sam bounced hard off that after Petra disappeared, so it fell on me. And I am—was—strong and pretty indestructible, so it just made sense to suit up and save the day. And then you came along and you were . . ."

"Always in trouble," I said, prompting him with a smile.

He smiled back. "Somebody had to save you. I

didn't mind so much. I didn't hate having powers and constantly stepping up, and I wouldn't have chosen to lose them. But . . . if it happened by accident? I'm not heartbroken."

"How long have you felt this way?"

"A long time," he said. "Since the move to Miami was seen as a success at least. Probably before."

In his Blaze days, he'd put a stop to my kidnappings by removing himself from the picture and moving to Miami. The logic had been that if he wasn't there to tempt the villains into kidnapping me, they'd lose interest. And for ten months, he'd been right. Unfortunately, Dr. Mobius had ruined my kidnapping-free streak. It had never occurred to me that Guy might have been unhappy in Miami.

"How come you never told me any of this?" I asked.

"What was I supposed to say? 'I have amazing powers and I'd be super relieved if I didn't'?"

"Sure," I said. "Or anything you want, really. We're at each other's places two or three nights a week, which I'm told means we're in some kind of serious committed relationship and that's the kind of thing you share."

"It wouldn't have changed anything."

"Still," I said.

Guy shook his head.

"What do you think you'd be?" I asked. "If you hadn't become Blaze?"

"I'd still work for Dad, probably. Actually, you know what? Petra would be working for Dad. She always had the head for business."

"You'd be a chef," I said, since I'd known the answer before I had asked.

He ducked his head forward and finger-combed his hair on the undamaged side of his forehead with his free hand, one of his bigger tells. "I had about ten brochures for culinary schools in my desk. I was filling out an application to one of them the night before the explosion, believe it or not. It . . . had to be put on hold."

"You're still a great cook. I mean, I know I don't taste half of what I eat, but the half I do taste is spectacular."

"Thanks." He laughed a little, though it trailed off to nothing. "If I'd had powers, you wouldn't have been put into that situation today. Any of those situations, really."

I studied his face. "And yet you don't want your powers back."

He shook his head, looking a little miserable.

"Guy, that's fine."

"Is it? You were put into a terrible situation because of me today and I couldn't do anything."

I shifted a little to get more comfortable, bracing my back against the wall. I could feel the two crap-cakes doing their work, but I wasn't comfortable enough to lean against Guy the way I wanted to. So I squeezed his hand a little, careful not to use my full strength. That would take some getting used to. "It's kind of a taste of my own medicine, if you think about it. How many times was it exactly the same situation with us switching places?"

"Too many times," Guy said.

I rested the back of my head against the wall and closed my eyes. "Except you never had to make a trade for me."

"I'm glad about that. It would have been an impossible decision."

"Are you mad that I did?"

Guy was silent for a long time. "It was the logical choice."

"That doesn't mean you're not mad."

"What use is being mad? You're right. They want the scientist alive because he's valuable even if Brook hands the Demobilizer over. Me, I'm just a useless wannabe chef."

I opened my eyes and nearly started laughing at that.

"What?" he asked, catching the movement.

"Do you realize how much I consider a wannabe chef the farthest thing from useless? Even without your powers, which I really don't care about one way or the other, you being 'a useless wannabe chef' is still like the most perfect thing to me ever."

Guy paused for a long moment and unexpectedly began laughing, groaning a little when it obviously hurt his head. "I see where your priorities lie."

"You, then food, then kicking ass," I said.

He tugged on my arm to pull me closer so he could kiss me. The angle was a little awkward thanks to the fact that I couldn't move too much, and he smelled like iodine, but it still felt pretty close to perfect.

Until the door swung open. Right, I thought as we pulled back from each other. We were definitely sort of in public and could be interrupted at any moment by Medical staff. Like Kiki, who shook her head and smiled ruefully at us.

"At least you're both cute," she said.

I blinked, wondering if I was more tired than I thought. It had been like watching a badly dubbed foreign film. Her lips didn't match the words very well.

"What's the matter?" Guy asked as I pushed myself off of the cot.

"It's my—it's Mobius," Kiki said.

"Is he okay?" I asked, more as a reflex than anything. I had hit him kind of hard, after all.

Another spurt of annoyance, but Kiki nodded. "He'll heal. There's just a . . . snag."

"What kind of snag?" I asked warily.

"He's able to create an antidote to the Demobilizer," Kiki said, and my stomach jumped. I looked at Guy, whose face had closed off. "It could fix Guy and Vicki and restore their powers in full."

I decided to give Guy a moment to process that and turned Kiki's attention on me instead. "Okay, so what's the problem?"

Kiki made a face, and I suddenly knew *exactly* what the problem was. It just figured.

## CHAPTER 17

**"I** won't do it."

I made it a policy not to hit the elderly, but right now, looking into Mobius's horror show of a face, I really, really wanted to break that policy. And only part of that was anger over the fact that once he'd kidnapped me and turned me superhuman without my consent. Mostly it was because he was a stubborn old goat and it was my friend he was hurting.

"You *will* do it," I said, folding my arms gingerly over my chest and giving him my best glare. "You owe me."

Medical put Mobius in one of the cells since he technically was a mad scientist and that fell on the villain side of the spectrum. Sure, he was the second grandfather to the company founder's granddaughter, but nepotism only carried you so far. I wanted nothing to do with him whatsoever, but Kiki had pointed out that if he wasn't going to listen to her, he wouldn't listen to any Davenport techs. And like it or not, Mobius viewed me as his finest creation. His Frankenstein's monster, if you will. Which was certainly fitting, as standing before him, I felt made up of a mishmash of anger, resentment, and general frustration.

"My darling Girl," he said, glaring up at me from under his stringy hair, "I don't owe you a thing."

"You ruined my life," I said.

"You seem to have turned out quite . . . adequate."

"Adequate? You and Rita Detmer put me in the middle of a giant conspiracy. You owe me. My friend died—" she'd gotten better, but still "—*I* nearly died, my other friend is still in a coma and may never wake up, and you made a normal life impossible for me. All because you and some crazy supervillain picked me to be your little pawn."

He sniffed. "Your chess metaphor is badly thought out, dear Girl. A bishop would never apologize to a pawn."

"This isn't chess, this is my life," I said.

"I made you strong." He eyed me up and down. "You've adapted even better to the Mobium than the previous subject."

"Whose life you also ruined." We had no idea where Brook was or what she'd done with the Demobilizer. That was a very scary shoe we were waiting to have drop. Probably on top of our heads, with our luck.

"Ruined or not, you seem to have turned out quite well, dear Girl." Mobius remained sitting in the little wheelchair they'd given him. He had a pleased look on his face that made my skin crawl. His cell was the last place I wanted to be, but Kiki had a point: we needed the antidote. She had a team of Davenport scientists working on it, but according to her, Mobius's brain operated on an entirely new level. The fact that he'd created a substance that could kill so many types of powers while leaving the original host in one piece and human was apparently a scientific breakthrough beyond anything Davenport could hope to put out in the next ten or fifteen years.

"Great," I'd said when Kiki had brought it up. "So you can't replicate it, either."

"Somebody with knowledge of it might be able to, if they were familiar enough," Kiki had said. "Like Elwin Lucas."

So even if Brook didn't hand over the Demobilizer, Tamara Diesel potentially had a way of making more on her hands, provided she could motivate Elwin Lucas properly. She'd have no trouble with that. I'd seen firsthand how good she was at providing incentive.

So now I stood in front of my tormentor, something I'd never wanted to do ever again, and glared at him as he looked me over earnestly, proud his experiment had gone so well.

"The Mobium was an accident, you know," Mobius said, pushing his fingertips together to form a steeple with his fingers. He ignored the death glare I shot at him. "Obviously I had no intention of making it. Can you imagine? A world with superheroes is bad enough.

The ability to make more? Absolutely dreadful. Worst idea I've ever had, not to destroy those notes before Lodi found them."

"You seemed to have no problem using it on me," I said.

"You served a purpose. And you proved to be an amazing specimen." He wheeled closer. "You are a gift to science, Miss Godwin."

I took a step back. "Make the antidote," I said.

Mobius's face went even more ghoulish. "The thing I hate most in this world is superheroes. Why do you think I would ever assist you in returning more of them to the fold?"

"Your granddaughter has powers," I said.

"Precisely." He smiled, revealing yellow teeth that definitely needed a dentist. They'd been like that before his captivity with Elwin Lucas, though. "Why do you think I created the Demobilizer in the first place?"

This time my step back was out of shock than a desire to protect myself. "You made it for Kiki?"

"Her grandmother has Villain Syndrome, and her father, that unfortunate layabout, suffered from the same. My daughter was sacrificed to that man's sickness. I will not allow my granddaughter to fall prey to the same."

My throat closed up. Kiki had told me about her father, Marcus Davenport. I knew he was dead and I knew he'd gone crazy because he had Villain Syndrome, a unique brand of dementia that affected some villains. They wanted to save the world by destroying it, essentially. Rita Detmer, the world's first supervillain (and Kiki's grandmother on the other side), was the most famous case. But I didn't know Kiki's mother had died because of it. Somehow or other, Mobius had lost his daughter to a supervillain's machinations. It didn't make him a good guy, but he hadn't deserved to be held captive and forced to create things by the evil Lodi Corporation, either.

"Does Kiki know you did this?" I asked, looking toward the two-way glass on the other side of the room. Kiki was on the other side of it. Somehow I knew the answer to the question would be no.

"This was the first chance I have had to see my granddaughter in a long while, Girl," Mobius said. "But everything I do, I do for her. She's all I have left."

"What about Brook?" I asked. "You took her from Lodi when you escaped. She must have meant something to you."

"You and Brook are my creations. Of course I have some manner of affection for you."

And just like that, I was back to feeling grossed once more. "Great," I said. "Well, I don't think of you as a father figure. Unless that prompts you to make that antidote."

"I won't help this insipid corporation ruin more lives," Mobius said. I could hear his heartbeat, so even without looking at the stony set to his features, I knew he was absolutely telling the truth. Nothing I could say would change his mind.

"Your Demobilizer hurt my friends," I said, trying, anyway.

Mobius leaned back in his wheelchair. "That's fair," he said with a small nod. "As much as it pleases me to hear that there are two fewer superfreaks on the street, there is the small matter of reparations for the pain and suffering I have caused you. Therefore I will promise you this: I will not make any further Demobilizer, save for what is needed should my granddaughter require it one day."

"That doesn't help my friends now," I said, wanting to deck him.

"We must all get used to disappointments in this life."

"With you, disappointment seems to be the only thing I get." I didn't storm out because that would be immature, but I didn't bother letting the door shut quietly behind me. Thankfully, the hallway was abandoned since everybody was in the observation room. It gave me a few precious seconds to gather myself. My hands shook, but there wasn't really anything I could do about that.

One quick breath to brace myself, and I stepped into the observation room. As expected, Guy looked frustrated. Kiki's face was a carefully blank slate, but her presence felt like a shout in my brain. If I felt like I was breaking into pieces, she was a thousand times worse.

Everything that was happening was because of her.

"Hey," I said. "Don't blame yourself."

Kiki looked at me swiftly. "How . . . ?"

I shrugged. "Trust me, if there's anything I can tell

you from my Hostage Girl days, it's that no matter how sane or crazy the villain seems, their actions are never your fault. Even when they try to pin it on you."

Kiki didn't look reassured, though I didn't figure she would. Instead, she had her eyes narrowed.

Guy cleared his throat. "You okay?" he asked.

I nodded and batted distractedly at the back of my neck. The base of my skull felt funny, but given how tense I'd been while facing off against Mobius, it was to be expected. "Some things get better with age. He's not one of them."

"Are you okay emotionally?"

I leaned my weight against the railing beneath the observation window until I heard it creak. In the room, Mobius wheeled over to the desk and picked up an empty journal that had been left for him. The man really liked his journals. He made my stomach turn. "I hate that guy so much. Sorry, Ki."

"Your feelings are justified," she said, her voice neutral. "You gave it your best shot and didn't punch him. You were close, weren't you?"

"It was that obvious?" I asked.

Guy frowned. "You were close to punching him? I couldn't tell."

"I dislike him immensely. He's not going to help. But he did at least confirm that an antidote is possible, so there's that. Can I . . . am I allowed to roam for a bit if I don't leave the complex? I need to . . ." I gestured vaguely in the direction of my forehead. Mobius had made me furious to the point where I'd felt my blood pressure rise, and it was affecting my head.

Kiki handed over a badge. "Try not to run into Eddie. I'd rather not face a lecture."

"You don't want company, right?" Guy asked.

I gave him an apologetic look.

"Perfectly fine," he said. "I'll go see if I can bake something so you're not stuck with crap-cakes this whole time."

"Or you could try resting since you're no longer unbreakable," I said, giving him a quick kiss before I took the badge and left.

I considered for a moment dropping by to see Jeremy, as that was always oddly calming. But if I looked at his face, all I would think about was how he'd been injured because of something Mobius and Rita Detmer had set in motion. So instead, I wandered. Memorizing the layout of Davenport had been easy with my sense of recall—Vicki had walked me through once, and that was all it took—so I headed for the Indoor Arboretum, figuring that would at least be peaceful. After everything that had happened with Raze getting hurt at Mind the Boom, keeping Brook from killing Elwin at Wrigley Field, trading Elwin for Guy at O'Hara's, facing off against Dr. Mobius, I really needed a chance to be alone and sort things out.

I took a seat in the arboretum, away from the few trainees gathered to one side, and stared into the fountain in the center of it all. Artificial sunlight filtered through panels in the ceiling, illuminating the lily pads and water flowers growing in the fountain. Soft sounds of water burbling reached my ears, laying out a perfect blanket of peace in the air. If I'd stayed with Davenport, no doubt this little corner of tranquility would have become a preferred spot.

"Hey, mentor," I said without looking when I heard footsteps behind me.

Vicki sat next to me on the bench. "I'm not exactly your mentor without powers," she said.

"There's plenty you can still teach me." I cuffed her shoulder gently. Without his powers, Guy felt different, less like stone, but Vicki seemed the same, all sinewy muscle. It made sense. She wouldn't get far in an industry where quite a lot of people had to touch her for fittings and photographs if it was obvious she was a superhero by feel or sight.

But I could sense something was off. Not anything physical. She wore jeans with no shoes and a ripped tank top that I recognized as one of Jeremy's. Her hair was piled messily on top of her head and her makeup was as perfect as usual.

"Is it stupid to ask how you are?" I asked.

"I think I feel better than you look right now." She reached up and brushed her fingers through my hair. Of course, as curly as it was, all she did was wind up getting her fingers stuck in it, but she tried in vain to brush out some of the mess. "What happened here?"

"Good news: we're getting a new version of Wrigley Field."

"It'll be as cursed as the last six," she said. "You need a shower."

"And a nap. I have no idea what time it is or even what's going on. Been a long day."

"I should've been there," Vicki said.

"If you had, I'd have even more dust in my hair." Plain Jane famously wasn't bothered if a building or five was in her way. Davenport paid for the damage, of course, but I imagined Wrigley Field wouldn't have slowed her down at all.

She laughed, a noise without much mirth in it. "You may have a point."

"I thought you'd be in, like, Tokyo or Milan on a runway somewhere," I said, since there were two halves to Vicki and they were both inordinately busy. I had no idea how she juggled it all. Just thinking of being a superhero with a sedentary office job during the day made me feel tired enough.

"I took the week off." Vicki pulled one of her impossibly long legs up and wrapped her arm around it, resting her chin on her knee. "I just ran into Kiki. She said you tried to get Mobius to make an antidote."

"Not very successfully."

"Still. I appreciate that you tried."

"And Kiki appreciates that I didn't deck her grandfather. It's nice to be appreciated for the things I bring to the table." I stared at the fountain and the lily pads with their bright pink flowers. It was such a peaceful contrast to all of the calamity that I imagined was happening out above the surface between the forces of good and evil. This little slice of tranquility was always here for anybody who needed it, I realized.

Staying with Davenport wouldn't have been entirely terrible.

"I'm sorry I haven't been to see you before now," I said.

"You've been trying to save the day. I can get behind that. It shows good character."

"I have a good mentor."

Vicki laid her cheek atop her knee, some of her hair slipping out of its bun. Even though she wasn't at a photo shoot or getting ready to walk a runway, she still looked amazing. Losing her powers couldn't rob her of the things that made her Victoria Dawn Burroughs. It would be a matter of time if the same thing was true for Vicki Burroughs, Plain Jane.

"Have you been to see Jeremy?" I asked.

She nodded. "No change."

"He's stubborn. He'll wake up when he's good and ready and not a second before."

"Jeremy? Stubborn? I'd never have guessed." Vicki left her cheek resting on her knee. "Losing the power sucks, don't get me wrong. And I have done plenty of bitching about that—"

"Maybe I'm lucky I was so busy," I said.

She bumped her shoulder against mine, a gentle scold tempered by a smile. "Thanks, you. Anyway, as much as I want to bitch about this damn Demobilizer, I can't help but think that it would help Jeremy."

"Maybe. The powers might be the only thing keeping him alive," I said. The doctors had no idea what was going on with Jeremy, why he hadn't woken up. And nobody knew exactly how the little flickers of static discharge in the webbing between his fingers would manifest into actual powers when he was conscious.

"If Kiki's grandfather is as smart as she claims, he could probably figure it out."

"He's self-serving. Mad scientists tend to be like that."

"Maybe you *should* punch him."

"Not without pissing Kiki off," I said, shaking my head. "It also probably wouldn't help much, but it sure as hell would make me feel better."

Vicki cuffed me on the arm. "That's the spirit."

# CHAPTER 18

I hated waiting.

I especially hated waiting while stuck in a facility that held the dubious honor of also storing the man who had turned me into what I was. After I had been let out of Jessie's supervision and had subsequently gone on a trouble-streak that had ended with Brook absconding with the Demobilizer and Tamara likewise taking off with Elwin, Eddie wouldn't let me crash at the Nest again. So for three days, I stayed in Guy's apartment and dodged increasingly irate phone calls from my coworkers.

That wasn't much of a surprise. I was one of the few people in that office who could find the shortcut for Excel on her desktop, after all.

Of course, as much as I hated waiting, I also excelled at it. And I'd rarely had to wait on my own. Supervillains could be oddly good at small talk as we waited for Blaze to arrive and for the battle to start. Though she'd once turned me green in a move that later proved to be oddly supportive of my romantic choices, Venus von Trapp had given me tips to help me save an ailing African violet I'd kept (it had later been smashed by Captain Cracked, but before its untimely demise, I'd managed to nurse it back to health). So I was used to having all manner of strange people waiting with me.

Having friends instead of villains was even better. Guy still had his apartment in Davenport Tower, so I wasn't in a cell. And I really wasn't going to complain if Guy cooked shirtless because neither of us had anywhere to go. Though that only happened when he wasn't using hot oil.

I had to look away from the TV to check my text messages. "Vicki says she's not coming over for dinner because she's got a thing with . . ." I blinked at my screen. "Yeah, that actress is incredibly famous and also I'm afraid saying her name out loud will somehow summon her here. So just assume famous and go with that."

"Sounds like Vicki." Guy pulled the duck á l'orange out of the oven, making careful use of the oven mitts. He'd forgotten them the day before and now he had bandages wrapped around his left hand. Medical had said it would probably leave a scar; Guy had ruefully noted that maybe it was for the best, since now he would remember not to simply grab hot cookware.

Angélica and Kiki had shown up armed with a full set of oven mitts when they'd dropped by for dinner the night before. It had been a strange meal. Angélica wasn't any happier about being quarantined than I was, not with her gym having to be shut down. And Kiki had been slanting me curious looks all night, like I might know something more than I was telling. Since Brook hadn't emerged from the woodwork, and I'd been the last one to see her, that was probably fair. At least no other heroes had been attacked with the Demobilizer. So maybe she hadn't handed it over to Tamara Diesel and Elwin hadn't been able to replicate Mobius's results.

Every day that passed without news became more unnerving.

I turned my attention back to Guy since I didn't want to think about that. The duck smelled sinfully delicious. He'd tripled the recipe and had chattered on about different alterations he'd made to each batch. Luckily, he didn't seem to mind that half of my focus was clearly elsewhere. I eyed his chest and shoulders, sculpted from his weight-lifting regimen. I could map out all of the raised, horizontal scars, old scrapes that started at one shoulder and spread all the way across his chest. Most of them, he'd told me, had come from the explosion where he'd gained his powers, but there were fainter burn marks on his skin that had been a gift from Brook trying to destroy him in a rage.

Either way, it was all suitably distracting.

"Gail?" Guy said.

"Huh?" I blinked and looked up to find him smirking at me.

"My eyes are up here," he said, pointing.

I threw a piece of carrot at him and he laughed. "Want a taste?" he asked.

I had to hop up and lean over the counter to take the proffered sip from the spoon. "Needs more garlic."

"You think everything needs more garlic."

"It's good for memory or something. I think."

Guy obligingly added more garlic, making a noise in the back of his throat. "Having memory troubles, huh?"

I opened my mouth to make a joke and stopped abruptly as something niggled in the back of my mind. "I think I might be," I said instead.

The amusement dropped away from Guy's face. "What do you mean?"

"Stretchy McGee. Whoever she is, the one you shot with Raze's gun. I had that gun the whole time," I said. I looked down at the scars on Guy's chest and shook my head as a thought tried to surface and disappeared just as quickly. "It was tucked into my belt. I could feel it, but I just wasn't thinking about it. The Mobium ensures I'm going to use every advantage I possibly can. So why didn't I use it? Why didn't it even occur to me?"

"You were a little stressed at the time," Guy said. "I think that's forgivable."

"Yeah, and if it had been an isolated incident, that'd be one thing."

"There've been other incidents?" Guy tasted the sauce and added a pinch of salt. He finished basting the roast and pushed it back into the oven.

"Naomi visited me at work to talk about Mobius and not twenty minutes later we watched a ransom video with the same guy. And my brain didn't think, 'That can't be a coincidence.' Yesterday morning, way after my morning coffee, I wondered why I hadn't talked to Jeremy in a while. It took me a full three minutes to remember that he's in a coma."

"Again, you were stressed," Guy said, but he was frowning deeply. "I didn't know him nearly as long and sometimes I wonder if Jeremy's going to wander in and insult me."

"I wish he would. Wander in, not insult you. God, he could be such an asshole. Can be," I said, shaking my head. "But I think it's more than that. I mean, we don't know *that* much about the Mobium, and the man who could tell us anything about it is a) not willing to work with us unless it benefits Kiki, and b) more than a few coconuts short of a cream pie, you know?"

"You think the Mobium is breaking down? That's jumping to extremes right away, I think," Guy said. "Maybe talk to Kiki about it before you freak out."

I was worried he was going to say that. Kiki had enough on her mind with Dr. Mobius's horrible life choices pressing in on her, but she was also the closest thing Davenport had to a willing expert about my powers. "I'll let Kiki worry about all of these questions tomorrow. Right now, though, you should probably put on a shirt."

Guy grinned. "Is that what you really want me to do?"

"No, of course not, but I don't think you really want to entertain Naomi while shirtless and she'll be here in three . . . two . . ."

On cue, the doorbell rang.

"You know, powers or not, it's creepy when you do things like that," Guy said, and went to go put on a shirt as I headed to answer the front door.

As it happened, Kiki reached out to me first. I saw her text message after I'd stepped out of the shower, leaving Guy to finish scrubbing his back. *Got time today? It's not about Mobius.*

I texted back that I needed to talk to her, too, and went on about my day since she apparently had a full morning. Instead, I stopped by Naomi's new office to bring her the leftovers she'd left behind the night before. Like Guy and me, Naomi was being kept at Davenport, but at least they had work for her. She'd been granted full access to everything we'd found in the lair where Elwin had been keeping Mobius. While it was intriguing and she loved poking through everything, she'd expressed more than a little aggravation over dinner.

"All of this really deeply fascinating information and I'm not allowed to share any of it," she'd said, glumly poking at the baked Alaska Guy had prepared for dessert. "Do you know how much that hurts my little journalistic heart?"

I'd patted her on the shoulder. "If you need a distraction, Portia has texted me seventeen questions about Outlook today. It would cheer her up to hear from you instead."

"Oh, I bet it would," Naomi had said, rolling her eyes. My coworker had come on a little strong about how cute she found Naomi. "But in this case, I'll have to pass. Are you still working there? How come you haven't quit yet?"

"Because I'm starting to get the impression it's there or Davenport, and I really don't want to have to work anywhere near Eddie Davenport. The man is a raging prick."

At least he hadn't seen fit to visit me again. Angélica and Kiki seemed to be the main liaisons I dealt with from Davenport. Maybe Jessie had stepped in on my behalf or something. After the random and deep interest she'd taken in me, it had been a little weird to receive radio silence from her. But then, she was a strange individual altogether. I shouldn't have been surprised, maybe.

"Do you know your aunt is kind of weird?" I asked as I stepped into Kiki's office in Medical. Usually I saw her in the exam room, but she had an office full of paperwork and overstuffed bookshelves that I'd only seen once.

She had her back turned toward me, but she'd distractedly called, "Come in!" so she knew I was there.

She didn't turn toward me. "I'm aware. Has something happened with her?"

"Nothing recent. Just an observation. Also a strange

way to start a conversation, now that I think about it," I said. "Most people would just say hi."

"Hi," Kiki said, typing something into her computer.

It was a little odd that she hadn't looked at me yet, but she had a lot on her plate between Mobius and the Demobilizer and monitoring Vicki and Guy for any signs of trouble. "Am I interrupting? I can come back."

"No, I'm just checking something. Do me a favor and say, 'Aardvark.'"

"Uh," I said. That was a strange request. "Aardvark."

Kiki turned toward me. She pushed her thumb into her cheekbone and dug two fingers into her forehead like she was developing a headache. "I was afraid of this," she said.

Two things struck me at once. The first was the worry beneath her resigned tone, which was something everybody should be concerned about hearing from their doctor.

And the second was far more important: *her lips never moved.*

I heard her voice perfectly, but her mouth had stayed completely closed.

"What the hell?" I asked.

She stood and stepped around me to close the door, gesturing for me to sit. Numbly, I dropped into the chair. "Has anything unusual been happening to you lately? Nosebleeds, phantom pains, headaches?"

What was it with everybody's inability to give me

a straight answer lately? And those questions sounded like . . .

I groaned as my rather slow brain finally put it all together. "You're kidding."

"I don't think I am."

I put my hands over my face and left them there. One of the properties of the Mobium was its ability to absorb powers from other superheroes. Nobody was sure how it worked or how it chose the powers to absorb and adapt. And it usually took something out of me until I learned how to control it. With 'porting, it had been migraines. I'd absorbed powers before. But this? This was a nightmare.

"I cannot have psychic powers."

"I don't know what to tell you, Gail."

"Are you vocalizing that or is it in my mind?" I asked.

"I'll do you a favor and vocalize for now."

"How did this happen? I haven't even had that much exposure to you!"

"Yeah, of you and Angélica, you are not the one I would expect to get the psychic abilities. What . . . exactly is the problem with them? You've been wary of me from the beginning. I have to figure that's part of it somehow."

"Distrust, not dislike," I said, lowering my hands to rub them against my thighs in agitation. Psychic. It figured. It was true that I'd always been leery of Kiki, though I actually liked her. "The villain that started everything for me, he was psychic. He was controlling some kids on the train tracks, I was brave or stupid depending on who's telling the story, and I hit him with a beer bottle. He's the one that spread it that I must be involved with, you know, Blaze, kicking off the whole Hostage Girl lifestyle."

Kiki stared at me for a long moment, her mouth partially open in surprise. "That . . ."

"You couldn't pluck that out of my head? Psychically or whatever?" I asked.

She shook her head. "It doesn't exactly work like that. Or mine doesn't, so I'm assuming since I'm the original host, your psychic abilities don't, either. But I can understand your distrust of me now. Which villain was it?"

"Sykik."

"Yeah, that guy is trash. We're not all bad, I promise. Hell, most of us don't even want to see what people are thinking. It's . . . inconvenient."

Right. Inconvenient. Also known as invasive as hell.

"It is, at that," Kiki said, and I scowled because I hadn't said that aloud. "Sorry," she said. "Let's go into the exam room. I want to run some tests."

"This is a completely surprising twist that I never would have seen coming," I said dryly, as Kiki's first reaction to everything was to put it under a microscope. It fit with all of those science degrees on her office walls. I trailed after her into the exam room and dropped onto the cot.

"You know," I said. "I thought my mind was the only thing left."

"What do you mean?" Kiki was already logging into the computer.

"The villains, Dr. Mobius, whoever, they kidnapped me, they beat me up, hit me with pain toxins, turned me into what I am now. But I always had my brain. Except now I don't, really. Because now my brain's not completely mine, if I'm picking up other thoughts."

Kiki spared me a look, her eyebrows drawn close together. "Are you going to get philosophical because you can pick up telepathic signals from me?"

"It's either that or whine," I said. "I can do that, too, if you like."

Kiki bit her bottom lip and shook her head. This time when I felt a spurt of amusement, I was able to pick it apart from my own aggravation. It didn't feel intrusive, but it still rang distinctly of Kiki. How long had that been going on? It could have been weeks. Possibly months.

"How did you figure out that I'm . . ."

"'Psychically attuned' is my hypothesis." Kiki gestured for me to sit up, so I did. She checked my pulse, keeping her eyes on her watch as she timed it. "And something's been off, just a funny feeling. And then you started answering my thoughts instead of my words."

I thought back to our last couple of encounters. Guy, Kiki, and Angélica had given me such baffled looks. In retrospect, that made a lot more sense.

"Why telepathy?" I asked. "The powers I've developed are kind of arbitrary. Why this one?"

"They're not actually that arbitrary." Kiki wrapped a blood pressure cuff around my arm.

"Really? Because it feels pretty random to me."

"Your first developed power, outside of the regular effects of the Mobium, was Angélica's phasing ability." Kiki ticked this off on a finger. "At the time, you were being put through a heavy fighting regimen against a superior fighter. No doubt the Mobium adapted in order to level the playing field. It also gave you the advantage of being quicker."

"Being able to get away quicker," I said, mostly kidding.

But Kiki pointed at me like I'd stumbled on something important. "Precisely. And your next developed power, 'porting, effectively removes you from danger and places you in a position of safety. As it integrates into the Mobium, you've 'ported longer and longer distances."

"Until I wind up on my couch, yeah."

"A safe space. Your abilities have been uniquely tailored to—"

"Allow me to run away?" I asked.

Kiki nodded.

"Well, that's heroic." When the blood pressure readings popped up, I took the cuff off and held it out to her. "I feel like it's kind of working at cross-purposes, too. I've been fighting more since I got the Mobium. But my powers are developing more for the opposite."

"You're a contrary soul, Gail."

Well, she wasn't wrong.

Kiki pressed her palm against a panel on the wall and some kind of diagnostic equipment, as blindingly white as the rest of the place, emerged with a small whirring noise. She gestured for me to rest my chin on a little bar at the front of the scanner. Feeling like I'd stumbled into an optometrist appointment, I did so. At least there weren't those ugly giant glasses attached to the front.

"So how does psychic ability fit in?" I asked.

"It's probably pretty simple. You keep losing cell phones. How else are you going to get in touch?" Kiki touched a button on the side of the scanner, which circled my head a couple of times. It made an unpleasant vibrating noise echo through the shells of my ears and down into my jaw. I wrinkled my nose. "I'll have to look at the tests to make sure, but when I said you were psychically attuned, I meant probably just to me. Think of it as a psychic tether."

I looked sideways around the scanner at her without lifting my chin from the bar. She hadn't said anything about holding still, but I didn't want to push it. "Are you saying that the Mobium has enabled you to be my psychic emergency contact?"

"That's one way to put it. Sit back, I need to put this away."

"So you think it's just you and me, right? I can't go up to Angélica and read her mind?"

"Probably not. She's got a pretty strong mental shield."

"Damn."

"Why do you say that?" Kiki pulled out the same wand she'd used to check if Guy had a concussion a few days before.

"I'm positive she's got a stash of those dark chocolate coffee beans, but I have no idea where she's keeping them. And she's got some mystery boyfriend she's hiding. Which is fine, but I'm nosy and—" A tendril of shock shot through my brain, followed by a bunch of emotions I didn't expect. I broke off with a choking noise and whipped around to face Kiki, who had gone amazingly still and who was definitely not meeting my eye.

"Or not a boyfriend," I said. She shut down whatever emotions she'd projected at me, but not soon enough. No wonder Angélica had always been so secretive whenever she'd sneaked off to meet up with this mysterious lover of hers. "Um. How long has that been going on?"

"It started after Cooper."

Cooper had been the almost indestructible spy inside of Davenport that had wanted to kill me and had killed Angélica, however temporary that turned out to be. Kiki had brought Angélica back to life using the Mobium, and I'd thought things were weird between them. Guess I was really wrong about that.

But things about it made me wonder. Angélica had been so adamant about getting Dr. Mobius back in one piece. Given how much he mattered to Kiki, it was only logical. But why had they tried to hide it at all? Angélica always came home from her nights out smelling of the gym showers rather than whoever she'd stayed with.

"It's new," Kiki said when I asked that, aloud. "She would have told you eventually. If you hadn't, you know, decided to mind-link up with me because you keep breaking cell phones and beat her to it."

Well, when she put it that way. "Oh," I said. "Okay. Cool. Am I allowed to give her shit for this later? She really had me fooled. I had so many theories. I mean, this is better, don't get me wrong."

"You do whatever you need to do." She cleared her throat and I didn't need to be psychic—god, that would take some getting used to—to sense discomfort rolling off of her. "Let's get back to the testing."

"Sure," I said.

The tests proved endlessly fascinating to Kiki, but they didn't tell me much. Our minds were tuned to each other, which apparently meant we were on the same psychic wavelength. Strong emotions could be felt by the other in close proximity, as we'd discovered by accident, and Kiki theorized that they could also be transmitted greater distances, along with mental messages. Standing face-to-face, we could talk either vocally or mentally.

I much preferred the former. The latter creeped me out.

Kiki ran through a series of cognitive tests because I told her about my memory problems, and the results made her frown. "There's no way to be sure, but I'm not seeing any tumors or lesions on your scans. It's possibly it could be a sign of something as simple as stress or it might be a side effect of the burgeoning psychic ability. Do you have anywhere to be right now? I'd like to run more tests."

"No, but . . ."

"I'll order some food," she said, and stepped over to the room's intercom system.

"It's like you read my mind," I said, because I really couldn't help myself.

Kiki's look told me I only got to make that joke once, and I'd just used my only opportunity.

An hour later, Kiki had reams more data and I had a headache and a couple of sandwiches left. She'd physically tested every inch of me and she had tried every psychic trick she knew. I could block her from my thoughts, we'd discovered, and vice versa. She could put a picture in my mind, though it was blurry and indistinct. I hadn't been able to return the favor.

When the door slid open, I looked up, hoping that it was somebody coming to rescue me from being mentally and physically probed.

When I saw Angélica standing in the doorway, the smart-ass side of me took over. "Your girlfriend's here," I told Kiki, who was still bent over the monitor.

Angélica stopped, her gaze cutting between Kiki and me warily.

"Believe it or not, I didn't tell her," Kiki said to her. "Not . . . intentionally."

"I can't believe you didn't tell me. Say, are you guys going to be the Rocha-Davenports or the Davenport-

Rochas? I need to know what to put on the mono-grammed hand towels I'm getting you," I said, holding out one of the sandwiches to Angélica.

Unsurprisingly, she took it, but she gave me a stern look. "I will deal with you later," she said. "Ki, there's trouble."

Kiki whirled on the stool. Her aura in my brain, which we'd started working to develop, turned yellow with alarm. "Who is it this time?"

"Who's what this time?" I asked.

Angélica ignored me. "They got War Hammer."

"Wait," I said, on my feet before I even thought about it. "Who got Guy?"

Kiki and Angélica exchanged a look that I couldn't read, even being on the same frequency as Kiki. Angélica turned to me. "Not Guy. Sam. He came back when Davenport reached out to him."

"They could reach him the whole time?" I asked, offended. Guy had been so upset when his brother had vanished into the ether without a word. But Davenport had known where he was all along?

"That's not important," Angélica said. "What's important is that he's missing."

I caught a tendril of thought from Kiki's brain, likely before she could stop it, and turned to look at her. "He's not the only one, is he? Something's going on."

The look the two shared was more than enough confirmation.

## CHAPTER 19

**M**issing superheroes.

It just *figured*.

Guy's reaction to finding out his brother had returned and had subsequently vanished was to head straight for the closet, unbuttoning his shirt. He stopped halfway there with a puzzled, lost look on his face.

"What did Eddie say?" Guy said, looking at me as I sat on the edge of the bed, kicking idly at a pile of his shirts on the floor. He might be an amazing chef, but a neat freak he would never be. "There's a briefing, right?"

"I didn't go. Angélica did, though." I filled him in on what I knew. Davenport didn't have much, except that their biggest names on the roster were disappearing one by one. All signs pointed to the Demobilizer being involved, and nobody had seen Brook. She certainly hadn't been sighted with Tamara Diesel, whose goons had happily been running around fighting every hero they possibly could. It was a free-for-all worse than the time Atlanta had hosted the Olympics and the heroes and villains had treated the international competition as their own good vs. evil party.

When I was done telling him everything I knew, Guy dropped his head back, clearly trying to rein in his temper. "This has been happening for a while, hasn't it?"

"Yup." Our friends had all worked together to keep us in the dark. Guy didn't need the stress, according to Kiki. Angélica had thought keeping me off of Eddie's radar was for the best. This way he didn't send me in to single-handedly face off against the biggest villains on Tamara Diesel's roster.

"You're not ready for it," she'd told me bluntly. "The fact that you survived two encounters with that woman is enough of a miracle. Let's not push our luck."

I'd argued that I could help. Kiki had argued back that since Tamara by now knew my powers had come from the same man who had created the Demobilizer, it was better that I stay underground. The situation was too hot, especially for anybody as close to it as I was.

At least I wasn't alone in being annoyed by them. Now, twenty minutes later, Guy paced the room, something that was usually my shtick. "Sam's back," he said.

"Yes."

"And now they can't find him," he said, going on like I hadn't spoken.

"Yes," I said again.

Guy pushed his hands through his hair. "He's vanished before. It might not even be related to this. Hell, maybe he came back, decided it was too much, and left again."

"It could be."

"It might not even be Tamara Diesel. Maybe Brook found him and that Bookman trigger isn't as gone as she claimed. Maybe *she* has him."

I shook my head. "It feels too convenient for that. Tamara Diesel's crew is going after the heavy hitters. If anybody has Sam, it's her."

Guy didn't speak for a moment. "Kiki needs to convince Mobius to make that antidote. I need to rescue them."

He didn't sound happy about it.

"They have other people that can rescue them," I said.

"But he's my brother. I should be out there helping find him."

I bit my lip. "Are you feeling guilty over the fact that you still don't want your powers back?"

His miserable nod confirmed it. Since I didn't really have words for that, I reached out and grabbed his hand, linking my fingers through his. He sat down next to me, heavily.

"It's okay, you know," I said. "You sacrificed your personal life for years."

And his relationship with his brother, and he'd lost a sister. He'd given so much to the mask and, seeing him free of it, seeing how carefree he suddenly felt, was like a quiet pang in my chest.

"You shouldn't be too mad at them, you know," Guy said out of nowhere. I gave him a questioning look. "Angélica and Kiki. Not for trying to keep us out of everything that's going on. I understand why. It's the law of proximity."

"The what?"

"The closer you are to superheroes, the more likely you are to get screwed over."

Like Jeremy, I realized. Before he'd sacrificed himself to help take out Cooper, everybody surrounding him had superpowers. And now he was in a coma deep underground with static sparking between his fingers. The same held true for me. Four years being kidnapped by every villain in Chicago had dropped me square in the middle of Mobius and Rita Detmer's plan to save Kiki and had landed me with Mobium, which was hopelessly entangled in the latest crises facing the superpowered world. And Guy, just by being close to me, had been in prime position to lose his powers.

Law of proximity indeed.

"It's a little late for them to be keeping us out of the loop," I said. "We're already here, we're already screwed. You know?"

"Yeah, I know." Guy pinched the bridge of his nose.

We heard nothing new that night, but Guy didn't sleep well, no doubt worried about his brother. In the morning, he cooked breakfast and went to meet up with Angélica for training. Part of the acclimation period to adjust to his new powers and test his new-found lack of strength, I imagined. After he left, I debated grabbing a snack. For once, I was all caught up on my favorite soap opera, so I didn't need to check in on Chance's torrid affair with the evil Lucinda. Shrugging, I picked up my new phone—Guy had replaced the destroyed one, insisting that he didn't mind the cost and I shouldn't, either—and tucked it in my pocket before heading into the main part of Davenport Complex. The one nice thing about staying in New York instead of Chicago was that I had unfettered access to visit Jeremy.

His face was completely slack, with absolutely no change, when I stepped in. But his visitor caught me off guard.

"Gail," Kiki said, looking up from where she was reading Jeremy's chart. She gave me a small, sad smile.

"Hey, Ki. I didn't know you two were friends."

"It's a nice place to think. Nobody bothers me here. Mostly I read my thesis to him and update him on scientific subjects I imagine would actually put him to sleep if he was awake." Kiki's smile gained a little more humor. "They do actually put Angélica to sleep."

"I'm not surprised," I said, poking Jeremy and receiving a small shock for my trouble. "He's pretty nerdy. If it's true that he can hear us, he probably enjoys it on some level. At least you're making him smarter. He could use it."

By reflex, I glanced at his face. For a while, I'd tried insulting Jeremy, thinking if I found just the right combination, he'd awake in a spluttering ire and insult me back. It hadn't happened yet.

Kiki started to push herself up from her chair, but I waved at her. "You don't have to leave, not on my account."

I could actually feel a little of her indecisiveness as she mulled it over, which was strange. She finally nodded and settled back in. "Do you visit him much?" she asked.

"When my best buddy Marsh the security guard decides not to be an asshole and lets me come over. Sometimes I bring one of his handheld games," I said. "But the problem is that I'm getting too good at them, and I don't want to beat all of his levels. Just some of them. He needs something to live for."

"Braggart," Kiki said, her tone teasing. She ran her fingers through her ponytail, twisting them through her hair. "I wish I could do more for him."

"Do you think the Demobilizer would help him?" I asked. With every day that passed, it was obvious that we probably weren't getting back the Demobilizer Brook had taken. And Mobius would only make it to remove superheroes from the fold. I doubted very much he'd care about a coma patient, not unless it saved his granddaughter somehow.

From the way Kiki shook her head, tightly, she'd come to the same conclusion. "He's a brilliant man, but not a good one."

"Shame," I said. "Too bad we can't convince Mobius you're in mortal peril or something. He's helpful then."

My phone buzzed with a new text message from Raze, the twelfth that day. She really was not enjoying her convalescence, not when there were things outside to shoot and promised battles to be had. I fired back a text telling her to behave.

When I looked up, Kiki was frowning at Jeremy's face.

"Something on your mind?" I asked.

She jerked like she'd forgotten I was there. I raised my eyebrows at her. "No," she said. "No, I'm good. Just remembered something in the lab. If you'll excuse me?"

"See ya," I said, and Kiki hurried off, leaving me with Jeremy.

Immediately, I propped my feet on the bed. I'd get scolded if a nurse caught me, but I didn't care. I flicked through the magazine I'd brought until I found an article that would make Jeremy grind his teeth were he awake. "Time to wake up, buddy," I said. "Or you're going to hear all about what this article on perfecting smoky eye has to say. And trust me, it's a doozy. I think they paid the writer by the word."

I glanced at his face. No reaction.

"You brought this on yourself," I said, and began to read aloud.

I stayed for a couple of hours, though I didn't read the whole time. Instead, I talked, filling him in on everything. I was pretty sure I was fired since I hadn't been to work in a week, and that meant either job hunting or going back under Davenport's umbrella. It might not be all bad. Jessie Davenport seemed to like me enough to protect me from Eddie, and that was a handy friendship to have. Once they stopped locking us inside, Guy could go to culinary school like he'd dreamed, and Jeremy could wake up and meet Raze. She really could use more enemies.

The only movement from Jeremy during all these musings was from the little blue crackles between his fingers and occasionally around his ears. "Good talk," I said, patting his hand and grimacing at the zap. "I'll be by again soon. I hear blue eye shadow's making a comeback. I bet I can find an article with lots of purple prose. So you might want to wake up before then, Jer."

It was stupid to hope, but I glanced at his face one last time and left.

In the corridor, I heard Naomi call my name. I turned and watched her trot up, wanting to shake my head. Due to the house arrest, she was stuck in the Davenport Industries uniform, and it was weird to see her out of her hipster gear and in a pressed polo shirt. At least I'd had a few outfits in Guy's New York place and didn't have to suffer the same fate.

"Any other missing heroes I should know about?" I asked when she reached me.

She had the grace to look ashamed. "It wasn't my idea to keep you two in the dark. But still, my bad. And no, nobody else is missing."

That much was a relief.

"Sort of," Naomi corrected herself. "Have you seen Kiki? We were supposed to meet up to review some more of Mobius's notes and she's not answering my texts."

"She was visiting Jeremy a while ago, but she took off. Have you asked Angélica? She might know, on account of them being . . ." I crossed two fingers.

Naomi laughed. "Finally caught on, have you?"

That reaction made me somewhat grateful that at least Guy hadn't known about the relationship, either. Perhaps Naomi was the only one that knew. Her observation skills could be their own superpower, really.

"I'll text Angélica," Naomi said, shaking her head at my sour look. "Thanks, Gail."

"No problem," I said, and we headed our separate ways.

I made it to the end of the corridor when the walls and the floor tilted sharply to the left. Static rushed into my ears and filled my head. I hit the floor in an uncoordinated pile.

"Gail!" Naomi's footsteps sounded like thunder. Her voice rang like bells.

"Gail—" It wasn't Naomi talking. This voice was blurry and distorted and all of my thoughts were too far from each other to connect. "Gail—you get one chance—"

"Gail!" Naomi again. My world shuddered and everything in my head sloshed in response.

"—don't waste it—"

"Somebody help! She's having a seizure!"

"—make sure he gives you the antidote—"

"Help!"

"—and for god's sake, save me—"

The words began to blur. Feminine, I thought. Familiar. I opened my eyes, but all I could see was white. Images began to pour in my head, so fast and so overwhelming that the white blinked out, leaving me with nothing but darkness.

Mercifully, unconsciousness followed not too far after that.

I opened my eyes to find Dr. Mobius's ugly mug pushing into my face, and for one horrific second, I was back in that basement in the Chicago suburbs, being tormented by a mad scientist. A blink and I realized several things: I wasn't wearing a thin hospital gown, my arms and legs weren't shackled, I was in Medical, and there were several people in the room with varying degrees of worry shading their faces.

"Ugh, get away from me," I said.

He scooted backward in his wheelchair with a sniff. "As you can see," he said to everybody else in the room, "she is fine. Her seizures were not a result of my serum."

Guy immediately rushed forward and hugged me. "Are you okay?" he asked.

I rubbed my eyes, though my head didn't actually hurt. "What happened? Why am I here?"

"You fainted and had a seizure." Naomi gave me a flat look, but I could see relief underneath. Her heart was pounding. "How about you don't do that again, ever? You scared the ever-loving shit out of me, Girl. What *was* that?"

"I'm not sure." Seizures were new. Teleporting meant migraines, phasing drained my energy, psychic manifestations messed with my memory. What nightmare would this bring? "I'm hungry."

A crap-cake landed in my lap, courtesy of Angélica. I made a face at it.

"Do you remember anything about what happened? Did a light flash or something?" Guy remained kneeling in front of the cot so that we were eye level for once.

My mind was a blurry blank, so I shook my head. I remembered seeing Naomi in the corridor and I remembered talking to Jeremy beforehand. She was here, with Angélica and Guy, now. Looking around, though, made me realize that somebody was missing. "Where's Kiki?"

There was a pause as everybody looked at each other. "You were the last one to see her," Guy said. "She didn't say anything about where she was going, did she?"

I shook my head again. "She's not answering her phone?"

"She left it here. The last thing on it is a text from her aunt," Guy said. "We think. She deleted it."

Something poked at the edge of my brain, trying to break through the confusion. "That's weird. Nobody goes anywhere without their cell phone unless they're me. And that's usually because I broke it."

"Yes, but not everybody is as irresponsible with their possessions as you appear to be, Miss Godwin," Mobius said, which I felt was a little unfair. He'd once stolen my phone, after all. And he was the reason I'd once been hit by a car, too, which had been the fate of my last phone. I opened my mouth to tell him as much—and swayed on the spot.

Dr. Mobius reached out to prod me with one of his bony fingers. "Tell me where my granddaughter is," he said.

"Shut up," I said. His voice grated at my ears. It was a little distracting, but I was more concerned by the fact that an image had shown up in my head, unbidden, of a warehouse. I'd never been there, but it was in my head, feeling vaguely *wrong*. Like the colors were slightly off.

Dr. Mobius drew himself up like an offended peacock. "I will have you know that you have no right to speak to me this way. I am a respected—"

"Shut *up*," I said again. I pushed Guy's hands back and clutched at my forehead. The warehouse faded from my mind, replaced with another image that was just as clear and just as off as the first. Street signs. My nose twitched, picking up the smell of water. The Lake, I realized. Lake Michigan. I was hallucinating someplace in Chicago.

"Gail?" Naomi asked worriedly. Her voice no longer sounded panicked, like when she'd been shaking me in the corridor, not like the calm voice in my head.

The voice in my head.

My eyes snapped open as I finally put it all together. Kiki. She'd somehow used our mental bond to transmit information to me, things she'd seen with her own eyes, which was why they felt so foreign to mine. I could see it all clearly now: a text from Jessie that she'd deleted, images of her walking to the address Jessie had given her, the image of the warehouse, Kiki's voice urging me not to waste the opportunity.

It made me sick to my stomach, and furious. I breathed through my nose. Kiki, you *idiot*, I thought at her. Maybe she'd pick that up through the bond.

"Gail?" Naomi said. "What is it?"

"I know where Kiki is," I said. I took a deep breath and licked my lips, which had gone dry. "Tamara Diesel has her."

Vicki rolled immediately to her feet, Angélica's hands twitched, and Dr. Mobius's face drained of all color. I looked steadily at him, hoping that Angélica didn't mention to anybody else that my heart was pounding.

"And I'm not telling you where," I said, meeting Dr. Mobius's gaze and holding steady. "Not unless you make the antidote."

# CHAPTER 20

It was a toss-up who looked angrier as we entered the lab: Dr. Mobius or Angélica. Guy, Naomi, and Vicki just seemed baffled. Watching others be kidnapped tended to make me lose my head, and here I was coldly demanding the antidote from Dr. Mobius in exchange for information on his granddaughter's whereabouts. They knew it was out of character for me, but I was banking on Dr. Mobius not discovering that.

"This is abominable behavior for somebody who prides herself on being a good person," Dr. Mobius said as he wheeled himself to the front of the lab. He said "good person" with a sneer. "Perhaps you're no better than the villains you claim to dislike, Miss Godwin."

"I need seven doses," I said, keeping my voice even though the back of my throat felt oily. "Five for the hostages—including your granddaughter—and two for . . ." I gestured toward Vicki and Guy, even though I knew Guy didn't want the antidote.

"I will make six permanent cures for the Demobilizer, and no more," Mobius said.

"Seven," I said. "And I'd work quickly, if I were you."

The sooner he finished, the sooner we could save Kiki, but he didn't need to know that I was just as anxious as everybody else to rescue her. She'd sent me a mental image of the warehouse interior, the last thing I'd seen before I passed out. Studying it in my mind's eye now, I could see shelves of crates surrounding the open center of the floor plan. Several cages were on prominent display under spotlights, and each contained a familiar figure. So Tamara Diesel *was* collecting depowered heroes. To do what with them, I had no idea. She probably wanted to parade them around Times Square and crow about world domination, since Times Square was just about as gaudy as she was. They were all in costume and still masked, so apparently she was still playing by the rules. Heroes and villains respected the mask above all else. But it was only a matter of time before she unmasked or, worse, killed them all.

"How long will this take?" I asked.

"It takes as long as it takes." Mobius shot me a venomous glare and ducked down to work.

Out of the corner of my eye, I could see Angélica's temper beginning to bubble over. I didn't protest as she grabbed my arm and dragged me over to the far corner of the lab, though I did wave at the others to stay put. I didn't need Mobius getting suspicious.

"What the hell do you think you're doing?" she asked in Portuguese. "You're putting Kiki in danger."

"Trust me, I know." My Portuguese wasn't great, as I'd mostly picked it up thanks to Angélica yelling at me about the dishes. But I could hold a very rudimentary conversation, if necessary.

"And you're okay with this?" Angélica asked.

"I am definitely not," I said.

"Then why are you—" Angélica stopped, eyebrows low as she did the math in her head. "This is her idea, isn't it? She did something with . . ." She wiggled her fingers at my forehead.

"Technically, I think it was my idea, but I was joking." An offhand comment while we'd talked in Jeremy's room didn't mean I was being serious. Knowing Kiki had taken it and run with it only made my stomach hurt. "She didn't give me any warning. Just: wham."

Angélica dipped into several other languages to curse. She remained facing me as she did it, though, which sold the act that she was furious with me. I didn't know how much attention Mobius was paying us, but we had to be careful. "How much danger is she in?" she asked.

"Raptor's with her, so that's something. But Kiki told me not to waste this and she has a point. He's not going to cooperate any other way."

"I'm going to wring her neck." Angélica stomped away, muttering under her breath about foolish old men and their idiot granddaughters. I stayed in the corner and kept an eye on Mobius. Whatever he was doing smelled rank, which didn't surprise me. The man was incapable of being anything but disgusting. Occasionally he would raise his head to shoot hateful looks at me. I didn't let them get to me; they weren't as devastating as the countdown clock happening in my head. Every moment this took was one more that Kiki and Jessie and Sam were in danger.

And once we had the antidote, then what? Were we going to storm the warehouse, dose everybody, retrieve our fallen friends? Tamara Diesel no doubt had gathered allies in droves, likely to laugh at the misfortunes of the poor heroes they'd captured. Those were going to be impossible odds.

When Dr. Mobius seemed completely wrapped up in his work, I grabbed an unused tablet and stylus, tracing what I could of the warehouse from memory. Surreptitiously, I passed it to Vicki, whose eyes narrowed. A moment later, she handed it to Angélica, grabbed Naomi by the shoulder, and left. She came back in her Plain Jane outfit, the mask secured as ever at her hip. By that time, Mobius had something boiling that smelled like rotten eggs and Guy was struggling not to gag.

Reaching out mentally to Kiki proved fruitless. I wasn't even sure I could do it, or if she had been given the Demobilizer already. Had Elwin Lucas created it for them, or had Brook handed it over? I hadn't seen her in Kiki's image, but that didn't mean anything. She could've stepped out to kick a puppy or something. Or something bad might have happened to her. Neither option really appealed to me.

"Done," Dr. Mobius said, jerking me out of my reverie. He finished pouring his concoction into a row of test tubes. I stepped forward, finally giving in to the urgency that had been pushing away at the back of my mind.

I faltered when I counted the test tubes. "There's only six."

"Which is how many I promised I would give you."

My hand clenched into a fist.

"That's fine," Guy said. "Vicki can take the sixth dose. I don't mind."

Mobius shook his head. "Miss Godwin wants to leverage my feelings for my granddaughter against me? She shall suffer the consequences. This dose goes to the redhead or . . ." He picked up the test tube and let it slip through his fingers an inch.

Instantly all of us lunged forward, and his smile told me he had us exactly where he wanted us. I couldn't attack him, not without damaging some or all of the antidote, and he knew that.

"Why?" I asked.

"I am not your puppet," Mobius said. "The girl wants it. He doesn't."

"The girl," Vicki said under her breath, "is a grown-ass woman who would have no problems kicking your ass with or without powers."

Angélica shot her a look: not the time.

I met Guy's gaze. It was obvious to me how much

he *didn't* want to drink the antidote. But he took a deep breath and stepped forward.

"Guy," I said.

He took the test tube. "For Kiki," he said, and underneath I heard the silent *and Sam*.

"If he dies, I'm never telling you where Kiki is," I said to Dr. Mobius. "I hope you know that."

"You have a very skewed view of being a hero," was all he said.

Guy took a whiff of the test tube, wrinkling his nose. He shared a look with Vicki and then with me, tipped his head back, and gulped it down in one go. "That," he said as he set the test tube on the counter, "was deeply unpleasant. I really don't recommend—" He broke off to cough and collapsed on the floor.

"Guy!" I rushed to his side. He curled up, coughing, his face even redder than his hair, body twitching and shuddering.

Angélica hauled Dr. Mobius up by the front of his lab coat. "What did you do to him?"

"It takes a moment!" Actual fear entered the doctor's voice, a testament to Angélica's strength. "His body is adjusting to the return of its full abilities. Do you think it's a simple walk in the park to lose and gain powers the way he has?"

Guy's body continued to convulse with giant, wracking coughs and he pounded his fist into the ground like he couldn't breathe. "Call for Medical!" I said.

But Guy stopped coughing and flopped onto his

back, sweat soaking his forehead. He gasped, chest heaving.

"Are you okay?" I asked.

He nodded, squeezing his eyes shut.

"And your—how do you feel?"

Guy nudged me back so he could climb to his feet. He clenched his jaw and slowly, carefully, began to hover a foot off of the floor. "I'm a little shaky," he said, "but my powers are there. Get the rest of the antidote ready."

"Where is she?" Angélica asked me.

"Chicago."

Angélica looked first at Guy and then at me. "Got armor?"

"I can get some," I said.

"Get to the 'porters. Ten minutes." Angélica looked at Vicki. "Keep an eye on the good doctor until we get back?"

"With pleasure," Vicki said, glaring at Dr. Mobius. I didn't miss the way her eyes lingered on the empty test tube, but she gave Guy's shoulder a reassuring squeeze as he passed.

"You have armor?" Guy asked as we jogged down the hall.

"I have a suspicion there's something for me back at the apartment."

"In that case." Guy scooped me up like it was the good old days, took two running steps, and leapt into the air. It was always strange to fly indoors, but he was faster in the air than he was on the ground. In less than a minute, we were back at his apartment.

A box was sitting on the table, waiting for me.

"What the . . . ?" Guy looked around but there wasn't any sign that his apartment had been broken into. "How . . . ?"

"Behold the power that is Audra Yi," I said. Jessie's assistant-slash-valet was truly a terrifying woman as far as competence went, and I'd learned not to question it. Audra had once offered me her card and had promised that if I ever needed anything, I only had to ask. Kiki had done the asking for me in this case, but Audra probably hadn't even blinked. Not if Tamara Diesel and her cronies had Jessie in a cage. Kiki had to be the most prepared hostage I'd ever met. It didn't make it better that she'd given herself up, but I did respect her a little more for it.

While Guy flew up to the bedroom to dig out his own uniform, I opened the box and stared. Last time they'd given me gear for a mission like this, it had been body armor, similar to the tactical gear soldiers and mercenaries wore. This . . . was something entirely different.

This had a mask.

It sent a peculiar feeling through me as I held it up, as I'd only worn ski masks and nothing tailored. People asked what mask I was, what mask I'd taken up, and the truth was none of them. I hadn't wanted a mask. But here I was, looking down at the advanced microfabric mask in my hands. All along it had been unavoidable. The minute Dr. Mobius had infected me, this was where my path had been leading—and I really did not have time for an existential crisis right now.

I shimmied into the uniform, hands shaking as I tried to hurry. The top was somewhere between bronze and dark gray, shimmering a little as it caught the light, with scale-like pieces that interlocked over the top layer of the armor for extra protection. The pants were dark, the boots went halfway up my calves, and the armored fabric stretched across my torso. It could stop bullets, but it let me move freely.

I pulled the mask over my face. Like Guy's, it was a full face mask; Raptor's mask left the bottom of her face bare, but this didn't have the same design. It did have the little backward tufts near the crown, but nobody would mistake me for the Raptor. There was no logo across the chest.

Guy stepped out of the bedroom and both of us froze. He was back in his Blaze outfit. No more chest piece and helmet and no weapons. Just his black-and-green ensemble that made him look fighting trim, with the scarred boots and the battered mask clutched in one hand.

"Whoa," he said.

"Same."

He paused. "Can you even see in that thing?"

"Perfectly," I said.

"Good enough for me." He launched himself off of the second floor and scooped me up on the way by. "Let's go save our friend."

## CHAPTER 21

What was it with supervillains and empty warehouses?
Did they get some kind of two-for-one deal on them? Just
once, it would have been nice to see some supervillains
work out of a five-star hotel or something. Someplace
where after everything was done, a massage therapist
or two was guaranteed to be on hand.

At least we knew we were on the right path.
Tamara Diesel wasn't trying to be stealthy, but there
also weren't giant neon signs pointing to her lair. The
only obvious sign was the smashed security cameras
along the road. "So Davenport won't hack them and
spy," Angélica had said as we'd raced along. I phased a
few steps behind her as we darted around abandoned
warehouses by the docks, past the disabled cameras. It
might have kept Davenport out, but it did us a favor,
too. If we could get past Tamara Diesel's sentries, they
wouldn't see us coming.

Angélica had half of the antidote in unbreakable vials strapped to her thigh. The other two doses were tucked in little slots on the sleeve of my new uniform. I could feel the liquid sloshing as I phased in a pattern designed to avoid sentries. I recognized a couple of the lookouts: Captain Cracked flew overhead on his hoverboard, and Scorch spread the smell of burning as I sneaked past him. Guy flew close to the ground, darting between buildings and sticking to shadows as much as he could. It was kind of a miracle that we weren't noticed, though, because Angélica wore her uniform from her own days on the front line.

Vicki had told me once that it was red and memorable. She had really failed to impart just *how* red. Vividly crimson thigh-high boots, pants that were a couple of shades darker, and a top that left her arms bare and was somehow even brighter than the boots. She had black bracers around her rather impressive biceps, but I couldn't determine their purpose at all. She'd shoved her black hair under a gray beanie that I figured wasn't part of the original outfit.

She wore red sunglasses and a determined look as she ran. When she launched herself, phasing up to the fourth-story rooftop of a warehouse, I didn't question it. I followed after her. Granted, I aimed a little low and had to grab the edge to keep from falling off, but I pulled myself to safety and out of sight as Guy landed next to us. Together, we crept to the edge of the roof and studied the warehouse next door. I could see the street signs that Kiki had put into my head from this angle. It gave me an eerie feeling that wasn't quite déjà vu, but came damn close.

"Thoughts?" Angélica asked.

I moved to pull my mask up; Angélica grabbed my wrist and jerked my hand back down to my side. Right, no unmasking.

"It's hard to tell from this angle," Guy said. "The guards seem pretty relaxed. I don't think they're expecting trouble."

"You think we can sneak in?" Angélica asked.

"I think you and Gail might be able to." Guy tilted his head and I wished I could see his expression under his mask. I imagined he was frowning. "Stealth approach. Try to get the antidote to . . ." He looked to me.

"Sam's the closest one to the door," I said.

"If you give him the antidote, he'll react like I did. That could be enough of a distraction to get it to the others. They'll be focused on him," Guy said.

"So we go in, we activate Sam, and . . . what? Brawl?" I asked.

"*We* brawl." Guy gestured between Angélica and himself. "You—"

"Don't you dare say, 'Get to safety,' " I said.

"You do your best to find Elwin Lucas and get him out of there. Be careful, though, Brook might be wandering around. She'll know he'd be your primary target."

"Provided she's there at all," Angélica said in a dark voice.

It wasn't a great plan, but if we could get the antidote to the heavy hitters in the cages, we evened the odds considerably. Raptor alone could fight off Tamara Diesel, given how many times the women had clashed over the years. So we had a chance.

I peered at the building next door. It was weather-worn, years of exposure to the lake water and wind making it smell of mold and mildew. Four stories tall, it was open inside and, if Kiki's mental image was correct, full of ceiling-high shelves packed with wooden crates. Not only would it smell foul, I knew, but there would be plenty for heroes and villains alike to fling at each other. I'd have to be careful and keep an eye on every axis.

"So," I said as we studied the challenge that lay before us. "Your brother, your girlfriend, and my weird sugar-mama mentor walk into a warehouse . . ."

Angélica groaned and shoved the heel of her hand into my forehead, pushing my head back. "I'm with her on this one," Guy said when I looked to him for support, but he sounded amused. "Got any idea how you're going to sneak in?"

I studied the nearest wall. "There," I said, pointing to a shattered window near the top. It was about forty feet off of the ground and that wasn't going to be a pleasant fall if I missed. "If we can land quietly enough, it'll get us onto a shelf inside. We can sneak around along those until we reach the cages. They're laid out three on the other side, two on this side. Sam'll be on the other side if they haven't moved him."

"And Kiki?"

"In the cage next to Sam, if I had to guess. It's empty in the vision she sent," I said. "Windrider's on the other side of her."

"Well, when he gets loose, watch out for tornadoes."

"Gotcha."

"That leaves Raptor and Sharkbait on the near side," Angélica said. "You focus on them. Can you sense Kiki at all?"

I shook my head. I wasn't even sure how to intentionally use my mental powers, but it felt like only me inside my head. Kiki would've been keeping a mental ear out for me, wouldn't she? All it told me was that they'd probably given her the Demobilizer.

"Of course it couldn't be that easy," Angélica said, grumbling. "Blaze, you good on your end?"

Guy shrugged. His part of the plan involved laying low, waiting for Sam to get his powers back, and bursting in when all hell broke loose. I squeezed his hand as I pushed myself back away from the edge of the building. If I was going to hit that window without making a sound, I needed a running start. Angélica, much more used to her powers, merely trotted to the side of the building, took a readying breath, and phased right over. She hit the sill perfectly, balancing on the toes of those ridiculous red boots, and disappeared into the building without a backward glance. Once she was out of sight, I rolled my shoulders, bounced up on my toes a few times, and sprinted as hard as I could for the side of the building. I jumped and threw my weight forward, phasing and praying.

I miscalculated. I miscalculated badly.

Instead of landing as lightly as Angélica had, I missed the windowsill completely and phased right through the window, hurtling into the building. Daylight changed abruptly to darkness. I gritted my teeth and hoped whatever I slammed into had at least a little give.

Arms wrapped around my torso. Before I understood what was happening, I was phasing again, this time not under my own power. Angélica landed impossibly lightly atop the next set of shelves over.

Carefully, she set me down as I tried to get my breathing under control. She put her finger to her lips and began to creep along the shelves. Mercifully, they didn't groan under our weight, but my every sense remained on high alert. We were literally sneaking into a den full of supervillains. Somehow, this had become my life. It made me want to laugh a bit hysterically, but I swallowed that feeling down and followed her. The center of the warehouse was laid out in an open bay, but there were four rows of shelves to crawl across. We hopped lightly from row to row. Or rather, Angélica hopped lightly and caught me, as there was no way I could be accurate enough not to alert everybody within eight blocks that we were there. The smell of dust and mold made me want to sneeze, so I held my breath as best I could. Knowing my luck, I was bound to knock something over before we even made it halfway through the warehouse. At any second, some supervillain sentry could come soaring around the corner and see us in our bright bronze and red uniforms. Every shelf brought us closer and closer to danger. Every tiny noise we made was a gamble.

When the cages came into sight, I felt Angélica gasp, likely at seeing Kiki. She lay in the fifth cage, the back of her head pillowed on her hands, her feet crossed at the ankle. Completely relaxed. The rest of the heroes either paced or sat, arms folded over their chests. Jessie, in her Raptor gear, sat in a full lotus, eyes closed. She might actually be meditating, I realized. The cages didn't look enhanced—just good old steel and padlocks—so it was safe to say they'd been given the Demobilizer. Spotlights over each cage would make sneaking up all but impossible. We just had to hope for silence and luck.

Toward the back of the warehouse, I could see a couple of folding tables, one covered in snacks and a coffeemaker whose steam curled up into the air. Several men and women in dark clothing sat at the table beside it, hunched over in the cold, glaring at cards in their gloved hands. I didn't see Tamara Diesel or Elwin Lucas among them, but that didn't mean they weren't there.

Angélica gestured at the shelves on the other side of the cages and then at herself. I gave her a thumbs-up. "Wish me luck," she whispered, barely making a sound, and jumped.

One blink later, she was perched on the shelves above Kiki's cage. I gave her a little salute and began to climb down, ducking back among the crates to stay out of sight. The top two shelves proved a cinch, but right as I arrived near the bottom shelf, my boot scuffled off a loose board.

I watched it fall toward Shark-Man's cage in horror.

For as much as we made fun of the man in gray who protected San Francisco, he definitely had superior reflexes. He stuck his arm out of the cage and caught the board before it could clatter to the ground. His eyes, an unnatural shade of red, looked up and met mine where I was dangling from a shelf ten feet up.

Neither of us breathed.

A villain in an oversized blue parka threw his cards down on the table. Across the shelves, I could see Angélica gawking at us. Shark-Man's movement had drawn the attention of Windrider, Sam, and Kiki, too. Jessie continued to meditate. I waved frantically at the others and they did their best to resume acting naturally.

"I fold," the villain said, and all of the heroes in the cages and I let out a breath as one.

Shark-Man carefully set the board down as I scurried to the bottom level. "Who're you?" he hissed, turning back around to face forward.

"Not important. Take this." I shoved the first vial of the antidote through the bars.

"I'm not drinking something from a stranger," he said.

"As nice as it is to see lessons learned in kindergarten stuck, do you want your powers back or not?" I asked, watching the poker game and waiting for one of them to look up and notice me skulking behind the cage.

Shark-Man's entire body jolted. Eagerly, he turned and reached for the vial.

"Not yet," I said, though I handed it over. "Wait for the distraction."

Out of the corner of my eye, I saw a flash of red by Sam's cage that had to be Angélica sneaking away, too. Sam, in the original War Hammer armor—apparently he'd kept it, after all—tilted his head back and swigged the antidote in one gulp.

Unfortunately, our luck ran out at that precise moment. As he lowered the vial, Tamara Diesel rounded the corner. She drew up short. "Where did you get that? What is it?"

A yank of her hand and the vial flew across the space, landing in her palm.

Sam stared defiantly at her for all of a split second before he collapsed onto the floor of his cage, coughing and convulsing the way Guy had. Angélica decided this was a moment to take advantage of: she sprang at Tamara.

"On second thought," I said to Shark-Man, "new plan. Drink it now."

"But—" He waved at Sam, who was writhing at the bottom of his cage. He had a point, but I was a little distracted by the poker players surging to their feet.

"Just do it!" I jumped off the shelf, ran across the top of Shark-Man's cage, and launched myself after Angélica. The fighting wasn't supposed to begin until Sam's powers were back, but there wasn't any way I was letting Angélica face Tamara and her goons alone.

I landed on the balls of my feet and rolled, trying to jump up and knock Tamara's feet out from under her. She swept out an arm, flicking me away like a particularly annoying gnat. The telekinetic force sent me sliding toward the rent-a-villains racing at us. I scrambled to my feet. Crap. I hadn't even delivered the antidote to Jessie and I was supposed to be finding and rescuing Elwin Lucas, not fighting off lower-tier henchmen. But needs must, I supposed.

They piled on, trying to overwhelm me with sheer numbers. I knocked the first man over with a jab to the solar plexus before he could get his arms around me, kicked the second in the crotch, and phased, smashing my elbow into the third one's neck, all within the space of a few heartbeats. Unfortunately, the fourth fighter proved faster than I had anticipated. Her haymaker caught me on the chin. I stumbled back, head ringing and my chin a white-hot point of pain.

She swung again at the same time as an invisible force shoved against my side, flinging me across the open space in the center of the warehouse. My back slammed solidly into the bars of Jessie's cage. Tamara Diesel, who'd hit me, started to advance on me, only to be knocked to the side by a red blur. She let out a roar and chased after Angélica.

A second later, I felt something tug on the utility pouch at my hip and Jessie yanked out a small gray disc no bigger than a quarter. She slapped it over the lock on her cage. "Perfect, just what I needed. Much obliged."

I blinked at her in a daze. The reek of burning metal filled the air. "So you like the uniform?" she asked.

"Wh-what?" I asked.

"Looks like Audra got your measurements right. Also, you might want to duck," she said.

I obeyed. My opponent howled as his fist clanged solidly into the bars of the cage, and I used the distraction to drive my shoulder into his stomach, tackling him back. We toppled to the ground and I grappled for purchase. Just one solid punch and I could end this problem, I knew, but that was easier said than done when he was fighting back just as hard.

I could see a red blur darting around the edges of my vision, no doubt Angélica attempting to draw Tamara's fire and distract her from the fact that Sam, Kiki, and Windrider were all coughing as the antidote worked away. I risked a glance at Shark-Man: he lay in a gray ball on the bottom of his cage.

My opponent seized the opportunity and tried to lever his hands around my neck. I blocked him with my elbow and kneed him hard in the balls. When he curled up like a shrimp, I finally landed the punch that knocked him out.

An instant later, a *pop* shook the floor around me and sparks skittered at the edge of my vision. I gaped at the smoking remains of Jessie's cage door. "Thanks for the assist," she said, shoving it open. She grabbed the pouch from my belt and hooked it to her own. "Now get the hell out. I'll handle Diesel."

I scrabbled for the vial still in the slot in my sleeve. "Wait—the antidote—"

"I'll be fine. Go." She ran to join Angélica as the door burst open and a green-and-black blur sped inside, followed by Scorch, who spewed flame every which way. No wonder Guy hadn't shown up on cue. I could see Sam rising to his feet, the coughing spell over and his powers obviously returned, which meant I had other priorities. Angélica would assist Jessie and spirit Kiki away to safety, but my priority was to find Elwin Lucas.

Seeing no sign of him, I decided my best bet was the way I'd seen Tamara enter. She had to be coming from somewhere. Hopefully it wasn't the bathroom. I phased my way across the open space to avoid getting hit by any of the heroes and villains crowding on the dance floor. The sound of explosions followed me, which told me Jessie was having a blast.

Tamara had emerged from a door that led down a set of stairs to some kind of basement beneath the warehouse. Instantly, foreboding set in. The walls were scratched and dirty with age and neglect, giving the whole thing a very horror-movie feel. I crept down a rickety set of wooden stairs lit by a single uncovered bulb with a flickering yellow filament. Fighting upstairs rattled the floor, covering any sound that anybody would make. Dampness clung persistently to the air and it smelled of rot. But underneath that was a very familiar scent that I wouldn't be able to smell ever again without thinking of Vicki's stricken look as the last of her fire died.

Apricots.

Whatever was down here, it was chock-full of De-mobilizer.

"This is just awesome," I said, thinking of the lair under the business park where Elwin had kept Mobius captive. I reached the bottom step and found a long cinder block hallway awaiting me. It reminded me of something from one of Jeremy's video games, which he'd cheerfully liked to call "the creepy-ass murder hallway."

Overhead, something boomed, shaking the floor and sending little curls of dirt raining down from the ceiling. I headed down the hallway at a faster clip. It occurred to me that with the battle for good and evil going on over my head, I was in as much danger from the ceiling caving in as I was from whatever lay ahead. What a cheerful thought.

I reached the end of the hallway and leaned around the blind corner to check. I got the impression of a mad scientist lab: desks full of complicated machines, beakers with bright multicolored liquid, chalkboards full of formulae, an operating table.

Brook.

She stood in the middle of the room, wearing the clothes I'd last seen her in. She spotted me and her eyes went wide. Before I could lunge, though, something on my left moved. I felt a sharp prick of pain in the side of my neck and thought, *Oh, shit.*

# CHAPTER 22

The stab to my neck felt like a needle—I'd had far too much experience with those over the years not to recognize one right away—so I jumped back immediately. Before it even connected that I'd just been dosed with something, I was already mid-punch. My fist drove right into cartilage and flesh.

I heard an enraged yowl. Elwin Lucas hopped back, dropping a syringe on the ground. Blood gushed past the hands he'd slapped over his nose. I grabbed him by the collar of his lab coat and yanked him down to my level. "What did you just do to me?" I asked.

He looked absolutely terrified for a split second. The blood dripping off of his jaw and onto his polo shirt helped sell the impression. Until my fingers began to tingle. It spread like wildfire, racing up my arms, pinpricks that covered my chest and neck, gathering behind my cheeks and my forehead. Everything in the room promptly lost all sense of permanence, melting and warping together into some kind of nightmare. Nausea sprang up to tango with the dizziness.

"What the hell?" I asked. When I tried to step forward, I lurched and hit the wall, pain singing up my arm. "What's happening to—"

Far too late I realized it: Elwin had given me something that even the Mobium couldn't combat. It was the last clear thought I had before an empty gray haze swept in over the limbs-falling-asleep sensation covering every inch of my body. The last clear image I had was of Brook.

And the reinforced shackle chaining her to the workbench behind her.

Being the once and future Hostage Girl meant I'd woken up in a lot of strange places, usually in various states of debilitating pain and confusion. On operating tables, roped to lightning rods atop skyscrapers, dangling over pits of acid. There'd been one time with an active volcano that I wasn't in any hurry to repeat ever.

But never on a street corner, and barely ever standing on my own two feet. Never standing on my own unassisted, at any rate. And sunshine was rare, too. Even though it was cold—and by that I meant *cold*. Suddenly I could experience every bit of November in Chicago that I hadn't felt all month. I knew this should feel strange, but I didn't know why.

I opened my eyes and immediately looked down at

my hands. They shook with the cold, but there were no shackles.

The same could not be said for Brook.

Still confused and not sure why, I drank in the details: she stood in front of me, her hands bound together with regular handcuffs—something felt wrong about that, but I didn't know what—and I was standing outside on a street corner I recognized downtown. There was slush and partially melted ice beneath my boots, and I was still in uniform. People walked by me as though this was completely normal.

I tried to speak, but all that emerged were slurred syllables that definitely weren't English.

"One moment," a voice behind me said. "I need to pay the driver."

I turned my head, which seemed to sap most of my energy, and saw Elwin Lucas handing a few bills through the passenger window of a cab.

When I turned back, Brook was glaring at me. "His serum counteracts the Mobium. You'll never be able to fight him off. Not without passing out."

Shit. Brook took a step back as Elwin took his change from the cabbie. The driver shot me a strange look and pulled away from the curb. Elwin Lucas, who'd ditched his lab coat and whose nose looked red and puffy, stepped over to Brook and me. Something inside me struggled, like I wanted to fight him, but my body stood there uselessly. I could taste a pervasive sense of wrongness. Whatever Elwin had given me, it overpowered everything else. I felt like a mindless drone, trapped in syrup.

"Welcome back to the land of the living," Elwin said. He looked at Brook, whose jaw had clenched even tighter. Her dark eyes were promising a great deal more murder than I found comfortable, given my proximity and the fact that my limbs did not seem interested in cooperating with the rest of me.

"Go to hell," I said, surprised the words came out coherently.

Elwin grabbed my elbow, giving me no choice but to begin walking, though the very action alone made me dizzy. We were heading toward the Willis Tower, I realized vaguely. The chemical in my blood counteracting the Mobium made it difficult to stay on my feet, much less try to talk, but Elwin pulled me along at a good clip, Brook following behind us. My teeth began to chatter.

Elwin pulled me into the lobby and to the bank of elevator bays, flashing a white badge at the security guards. Though there were people around, he yanked me close to his side and I smelled the faint remnants of the apricot scent on him under a healthy layer of fear-sweat. Whatever he was doing right now, he was almost out of his mind with terror.

In the elevator, he pressed the button for the forty-seventh floor. He was marching me directly into Davenport. Well, that took a certain amount of nerve.

The three of us had the elevator to ourselves. Elwin turned the front of his body away from the security camera in the corner and subtly lifted up the corner of his shirt. I saw the matte-black flash of gun handle and wanted to close my eyes. "You're a returning hero bringing back a prisoner and a scientist you captured," he said. "Deviate from the plan or try to signal anybody, and I shoot Ms. Gianelli. I'm very fast, you know. I spent a lot of time in the Lodi gun range."

I wanted to despair. All my superpowers, and I was being brought down by a gun.

We reached the forty-seventh floor and Elwin shoved Brook at me. Thinking of the gun tucked into his waistband, I couldn't do anything but close my hand around Brook's elbow.

She was shaking.

Elwin pressed a keycard into my hand: Kiki's. My stomach sank. Kiki had access to all of Davenport, which meant that if nobody questioned us, Elwin could likely get whatever he wanted. I had to figure out a way around this without getting Brook shot, but my body was barely responding. Whatever Elwin had given me had made me even weaker than my Hostage Girl days.

Relief flooded through me when I saw the security guard in the waystation. After all the crap Marsh had put me through every time I wanted to 'port to New York, there was no possible way he'd wave me through with the wrong credentials. This plan would be foiled before it even got started, and all thanks to the world's crankiest security guard.

Marsh looked up from his computer, took in my uniform, eyed the two people flanking me, and waved me through.

"Seriously?" I wanted to ask him as I scanned the badge. If I survived this, I was coming back here and kicking Marsh's ass just for being a pain in mine.

The 'porter took us to Davenport Tower without complaint. In her line of work, I imagined, there were a lot of strange things that needed to be transported between stations. A uniformed hero bringing back a villain and a scientist barely even rated a second look. It made me want to scream, but I couldn't even get my body to do that much. Hell, I thought. I'm in hell. This is hell.

From the look on Brook's face, she'd lived through years of something like this. When I got control of my body back, I was going to either murder Elwin myself or stand to the side and let her do it.

In Davenport Tower, Elwin grabbed my wrist and stepped close. "Take me to Mobius," he said.

I had no idea what the protocols were, but the first time I'd been taken to the Davenport Complex—after fighting the very woman who stood in shackles next to me—Vicki had delivered me directly to Medical. So unfortunately, doing the same to Elwin and Brook wouldn't be seen as unusual.

"Why are you doing this?" I asked, forcing the words out through the hazy barrier that came between my thoughts and actions.

"Money, why else? If Davenport had just paid the ransom, I would've happily handed over the lunatic and the Demobilizer and none of us would be here, would we?" Elwin shoved at my elbow to make me move faster. "I could be on a beach right now."

"That's it?" I asked.

"What?"

"It's usually that the bad guy wants world domination or something sinister. You just want money?"

"Lodi was a job, not my life's work. I shouldn't be treated like a criminal just because my employer did a few bad things."

Brook began to shake harder. "You kept me in a cage and experimented on me for years!"

"I was following orders. I'm owed my due."

"You're owed a kick in the balls," Brook said, and I couldn't disagree. She looked at me, her own movements sluggish. "I didn't give Tamara Diesel the Demobilizer."

"Stop talking," Elwin said.

"They ambushed me. At Wrigley." Sweat gathered on Brook's forehead as she fought the effects of whatever we'd been dosed with. "I know you won't believe me, but all I want is to find Petra. Davenport can have this bastard."

Assuming he didn't get away with whatever he had planned.

He put his hand on the gun. "I *said* stop talking," he said.

Time to distract him. If he shot either of us, we'd bleed out before the drugs wore off and the Mobium could save our lives. "If you're after money, what do you want with Mobius?" I asked, hoping to distract him. Elwin Lucas might be human and amoral and awful, but he no doubt had the same weakness most villains shared: pride.

"Ms. Diesel offered me a lot of money to make more of the Demobilizer."

"You can do that?" I asked. It was getting easier to talk, but the rest of me still felt trapped in syrup.

Elwin scowled. "I'm working on it. But the Demobilizer is useless if there's an antidote to it."

"So you want to kill Mobius," I said, a cold trickle of fear working down the back of my neck. Where was everybody? Why was nobody stopping us? Were they all still at the fight?

"The stubborn idiot won't have shared his formula with anyone and nobody else is smart enough to replicate what he can do." Elwin's voice took on a boasting note as we made another turn that would bring us closer and closer to Medical. "I'm doing the world a favor. He's a monster, you know."

"He's not the only one," Brook said.

Of course we weren't lucky enough to be stopped by the receptionists in Medical. They saw the credentials and the uniform—Jessie sure had a lot of pull around Davenport that even a knockoff of her uniform got this much respect—and didn't question my assertion that the prisoners needed to be kept with Dr. Mobius for their own safety.

When I hesitated, Elwin looked hard at me and then hard at Brook. Again, I was being forced to make a choice. Brook was a villain, yes, but she was doing her time in prison and she was trying to turn her life around. Mobius was a villain as well that had done irreparable damage to my life.

Neither of them deserved to die, though.

I needed to stall somehow. But right now, there wasn't a way to do that, not without Elwin whipping out the gun and shooting Brook and now possibly the receptionists. My stomach sinking low, I walked toward the cell where they were keeping Mobius.

The badge let me right through. I stepped in, struggling as hard as I could against the drugs, trying to fight it off—

"Oh, hey!" Vicki's voice chirped out. "Jessie, you're—you're not Jessie."

I'd never even considered that Mobius might not be alone, I realized, even though Angélica had asked Vicki to keep an eye on him. And keep an eye on him she had. Dr. Mobius sat on his hospital bed, peevishly glaring at the cards in his hand, while Vicki sat in the chair next to his bed in her Plain Jane uniform. They had a little tray in between them. It looked like they'd been playing for popsicle sticks, and if the stack next to Vicki was anything to go by, I should never, ever play poker against her.

She rose to her feet when she saw Brook and Elwin, her eyes cutting immediately to the handcuffs on Brook's wrists. It was Mobius's reaction that I found more interesting. He blanched, all the color leaching from his skin. Whether he was gaping at Brook or Elwin, I had no idea.

"What's going on?" Vicki asked. In a move that seemed instinctual, she drew the Plain Jane mask on and stepped between Dr. Mobius and us. To do what,

I didn't know. She was as human as Brook and I were at the moment.

"He's gonna kill Mobius," I said, forcing the words out as fast as I could.

"Gail?" Vicki asked, turning toward me in surprise.

That proved to be a giant mistake.

Without any warning, Elwin yanked out the gun. I shouted, trying to fight off the drugs and race for him, but I wasn't fast enough. He pulled the trigger, aiming right at Vicki's forehead, and from that distance, there was no way he could miss.

He didn't miss. The gunshot sounded like a sonic boom, reverberating off of the walls as I watched in complete horror, unable to do anything. My brain could process it, but everything else froze in shock. He'd shot Vicki. He'd opened fire and shot my very human friend right in the forehead. He'd killed Vicki Burroughs.

Vicki, though, only took a staggering step back and said, "Ow."

And as I blinked, she shook her head, put a gloved hand to her forehead, and charged. She tackled Elwin hard, grappling for the gun. Her powers, I realized as I tried to force my body to move, to help out somehow. She must have convinced Mobius to make more of the antidote. She'd been shot in the head and hadn't died. She had her powers back!

But for somebody who was supposed to be super strong, she sure was struggling to get the gun away from Elwin. He was a full-grown man, but he shouldn't have been any trouble for her. I tried to drop to my knees, to grab Elwin's wrist and force the gun out of his hand, but my limbs wouldn't cooperate.

Vicki got a lucky elbow in, making Elwin grunt and drop the gun. I moved toward it, fighting to make my limbs function, but Brook got to it first. She scooped it up, holding it awkwardly since her hands were cuffed, and took a step back. I saw her gaze lock on Dr. Mobius and fear raced through me. "Brook, don't—"

"They did this to me," she said. The gun shook in her hands, but it wasn't pointed at him. "Both of them."

"Brook, think of—"

I never got a chance to finish that sentence because the door slammed open and guards in Detmer uniforms swarmed in to save the day. They pulled Vicki off of Elwin, shoved Brook and me against the walls, and mercifully relieved Brook of the gun before she could shoot anybody and revoke the deal she'd made for a shorter sentence.

Vicki whipped off the mask, her face and hair sweaty. "About time you boys got here," she said, breathing hard. She looked at me and held the mask up. "Good thing this is bulletproof, huh?"

# CHAPTER 23

It was almost anticlimactic, after that. Elwin was carted away. His plan, I found out later, had been to sneak in, kill Mobius, and sneak back out to continue making the Demobilizer for Tamara Diesel until she made him rich enough to retire to his own private island with lots of security. He might have gotten away with it if Vicki hadn't been there and if he hadn't been forced to use the gun.

"Guns," Vicki said with a scowl. "Definitely cheating."

Mercifully, it had been obvious that something was wrong with Brook and me. Perhaps out of some heretofore unknowing feeling of gratitude, Dr. Mobius had checked us both over and had declared that we would be fine. I'd protested that, but he pointed out that he'd used the same serum on me once before, the morning he had freed me from my captivity with him, and I'd been fine then. So we weren't in any danger. Probably.

Sitting still and letting the effects wear off, though, felt like torture, especially since I could barely move or speak. They carted Brook off and left me sitting in a room in Medical with Vicki. As best as we could tell, I'd lost less than an hour to the serum that Elwin had dosed me with, but the battle had apparently raged on for quite some time in my absence, and nobody had noticed I'd vanished. Tamara Diesel had slipped away, off to destroy the world another day, no doubt, but there were plenty of villains on their way to Detmer. And the powers had been restored to the major heroes that had lost them, thanks to Mobius's antidote.

If there was more Demobilizer in Elwin's underground lab, it was now property of Davenport Industries, for better or worse. I wasn't sure that was much better than Tamara Diesel having control of it, honestly. Either way, Elwin was going to prison for a long, long time.

"Man, am I lucky he hit the mask and not somewhere else," Vicki said as I sat on the cot and stared at her. "Bullet holes don't exactly go over well in the fashion industry. Nice to know I can still kick ass without my powers, though."

"But *you* were bulletproof before you lost them," I said.

"So?"

"What use would you have for a bulletproof mask?"

"Gail, do you know how much this face is worth? The mask is more than just a beacon of hope to humanity everywhere—it's extra insurance."

I had to laugh at that. "I'm glad you didn't die," I said.

"Me, too." She checked her phone. "Looks like your boyfriend's on his way back. He wants to know what happened to your phone."

As far as I could tell, Elwin had tossed my phone. Hopefully a search of the warehouse would turn it up. "At this point, your guess is as good as mine."

The serum finally started to wear off, letting me have some movement back, when the door flew open. Guy burst through, half flying in his hurry to get to me. "You're okay!" he said, scooping me up and swinging me around.

"Relatively uninjured, too," I said. "No head wounds or anything. Just drugs that I hope I never see again."

"You and me both," he said, and I tugged him down for a kiss that went on until Angélica stepped in and cleared her throat. I felt a spurt of amusement from behind her, which told me Kiki was there and that she'd gotten her powers back.

I glared at her.

"Hey, my plan worked," Kiki said. She was a little pale, her shirt streaked with dirt. As somebody whose powers were entirely psychic, I imagined she didn't get out to fight much. "Besides, Jessie was there. My aunt wouldn't have let anything happen to me."

I glared harder. Angélica crossed her arms over her chest and stood next to me. Faced with the two of us, Kiki visibly faltered and hung her head. "Okay," she said. "I won't do that again. I'm glad you were able to get my message, though."

"I've passed out twice today," I said. "Just so you know. One of those? Your fault."

Instead of apologetic, Kiki looked fascinated. Mercifully, Angélica pulled her away before she could start asking questions. Damn scientists. Should I worry that I was now telepathically linked to one? Did that kind of intellectual curiosity rub off? I'd have to figure that out later. At the moment, I had more pressing things to worry about. I felt my sleeve and breathed out in relief when I felt the bulge in the pocket. Elwin had searched my other pockets, but he hadn't noticed that one.

"Where's Jessie?" I asked.

"Taking Captain Cracked and the others to Detmer," Guy said. "Your buddy Scorch said to say hi, by the way. We ran into him at the fight. Why do you ask?"

I fumbled with my sleeve since the serum was wearing off. "The antidote—Jessie didn't take it," I said.

"Let me," Angélica said, reappearing at my side. She pulled the vial out. "Yo, Vicki."

Vicki caught it, fumbling a little. "Cheers," she said, and I realized that she actually *hadn't* been that upset about Mobius picking Guy to get his powers back. Like she'd been expecting this the whole time. She downed the antidote and I turned to Guy and Angélica in confusion.

"One of the hallmarks of being Raptor?" Angélica said. "No powers."

"What? But—but—*how*?" Jessie was a terrifying opponent in broad daylight, and I'd had the misfortune of going against her in an abandoned building by the docks in the middle of the night. And the entire time she hadn't had any powers?

Actually, it made a lot of sense, given how many gadgets she had. And Angélica had always cautioned me not to hit with my full strength whenever I was sparring with her.

"You knew the whole time," I said to Guy and Angélica as Kiki crouched over the coughing Vicki. "You knew we had enough of the antidote. Why didn't you say something?"

"Mobius wanted to hurt us. We had to let him think he was getting away with it." My incredulity must have shown on my face, for Angélica patted my arm. "Why don't you take a nap? You've had a hard day. Though you might need to wait. Kiki wants a sample of your blood."

"Of course she does," I said, already rolling up the sleeve to my uniform.

It would have to wait, though. Apparently, according to Vicki, the only way to celebrate the return of powers was to set something on fire and fly through a wall.

Fitting for Plain Jane, really, but the staff in Medical weren't exactly happy with us right then.

I took the next day off of work. I had probably been fired, anyway, so it really didn't matter. Dealing with supervillains and hostage situations one day and returning to work on spreadsheets the next had been a reality for me for four years, but now that I was the one underneath the mask, it was time for a change. I didn't want to think about it, so I didn't. Instead, I focused on the fallout that the Demobilizer had caused. Or rather, I nagged Guy.

"I'm fine," he said for the fourth time over breakfast the next morning.

I gave him a look.

"Really. I am. What can I do to convince you?"

"You were so happy not to have powers," I said. "You were, like, making plans for culinary school. It's the most excited I've seen you since you found that new farmer's market."

He took a long sip of coffee and flipped the third omelet onto my plate. Whatever Elwin had given me had made me hungrier than usual. I hoped that would go away soon, too.

"You haven't been happy," I said. I dug in, but carefully didn't speak with my mouth full. "I know we haven't been together that long, but I could tell you were miserable, Guy."

"It is what it is." Guy sat down with his own omelet. "But maybe you have a point. I . . . wasn't happy. I don't like being War Hammer."

I looked at him, expectantly.

"It's that damn chest plate," he said. "It chafes. I don't know how Sam does it."

"I knew it!" I said, pointing at him. "I knew you hated it!"

He laughed a little helplessly. "Well, the good news is that I don't have to be War Hammer anymore."

"No? Does that mean Sam's done finding himself?"

"Yeah, it turns out getting his powers taken away put a few things in perspective for him, too. I talked to him last night." Guy's fingers twitched on his fork. He'd finally gotten a haircut, so his hair didn't fall into his eyes for once. The morning light made his eyes spectacularly green as he looked at me. "He was in Mexico for a while. He said he liked the warm weather. I suggested maybe he should put in for a transfer."

"Do you mean . . . . ?"

"People have been asking where Blaze is," Guy said. "I think the answer to that is going to be Chicago from now on. Sam can take over my job at Dad's office in Miami. It's not like I do anything but fill a desk and look pretty, anyway."

"But you do such an amazing job at looking pretty," I said. "You are definitely the hot one in this relationship."

His ears went red. "Now that's a downright lie."

"Aw, you think I'm pretty. So what are you going to do in Chicago?"

"*Pretty* is putting it mildly. And I was thinking culinary school," Guy said.

I raised my eyebrows.

"It's better for me to have the powers," he said. "Not being able to back you up? That sucked. But I don't need to sacrifice everything in my life. I can find a way to make something work, right?"

"Selfishly, I am going to support any and all endeavors you make that involve food." But I smiled and grabbed his hand. "Since I'm pretty sure I lost the job I probably shouldn't have gone back to in the first place, though, I won't be able to support you in the manner to which you've become accustomed, just to warn you."

"I think I can handle it," Guy said, laughing. He kissed the back of my hand. "I suspect you'll be plenty busy with other things."

"What do you mean?" I asked, squinting.

He refused to explain, though, only smiling when I badgered him and poked at the spot on his side where I knew he was ticklish. When I got up to do the dishes, he followed, leaning his hip against the counter as he sipped his second cup of coffee. "Sam wants to help Brook," he said.

"He wants to start looking for Petra again? Didn't that destroy him the first time around?"

"It's a mystery that I think all of us want solved. Brook more than any of us. She deserves some closure in something after what Lodi did. It can't have been easy on her, being held by Elwin again."

I shoved a dish into the water with a little too much force. "Douchebag didn't even care that he'd been complicit in torturing her. He only wanted money."

"Davenport's lawyers will hang him out to dry."

"I hope so." But it wasn't enough. Remembering the devastation and fury on her face as she stood over Elwin at Wrigley Field, and knowing that she'd wound up under his power once again, made me realize that I'd never fully be satisfied. Prison wasn't enough for that monster. I finished up the dishes while Guy checked the news on his phone, but the antsy feeling in my chest hadn't abated. I needed to hit something.

"I'm going to go to the Power House. Want to come with?"

"I promised Sam I'd help him out with some stuff. Good luck with your security guard friend."

From the way he ducked when I stepped into the lobby at the way station, I didn't think I'd have a problem with Marsh the security guard again. After he'd been responsible for a massive breach in Davenport, I had the power to get him fired, and he knew it. At least it would be easier to pop into New York and visit Jeremy now. I shot one final malevolent look at Marsh and headed downstairs to catch the train. I could phase my way across Chicago, but I wanted to save my energy for a punching bag or five.

Three had been piled in the corner, busted to pieces, so clearly Angélica had already been here to work through her own issues. I picked a relatively intact bag and worked methodically through combinations, finally letting loose a little of the frustration I'd been suffering ever since Elwin had dosed me.

An hour later, I'd worked up a sweat and the bag swung wildly as I pounded away. A single hand stopped it and I bounced back on my heels, breathing hard.

Jessie Davenport raised both eyebrows at me. "Brought you lunch," she said, holding up a fast food bag. Grease had turned splotches of it transparent, and

I felt my mouth watering when I caught the smell of delicious salty food.

"Thanks," I said, and she tossed the bag to me. I set it aside so I could unwrap my hands. "You've been spending a lot of time in Chicago lately."

"I have some interests in the area. Is there some place we can sit and talk?"

Angélica wouldn't mind if I used her office, so I led the way and cleared paperwork off of a couple chairs for us to sit. In addition to having the world's largest shoe collection, my roommate excelled at avoiding all semblances of neatness whatsoever. That had been eye-opening when we'd moved in together.

"So no powers, huh?" I asked as we dug into our burgers.

"None. No chance of getting Mom's Villain Syndrome, either, so that's an upside."

I eyed her. "Powers or not, you're insanely terrifying in a fight."

"I worked hard at that," she said, nodding seriously. "I spent years building up that skill. My father didn't have any powers, either, but he needed to keep up with the rest of the Feared Five. All of whom *did* have powers. He didn't want to just be the bankroll."

"And you took over," I said, as I knew that much from history. The Feared Five had been the first superhero team. There'd even been a Gail on that team, but I hadn't been named after her the way I'd thought for most of my life. That had just been a coincidence. "People think the Raptor is immortal."

"They also think the Raptor is male," Jessie said with a smile.

"True."

"In a way, the Raptor is immortal, I suppose." Jessie popped a fry in her mouth and chewed. "And adaptive. My father spent his entire life making the Raptor stronger. I followed in his footsteps. At times, the lack of powers can be a benefit. But often, it's a deterrent. I think it's time for the Raptor to adapt once more. This time, as a powered hero."

I blinked at her, trying to figure out what she could mean by that. When my brain finally put it together, I wanted to slap my forehead. "You want the Mobium," I said. "Oh, that makes sense, but I gotta tell you, it's more trouble than it's worth. And convincing Dr. Mobius is going to be impossible, unless you do Kiki's gambit again. And I'm pretty sure that was a one-time thing that . . ."

Jessie started laughing hard. Confused, I trailed off.

"I should be flattered," she said as I stared at her. She wiped away a tear. "I should be. Like, my age doesn't even factor into it for you."

"What?" I asked.

"Gail, I'm fifty-one. My father didn't even make it to fifty before he gave up the suit. My body is a mess and the villains are showing up harder and faster these days. I'm not talking about getting Mobium for myself. I'm talking about passing the suit on."

I gawked. I'd heard perfectly, but the words weren't connecting in my brain. "But," I said, when it became obvious that she was expecting me to say something. "But—you have kids. Your son, he—"

"He doesn't have powers. And Raptor's a heavy mantle to bear. I don't want him in this life. My daughter, either." Jessie gave me a serious look. "I want to pass it on to you."

"But *why*?"

"Well, most importantly, Audra thinks it's a good idea, and I've learned over the years that she's smarter than me." Jessie wiped a dab of ketchup off her fingers with a napkin. "You're smart, you're durable, you're willing to learn. You've got a good heart. You've already shown me you can make alliances with heroes and villains alike. And when it comes down to it, you can make difficult choices and you're capable of seeing the bigger picture when you need to."

I squirmed in my seat.

"But really," Jessie said, "I'm picking you because making you the next Raptor would piss Eddie off beyond belief."

Suddenly, it all made sense. I'd been puzzled by Jessie's random visits to Angélica's gym to spar with me and watch me train. The carte blanche she'd given me to borrow armor and vehicles from her armory. The fact that she'd had a log-in for me in her computer systems. The Raptor-like uniform she'd had tailor-made for me.

Jessie Davenport had been grooming me, and I hadn't even noticed. Which, really, should be all the argument she needed against me being the next Raptor, and I told her so.

She rolled her eyes. "Observational skills can be taught. I'm asking you to come be my apprentice, not put on the cape and go out to New York tonight. It'd be a full-time job. The Raptor has a venerable history and we'd need to make the transition seamless, so it would take time."

"When you say a full-time job . . ." I said, feeling weak.

"I mean you'd earn a paycheck, with benefits. Audra drew up a packet. There's a signing bonus."

"Are you insane?" I asked before I could stop myself.

"No, just really, really rich." She reached into the bottom desk drawer and dropped a thick white envelope in front of me. When had she even put that in there? "I've already had a talk with your roommate. I may be giving up the Raptor, but Audra comes with me, so you'll need somebody to manage your life. Angélica's already doing a pretty good job, from what I can tell."

She wiped her hands clean on a napkin, balled her trash up, and tossed it in the garbage. "Give it some thought, and let me know what you decide. Audra's waiting for your call," she said, and she left me there, sweaty from working out and holding what I imagined to be a pretty lucrative job offer.

**T**he worst part was that I was gobsmacked, but absolutely none of my friends were surprised, Guy chief among them. When I called him, he only laughed. "I saw the writing on the wall months ago," he said. "It's not a bad idea. You're never going to stay out of the field, you know."

I sighed. "I tried my hardest!"

"You're trouble. I love you for it, but you're trouble."

He had a point. "I love you, too," I said. "I'm going to go think about it."

"Say hi to Jeremy for me."

It took me a couple of hours of talking into the silence of Jeremy's room before I could really wrap my brain around it. Going through the paperwork made my mind boggle. No wonder Jessie had said Audra was smarter than her: she'd thought of every angle in the paperwork. There were schedules, anticipated conflicts, financial projections. The only reason the kitchen sink had been left out probably had to do with weight limits or something because the paperwork definitely had everything else.

"This is ridiculous," I said to Jeremy's impassive form. "I am crazy for even considering it."

And I *was* considering it. Angélica had pointed out that even if it didn't work out, even if I didn't become the Raptor, training with Jessie was an opportunity I shouldn't pass up.

I looked at Jeremy's prone form and poked his thigh with the toe of my sneaker. "I get an offer to be the world's most famous superhero's apprentice and you're sleeping. Lazybones. You need to be awake so you can mock me for even considering not taking this job. Raptor used to be your favorite superhero."

A little flare of static bubbled up the tip of his index finger. Other than that, no change.

"Fine," I said. "See how you like it when I become the Raptor, and you miss it."

And I was, I realized. I was going to take Jessie up on her offer. I'd liked the armor she'd given me, even if I hadn't been nuts about the color. And wearing a mask . . . it really had been inevitable. Still my hand shook a little as I picked up the phone to call.

Right as I unlocked it, though, a text message arrived. I read it with a frown, and then an idea began to form.

I'd take the job, I decided, and hopefully Audra wouldn't side-eye my conditions too much.

# EPILOGUE

**T**wo weeks later, I grimaced as one of my boots caught the edge of a puddle, splashing icy water all over my uniform pants. The cold didn't bother me, but the damp would stick around for hours, and that was aggravating. It couldn't be helped, though. I was already late. Making sure I knew how to use the suit had taken longer than either Audra or Angélica had anticipated.

"It's a loan only," Audra had said.

"Which means don't break it," Angélica had translated for me.

I looked between the two of them. How Angélica had managed to mimic Audra's unimpressed look in the space of a few hours was still perplexing to me. She had her own arsenal of those, but she had Audra's body language down perfectly. "You were just telling me that Jessie breaks the suit all the time!"

"That's Jessie. She breaks the suit doing serious things and fighting serious villains."

"This is a serious villain. Well, no, okay, she's not,

but I owe her one," I'd said, stubbornly, and Audra had given in with a sigh.

Their caution would probably save me trouble down the road, but right now it made me late. And the person I was meeting wasn't always smart about dressing for winter. So I hurried, phasing from rooftop to rooftop. I reached my destination eight minutes late, and found her hovering despondently in the air, listlessly kicking her feet.

She'd upgraded to her winter outfit at least, so that was a small mercy.

I crouched in the shadows and studied her for a moment, evaluating. In the end, the rocket boots were the best strategy. I reached into a pouch, scowling as I picked the wrong one and had to withdraw my fingers before I activated a taser disc and shocked myself again. The correct pouch netted the little device I needed, which I lobbed at Raze's left boot.

It hit with a *fzzt* and a shower of sparks. Raze yelled as she dropped about ten feet and transferred all the power to her right rocket boot. As she decelerated, she yanked one of her guns out and swung it about wildly. "Who's there?"

I leapt up onto a balcony railing and remained crouched, doing my best not to wobble.

Raze's jaw dropped. "Raptor? Oh, shit, sorry, I'll go. I didn't realize this was your territory, your Raptorness. I'll go right away—"

"Gail Godwin sent me," I said, trying not to grimace at the way the voice modulator made me sound. Creepy kidnapper had never been my aesthetic. I'd have to talk to Angélica about that.

"Sh-she did?" Raze's face had gone bone-white.

I grinned. "She couldn't make it. She sent a hero worthy of fighting you in her place, she said."

Puzzlement reigned supreme over Raze's face, even with her bulbous helmet blocking most of it. She edged her fingers along her half cape. "Gail said that?" she asked, her voice rising to a squeak at the end. "Really?"

I shrugged.

"Oh my god. I knew it! You're going to fight me? Like, for reals?"

"I can leave, if you want me to," I said, standing up as though to go. It nearly knocked me off balance. I had no idea how Jessie always clung to those narrow ledges.

Before I could turn, though, Raze shot at me. She missed, but it was close enough to sizzle at one of the backward tufts on my cowl. "I'm not going to miss fighting the *Raptor*," she said.

"Good enough for me," I said, and jumped off the balcony at her. She let out an actual yodel and dove at me in return.

An hour later, we'd destroyed a few rusty cars and had busted up some walls in foreclosed buildings (there was a reason I'd picked the area that I had). I was covered in bruises and sweating, but Raze's smile as she flew off had been worth it. No doubt she'd be blowing up my phone—hopefully not literally—with a wildly exaggerated account of the time she totally kicked my friend the Raptor's ass. I'd owed her one since she'd taken a bullet helping me out. And it was good training.

Good training that left me starving. I made my way back to where I'd left my new car, pulling out my phone to text Guy that I was finally on my way over to his place—after I dropped the armor off, of course.

The phone shocked my hand.

Cursing, I dropped it. Had something gone wrong with the suit? Raze had landed a couple of surprisingly heavy hits. Maybe one of the myriad devices I was learning to use had somehow supercharged my phone. Annoyance rose up. If I had to get a new phone because of this, that was just going to be a pain. At least it hadn't cracked when it fell on the concrete.

Warily, I bent over and reached for it, hoping it wouldn't shock me a second time.

It didn't. Instead, it exploded into a shower of blue sparks and static. I yelped and scrambled backward. Currents of electricity engulfed my poor phone, shaped like a mushroom cloud and glowing. I scurried back farther when the glowing cloud of static grew. The static fizzled and popped and crackled, filling the air with the overpowering scent of ozone. A blue cloud that sparked with energy sprouted outward from the phone, crawling along the concrete until it was waist-high and spreading lengthwise.

My brain pointed out that I should run, and run fast. Audra hadn't told me about anything in the Raptor suit that could do that, which meant this was clearly something else. But I remained rooted to the spot. The static burned the weeds struggling up through the cracks in the pavement, little puffs of smoke. At its center was a globe of blue light so bright that I couldn't look directly at it, but I also couldn't look away. It was beautiful and mesmerizing and terrifying.

I had just enough time to wonder at this before the bright cloud abruptly turned white and burst outward. A concussive wave knocked me back, shattering streetlamps and plunging the street into darkness. I could barely make out a body in the dark where my phone had been. Male. Tall. Wearing what looked like smoking hospital scrubs. And when my brain finally processed what my eyes were seeing, I grabbed the flashlight out of my utility pouch and shoved my cowl off.

The man coughed as I shone the light in his face. He was covered in sweat and he had a couple of shiny burns on his face. He lifted a hand to block the light and I saw a little blue spark travel up the length of his pinky. He was out of breath and he absolutely shouldn't have been lying on the street in Chicago, not when he was supposed to be in a coma in New York.

"So," Jeremy Collins said when my mouth bobbed uselessly, no sound coming out of it. "What did I miss?"

## ABOUT THE AUTHOR

**LEXIE DUNNE** is a lifelong winner of the coveted trophy for participation and author of the Superheroes Anonymous series. By day a mild-mannered technical writer and by night a writer of masked crusaders, she hails from St. Louis, home of the world's largest croquet game piece. Follow her on Twitter @DunneWriting.

www.dunnewriting.com

Discover great authors, exclusive offers, and more at hc.com.